To Janice

FREEING LUKA

THE CLECANIAN SERIES: BOOK TWO

VICTORIA AVELINE

Victoria Aveline

First paperback edition July 2020

Cover design by *Mayhem Cover Creations*

ISBN 978-1-7346788-1-9

www.victoriaaveline.com

Freeing Luka

The Clecanian Series: Book Two

Victoria Aveline

1

Am I being carried? Alice thought dreamily. Her eyes were still closed, but the fog of sleep was lifting. As it did, panic started to settle in its place. She mentally scanned her body, not yet able to move but gaining more awareness with each minute. Someone very large was indeed carrying her. Her head pounded as she tried to recall...anything. Where she was, how she'd gotten there, and whose fingers were digging into her thighs and ribs.

The last thing she could remember was taking the garbage out at work. She'd been exhausted after a double shift at Molly's, an old dive bar in her small college town.

Think! Think!

An image of something large and green rushing her in the alley behind the bar flashed in her mind, and she struggled to hang on to it. Her blood ran cold when she recalled the creature in more detail. It'd been a monster. Green, with scales instead of skin. More upright lizard than man. Alice remembered screaming, throwing the bag of garbage at the creature and running, then…it was all black.

It must've caught me.

Panic and fear took hold. She tried to open her eyes, but her lids only twitched in response. Her heart rate picked up speed and her breaths became quick and shallow. Luckily, whoever was holding her didn't seem to notice, or if they did, they didn't say anything.

Pleading with her thundering heart to quiet, she strained to listen for clues indicating where she was and whom she was with. The sound of two sets of heavy footsteps echoed around her, and her cheek rested on a hard chest. She needed to get away.

Can I even move?

The instinct to wiggle her fingers and toes to make sure she wasn't paralyzed ate at her. She forced herself to remain still, knowing she couldn't risk it. Instead, Alice gently clenched and relaxed every part of her body she could, hoping to appear more or less still. Blood flowed through her numb limbs, making them tingle. The more she worked the muscles, the easier it became.

She inhaled, taking in the cold, stagnant air. It reminded her of being on an airplane. She'd only flown a handful of times, but the stale scent of crisp, filtered air always stood out to her. Was there no fresh air in this place either?

When she finally lifted her lids a fraction, she squinted at whoever or whatever was carrying her. Through thick lashes, she could make out the blurry image of…a man?

What the hell is going on? Where am I?

Just then, he began to speak, his deep voice vibrating through his chest. "Where are we taking her?"

"I'm not sure," she heard another gravelly voice answer. "The boss is in room six. I'll ask." The resounding thump of the new man's steps accelerated, then slowed. He spoke again in a hushed tone, "Or we could take her to twelve first. He doesn't know she's here yet. Who knows what happened to her on that ship, what condition she'll be in upon delivery? We could have a little fun with her first."

Alice stiffened. As the steps of the man carrying her slowed, she let out a mental plea that he'd stop whatever the other guy had planned. She swallowed, her throat working to lubricate her dry windpipe in preparation to scream.

Chuckling, he replied, "True, the Cae can be a vicious species."

Wrong answer!

Curling her fingers into her palm, she gathered every ounce of strength she had and shot her fist up, slamming into the man's chin. His teeth clacked together, and his head snapped back a second before he dropped her with a grunt.

A sharp pain lanced through her hip when she tumbled to the floor, but she forced herself to ignore it and run, screaming at the top of her lungs. Her steps were clumsy, and her vision was blurry. Whatever drug she'd been given was still working its way out of her system. She blinked rapidly, stumbling forward.

Muttered curses from behind her told her the men hadn't moved to follow her yet. "That pishot made me bite my tongue!"

"Yeah, you'll need a healer for that," murmured the second man in an amused tone.

When her sight cleared, she found she was in a hallway lined on either side with heavy metal doors. The pristine floor, ceiling, and walls were white and bare, save for the imposing metal doors on either side of her. The odd air. The clean white surfaces. The metal doors. Was this a prison, or a hospital? Adrenaline spiked and she increased her speed.

Hearing heavy footsteps behind her, she screamed louder, ignoring the searing pain shooting through her vocal cords. They'd implied "the boss" wouldn't want them to do whatever they had planned. They'd also mentioned he was waiting in room six. If she could find room six, at least she'd be safe from the two men behind her.

While running, her frantic gaze landed on the doors, searching for a number. The symbols she saw were foreign. She couldn't even place which language they might've belonged to, and yet the men had been speaking perfect English, so it was unlikely they were in a foreign country.

What the hell is going on here?

A few feet ahead, a stocky man stepped through a heavy door and scanned the hallway. When he spotted her, his eyebrows drew together in confusion, and then he shot a furious look behind her.

Two sets of hands suddenly gripped her upper arms, jerking her backward.

"What's going on here? Why is she screaming and running through the halls?" he yelled, his booming voice echoing down the hallway.

Alice needed him to know what they planned. "They wanted to take me to room twelve before bringing me to their boss!" she screeched just before a firm hand wrapped around her mouth.

The "boss" stilled. "Is this true?"

They said nothing, but the hands on her arms tightened so painfully that she cried out into the calloused fingers covering her mouth.

Their leader stepped into the hallway more fully. The mustard yellow of his coat clashed with the light orange of his shoulder-length, pin-straight hair. Alice wasn't sure if it was his utterly still posture or the anger displayed everywhere except his eyes that made a shiver run through her. There was something about him that made her want to lean into the painful hold of the men behind her.

"You will ease your hold on her and take her to room nine. Any damage I find when I inspect her later will be inflicted on you. Do you understand me?"

A loud roar reverberated from the room behind him, making the man flinch. Her stomach somersaulted as the sound of rattling chains rang through the open door.

"I need to get back to our visitor," he said, glancing into the room then back to his two flunkies. "Do you understand my instructions?"

She heard a low "yes, sir" from each of the men, and then she was being pushed forward.

As they passed the open doorway, she tried to glance in to see what creature the furious sound had come from. The briefest glimpse of a naked, chained man had her struggling and screaming with renewed vigor. The imprisoned man's eyes were completely black. He swung his head toward her, snarling and snapping his teeth.

They pulled her thrashing body past the room, then one of the men stepped into her line of sight, and her screams died in her throat.

Alice gazed wide-eyed at him, frozen in place. She blinked. Her eyes must be playing tricks on her. She couldn't process what she was seeing. He was a man, but not entirely. Murky brown wings flared behind his back, and sharp fangs flashed at her as he snarled, "Keep your mouth shut. You're hurting my ears."

Was he an angel? Angels shouldn't look terrifying, though, should they?

Mouth wide, she craned her head to look at the other guard, wondering if she was hallucinating. While most of his features were normal, he had white shining markings running around his face and neck. She hadn't noticed them before through her half-closed lids. Shrinking away, she felt her knees buckle. He glared at her with bright yellow eyes.

A hoarse "what are you?" was all she could manage as they resumed dragging her to a door a short distance away.

In response to her question, the two men exchanged wicked grins and pushed her into the dark room. She stood where they placed her, dumbfounded. As they left, she heard an electric buzz, followed by the metallic scrapes of dozens of locks sliding into place.

After a few long moments, Alice's mind snapped to attention and she realized she was standing stock still in a pitch-black room. The darkness pressed in around her. With a start, she swept her hands out in front of her, and crept in the direction of the door.

She hissed when her knee hit a sharp edge. The sound of glass breaking from her right made her freeze.

Not willing to put trust in the soles of her worn Converse, she kept her feet planted then bent at the hip and groped forward in the darkness. A flat, solid surface met her hand a few feet in front of her. Blindly, she slid her fingers over the rough stone of the wall and stilled. Had her pinky brushed a smooth glass surface? She prodded the small, sleek area experimentally. All of a sudden, a harsh light illuminated the room.

Alice squinted, dazed by the sudden brightness, and tried to be patient as she waited for her eyes to adjust. After they did, she looked around the room.

Her shoulders relaxed in a moment of fleeting relief when she saw there were no chains. At least she wouldn't be shackled like the man a few rooms away.

Fragments of a broken glass of water lay around her feet in a puddle, and she carefully stepped around them. The sharp edge that'd hurt her knee belonged to a low table topped with a tray of food near the door. Alice's stomach rumbled as she looked at it.

Clutching her middle, she tried desperately to remember the last time she ate. The oddest sense that time had passed was present in her mind, but she couldn't account for any of the lost time. How long had it been since she'd been taken, and what had happened during that time? Her body was exhausted and sore from the short sprint, and her throat burned from her screaming. More than it should've.

She twisted and turned, inspecting her body, but didn't find anything out of the ordinary. No bruises other than the new dark ones forming on her arms. No atrophied muscles. Her legs, which she'd just shaved before work, were still smooth, and the small cut she always seemed to get when shaving around her knees was still fresh. Maybe she was just imagining the lost time, but her instincts said otherwise. Resolving to go down that rabbit hole later, she surveyed the space again.

The room itself, with its gray walls and long, thin lights embedded in the ceiling, wasn't completely unpleasant, but the locked heavy metal door and the lack of windows made it clear this was nothing but a sparsely furnished cell.

A sagging twin bed was crammed into one corner of the room, another small table was pushed alongside it, and what she could only assume was an odd-looking lamp stood on top.

Across from her was a doorway, through which she could see a small bathroom. A large, simple rug covered most of the floor in front of her, and a chair sat by the door.

Alice sank onto the bed's rough navy fabric, head in her hands.

What do I know? She tried to focus, her mind racing. *I know that one guy had fucking wings, and the other had yellow eyes. I know there are symbols I've never seen before on the doors. I know they all spoke English, and they didn't have an accent. I think I know that a green, scaly monster took me from work.*

Alice shook her head, incredulous. A few minutes ago, she'd thought she'd made up the green monster, that she'd hit her head and had a concussion or was hallucinating. Only now was she starting to accept it might've been real.

Alice remembered clearly that one of the men had said, "Who knows what could have happened to her on that ship?"

Sitting up a little straighter, she mused out loud. "The other one said the green guy was from a species called Cae. Species of what? Angels? Mutants? Am I in an X-Men bunker or something?"

But…a ship. What kind of ship? Her breaths quickened.

Her cell door opened, jarring her from the inevitable conclusion she was reaching.

She jumped back, grabbing the lamp from the side table. Alice glared at the man she now knew was the boss, and held the brown metal of the cordless lamp in front of her.

He stood in the doorway, hands resting in his pockets, and over his shoulder said, "Gishen, Sal, get in here."

9

The two men who'd dragged her through the hall a few moments ago shuffled through the door behind their leader.

"You can call me Helas," he said, eyeing the lamp in her hands. "Did they hurt you after I told them not to?"

Alice glanced to the two men glaring at her. *If looks could kill.* "No, they didn't." It was better not to make them hate her any more than they already did, she concluded warily.

Helas stared at her for a moment longer, then addressed the men. "You'll not touch her again. She's just become a very important part of our research."

Gishen and Sal looked at him quizzically.

"Research?" Alice interrupted, dread running through her. *What kind of ship was it?*

Ignoring her, Helas spoke to the men. "Luka recognized her."

With slackened jaws, both men's gazes ping-ponged between her and Helas.

"Someone here knows me?" Alice asked hopefully.

Once again, he continued to speak to the men while ignoring her completely. She gritted her teeth in annoyance. "Find a secure communicator and tell the other outposts what has occurred. Anyone who touches her will have to answer to me. This could be the breakthrough we've been waiting for."

Both men nodded and began to leave. The winged man didn't spare her a glance, but the other man's unreadable yellow eyes stayed trained on her for a few fleeting moments before he finally left too. When they were gone, Helas closed the door and moved to sit in the chair near the small table with food. He motioned to the lamp Alice was clutching in a death grip. "You can put that down. I'm not going to hurt you."

Alice snorted. "I think I'll hang on to it anyway. Maybe just until my arm bruises fade and I can leave this room without permission."

He raised his manicured brows, and the corner of his thin mouth lifted in a smile. "As you wish."

Now that she could see him more clearly, she realized he too had white tattoos, although his were much fainter than the other man's had been. Her forehead creased. There was still something off about him that she couldn't place. Were his eyes just slightly too large? The teeth he exposed when he smiled were small, but she could swear he had more of them than normal.

Again, she asked, "What are you?"

Surprisingly, he answered. "I am Clecanian. Lignas is my race. You're human, correct?"

"Yes. Are you human?" she asked, already knowing the answer.

"I am Clecanian," he repeated.

She licked her chapped lips, weighing whether she really wanted to ask her next question. His eyes shone as he waited for her to speak. *Is this asshole enjoying this?* "What's a Clecanian?"

"A Clecanian is a species made up of many races. We live on the planet Clecania. That's where we are right now."

Alice's palms were slick against the lamp, and a buzzing sounded in her ears. "I was on a spaceship," she mumbled absently.

"Yes, indeed. Brought here from Earth by a species known as the Cae," Helas said, coolly.

Anger at his uncaring tone caused Alice's mind to focus. "Why was I brought here? What research are you doing? Who is Luka, and how did he recognize me?" The name hadn't sounded familiar. She didn't even know a Luke. There was a guy named Luther who lived in her apartment complex. Had he been taken too?

"I don't have time for this," he said, but his relaxed posture made her question that. "I'll only explain what you need to know, and if you do what I tell you, I might be inclined to answer more of your questions later. Agreed?"

Alice glared at him. She was by no means stupid, but she knew she was sometimes naïve when it came to people. For the most part, she wanted to believe people were good. A year of serving drinks in a dive bar had taught her differently.

With the help of her coworker, Jen, she'd finally started to learn how to tell which men were harmless and which ones were dangerous. The drunk, handsy ones weren't great, but the ones you really had to watch out for were the quiet, polite ones—the ones whose charming smiles never met their eyes.

This affable-looking man might've stopped the other two before, and he'd been cordial enough with her so far, but she could tell by the coldness seeping from his eyes that he was a bad man. Probably the worst of them all. When cornered, angering men like this was never a good idea.

Play by his rules for now.

He must've seen the decision on her face, because he smiled and began speaking. "Our people, and the many races therein, are headed toward extinction. Males outnumber females twenty to one. Many attempts to have children are unsuccessful, and when they are successful, most of the children born are male. Our attempts to grow life using artificial wombs have failed. We've been searching endlessly for a race descended from our own that has compatible females."

Her head pounded. There was so much to take in. "You brought me here to become pregnant and have alien babies because you think humans are descendants of Cle…Clecin—?" Alice said, trying to keep the fear from her voice.

"Clecanians, yes." Helas corrected. "We have yet to be successful, but after today…I'm hopeful." He seemed pleased when Alice remained silent. "Long ago, Clecanians mated for life. There was only one person for another. If a Clecanian's eyes changed color, they knew the person they were with could be their true mate. If markings, called mating marks, appeared around both wrists, then they knew for a fact they'd found their true mate. Historically, true mates had the best chances of any couple to conceive."

Alice glanced down to his wrists instinctively.

"Don't worry, I'm not your mate." He chuckled. "There hasn't been a mating in over a hundred years. However, when you walked by the room I was in earlier, Luka, the male inside, had quite a reaction to you." Helas leaned forward, his grin widening. "He recognized you. His eyes changed."

Alice's recalled the eerie onyx of the snarling man's eyes and felt bile rise in her throat. "You brought me here because you think I'm his mate?" she said, glancing to the wall. How was she supposed to handle this news? Not only was he telling her that she was to be bred like an animal, but that the chained, roaring alien a few rooms away was supposed to do the breeding.

"I brought you here to be artificially inseminated and studied just like any other test subject. The fact that Luka recognized you is purely coincidental and highly interesting. I think you two have a better shot at creating life than any other beings in our facilities. And I think if you *do* turn out to be his mate, we'll have proven that human females should be considered a subspecies of Clecanians and taken seriously as a viable alternative to the females already living here."

Helas rose from his seat suddenly, causing Alice to stiffen.

"This is what we're going to do," he began matter-of-factly. "Every day, you will be taken to his room, where he will be chained. I'd like for you to sit with him so we can see whether extended proximity makes his mating marks appear."

"Why will he be chained?" Alice asked quietly, not wanting to upset her captor but needing to understand what kind of danger she'd soon be facing. "Is he violent?"

"He's been drugged since he got here. We were testing some new medications on him to make it easier to…" a cruel smile spread over his face as he searched for the right word, "obtain samples."

"Samples?" Alice started, appalled. "You can't mean—"

Helas smirked then began studying her room, as though the conversation was banal. "I can, and I do, mean samples of his seed. Luka is only half Clecanian. His mother was from another planet, Traxia."

The briefest flash of disgust passed over his face at the mention of Luka's mother.

"Members of our organization believe that tainting our ancient bloodlines with that of different species is…wrong. Although I agree, there is no denying that mixed-species Clecanians are walking among us, and with the amount of pure Clecanian births continuing to dwindle, our people are becoming desperate." He focused on Alice, his words spilling out of him now. "Only a few weeks ago I had a revolutionary idea. I decided perhaps there was a way to alter part of the biological information transferred through procreation. What if we could extract only the Clecanian pieces of DNA and combine them to produce a pure Clecanian sample from a mixed-breed individual?"

Alice felt her skin crawl. How could an alien species that'd made such advances in technology still have such antiquated views?

"Then all we'd have to do to create undiluted offspring would be to alter the mixed-species' diluted genetic material." Helas' chest puffed with pride, but then the corner of his mouth twitched. "I explained this to Luka, tried to convince him to stand with us and aid me in my endeavor, but he declined. He was unwilling, as so many who are brought here are, so I have been forced to do what is necessary to test my theory."

"So that makes it okay for you to rape him?" Alice whispered.

His smile stayed in place, but his right eye twitched, betraying his calm demeanor. "We do not touch him in that way. Weekly, we dose him with a drug that makes him feel overwhelming lust and clears his mind. He's chained, and then every few days he's allowed to relieve himself. We merely collect the sample."

Her shoulders straightened. "He hasn't consented. You know what you're doing is wrong. Don't pretend like it isn't." Alice felt a surge of satisfaction as she witnessed the twitch return to his eye at her words. She'd always been braver whilst defending others than when standing up for herself. For some reason, it came easily to her. See a patron talk down to a coworker, rage like an avenging angel. Get talked down to by a patron, shrivel into a self-conscious mess.

"We'll have to agree to disagree," he said after a moment. "In any case, his chains will act to keep you safe, as well. If he recognizes you as his mate while on these drugs, he'll try to get to you, and he won't have the presence of mind to be gentle."

Alice clutched the lamp tighter. An unfamiliar urge to inflict pain assailed her. This man was the kind who'd throw a person to the wolves and then ask for a "thank you."

He stood and crossed to her, his large frame crowding her. His stance was meant to intimidate and frighten; Alice hated that it worked. Cold sweat broke out over her skin, and she began to shake. The scent of rubbing alcohol and something else she couldn't quite place wafted over her, stinging her nostrils. "I won't allow him to touch you, and in return for my kindness, you will go in there every day and attempt to make his mating marks appear."

"How?" she asked in a squeaky voice as hundreds of terrifying possibilities flashed through her mind.

Helas' shrug was noncommittal. "If proximity doesn't work, you will touch him. If that doesn't work, we will have to think of something else." He allowed his smile to fade away, and at last, the coldness in his eyes matched the rest of his expression. "I am not asking."

She stayed silent and felt the pressure of tears forming behind her eyes. All she wanted to do was curl into a ball in the corner, but she forced herself to stand tall and not let him see her cower.

In an instant, his mask of aloof kindness was back in place. He stood and walked briskly to the door. Motioning to the small table, he said, "I'll have more food and water brought to you tomorrow. Sleep well."

After he left, Alice sank to the ground, her legs unable to support her weight. Pulling her knees to her chest, hot tears rolled down her cheeks, and the deep sobs exploding from her tore at her throat like sandpaper.

Her whole life had changed so drastically in less than an hour. She wasn't on Earth anymore, and if Helas had his way, the rest of her days would be spent in this room, either pregnant or trying to become pregnant.

There was no one to help her. No one to hold her while she cried. For all she knew, there were no humans on this planet at all. Alice would need to save herself somehow.

Tomorrow she'd be strong. Tomorrow she'd do what she had to do to survive. But just for tonight, she'd allow her pain and sadness to flow through her unrestrained.

Alice cried for what felt like hours until only dry, ragged sobs escaped her. She didn't try to rise from the cold concrete floor when her eyes slid closed. When she eventually drifted to sleep, she dreamed about the chained man.

2

Alice roamed around her room and scanned the bare walls for the umpteenth time. There was no clock. There was never a clock, but she couldn't help checking and rechecking. For all she knew, she could've slept for two hours or twelve.

There were very few things Alice was obsessive about. In most respects, she even considered herself laid back. Her house could be a mess without it frustrating her. Food could be slightly too cold. Wrinkled clothes weren't a cause for concern. But not knowing what time it was always made her anxious. It wasn't like she did anything with the information. She wasn't rigidly early or constantly late. She just liked the comfort of knowing.

It was complete and utter bad luck that her wristwatch had stopped working the day before she'd been taken. Or had it been an omen? At the time, she hadn't thought much of it. Just another electronic giving out after extended use. She always had her phone with her anyway, and the turquoise bicycle she rode everywhere had a watch mounted between the handlebars.

She began nibbling her short nails. Ripped from everything she knew, her whole measly existence on Earth, and she didn't even have the small comfort of knowing the time. At this point, she'd even settle for a sundial. Her steps faltered, and she narrowed her eyes, glancing at the ceiling.

It won't be the same sun. How long are the days on this planet?

She let out a short shriek into the empty room, fisting her hands at her sides. The one thing she could count on, the one thing that should've never changed, was now uncertain.

This is bullshit! she thought as she gnawed the cuticle of her index finger and continued pacing.

She was fixating on something that didn't matter. She realized that. The fact that there was no clock wasn't nearly as stressful as thinking about what might happen to her in here, but she couldn't focus on that for too long without dread starting to bubble up, and this was no place to have a panic attack.

Already, every small sound she heard made her flinch and sprint into the bathroom. Any minute now, they could come through the door to take her, and she still wasn't certain what she should do about that. Fight them tooth and nail?

Go along with it and search for an opportunity to escape, she told herself. There was no sense in fighting right now. It'd probably make things worse for her.

Trying to make herself busy, Alice tidied the already tidy room. She cleaned up the spilled water and carefully picked up the pieces of broken glass, none of which were large enough to use as a weapon, then looked around, annoyed there was nothing left to do.

The sound of approaching footsteps made her scramble toward the bathroom.

Grinding metal sounded before the door opened, and yellow eyes met hers. One of the men from yesterday glared at her. She knew his name was either Gishen or Sal, but he hadn't been directly addressed, so she wasn't sure which name belonged to him.

"Helas wants you to bathe. Knock on the door three times when you're done. You'll be given food *after* you're done with Luka." He moved to exit, not waiting for her reply, but she stopped him.

"Wait! I, uh…I don't know how to use it," she muttered, frustrated she had to ask her jailor for help over something that should be so simple.

She'd searched the small bathroom earlier after relieving herself to see if she could turn on the corner shower, but she hadn't found any knobs or controls. The toilet had flushed on its own, so she'd swept her hand under the round opening in the ceiling she assumed water would come from. Nothing had happened.

Yellow eyes shot her a cruel, condescending smile. "Stupid human. Did you try standing underneath the faucet? The floor has pressure sensors, and the cleansing unit will activate automatically."

She ground her teeth together and searched her blank mind for a good retort but found none. "Thank you...is it Gishen or Sal?"

He bristled. He must not like the fact that she knew his name. *Good.*

"It's Sal." He shot her another cold smirk. "But the only name you need to be thinking about today is Luka. He's been in a particularly violent rage since yesterday. I'm sure he'll be very excited to meet you."

Alice felt the blood drain from her face. One look at Sal told her he must've seen it too, and she cursed the fact that he knew how his words affected her.

"I'll be waiting outside. Don't take long," he said.

"Well, fuck you too," Alice mumbled, walking to the bathroom and stripping off her jeans and T-shirt.

Seeing the state of the clothing in her hands, she decided if she survived through the day, she'd attempt to wash her clothes at night. She might be caged like an animal, but she didn't have to feel or smell like one.

Cautiously, she placed one foot on the floor of the cleansing unit. Thick white foam poured from the faucet, rather than the water she'd expected. Alice swept her hand under the stream of foam and examined the fizzing substance tickling her skin.

"This must be what passes for a shower around here," she said to herself, noting that the grime covering her hand had vanished wherever the thick froth bubbled.

She stepped into the falling foam, spreading it around so it coated all of her exposed skin. After she was covered, she stepped from underneath the faucet, allowing the fizzy substance to slowly pop and crackle then melt away, leaving her skin clean.

Worst. Shower. Ever.

She did her best to finger-comb her tangled hair, but the drying foam and lack of conditioner made that downright impossible, so she smoothed it as much as she could and then stood frozen, gazing at the cell door. Sal had told her to hurry, but she couldn't seem to command her feet to move. If she didn't go, he'd come in. It was inevitable. She might as well meet her fate with her head held high.

Eventually, she found the courage to pound on the door three times then jumped back when it opened.

Sal studied her appearance. "Did you use the toilet?"

Alice grimaced at the personal question. "That's really none of your business."

Leaning against the door frame, he shrugged. "Suit yourself. There's no toilet in his cell."

She blinked, indignation for Luka roaring through her. "Why… How… Do you expect him to just go on the floor?"

He crossed his arms over his chest defensively. "He spends his evenings in a different cell and is only brought there during the day for testing."

She said nothing but shot him a withering glare. The distraction to her razor-thin nerves was welcome, outrage preferable to hysteria.

He held her glare for a moment, then stood aside, motioning for her to exit the room ahead of him. He didn't move out of the doorway, so she slid by, clinging to the wall as she passed the burly alien.

His large palm wrapped around her upper arm while they walked down the hall, and she had to bite her tongue to keep from complaining.

Anxiety started to crawl up her spine. *Is this my last day on Earth?* A crazed giggle burst from her, and Sal shot her a perplexed look. *Of course it isn't! My last day on Earth was who knows how long ago. This might be my last day on this shitty, damned, godforsaken— Stop. Stop. Calm down. No use falling apart now. Think about something else.*

"Do you know what time it is?" she asked, forcing her voice to sound polite.

He glanced sidelong at her with a scowl. "Why?"

"Because I like to know the time."

He focused ahead of him and was silent for a moment. "You should stop caring about things like that." His words were cruel, but they lacked venom, as if he were giving her hard advice rather than taunting her. All the same, the little bit of hope for normalcy she'd clung to dissolved.

When they reached the room a few doors away, Sal pounded on the metal twice in quick succession. Nausea rolled through her when the door opened and Helas appeared, throwing her a toothy smile. Today he wore another jacket in a lighter shade of yellow. Maybe it was an alien version of a lab coat. *Or maybe he has the worst sense of style in the universe.*

"Thank you, Sal. Please put her in the room," he said, moving out of the doorway.

Sal shoved her unceremoniously into the small cell, less than half the size of hers. In a flash, she hunched over, pulling her arms in protectively and balling her fists. Her eyes flew to the chained man kneeling on the floor only a few feet away. His large arms were shackled behind his back, and his head lolled in front of him. Was he asleep?

"Don't worry," Helas announced. "He's passed out for now. I'll wake him when I get to the control room."

She glanced at Helas, then back to the man. Even slumped, she could tell he was huge. His bare chest and torso were heavily muscled, and although he was kneeling, his head rose to her rib cage. He had to be well over six feet when standing.

Her breathing quickened, and her throat felt like it was constricting. She lunged toward Helas and the door. Luka was too large. What if he broke free?

Helas shoved her to the floor. "You will stay here. He's chained to the wall. If his marks appear, I'll let you out."

Luka grunted in sleep, and she stilled, eyes wide.

"Looks like he's waking up," Helas exclaimed, clapping his hands together. "I'd better get to the control room. I'll be watching." He pointed above the doorway to a small lens mounted on the stone.

Before she could move, the door was closed and locked.

Alice sat perfectly still in the corner of the room for long moments, watching the man and trying to control her breathing. Cold sweat broke out over her body.

He can't get free, she reminded herself, examining the taut chain connecting his shackled wrists to the wall behind him.

When she'd first glimpsed Luka, he'd been completely naked. Now, she was relieved to see, he wore soft, loose pants that hung low on his hips.

Her eyes were drawn to a large bruise running along his rib cage. Anger flared in her again. Had they kicked him? As she scanned his body, she saw his pale tattoos curving around other small cuts and bruises, some almost healed, some fresh.

She began to relax. This abused man, Luka, wasn't her enemy. She needed to remember that. He was a prisoner just like her. *Maybe he isn't as dangerous as Helas made him out to be. They were probably trying to scare me.* Even as she thought this, the memory of Luka snarling as his black eyes bored into her crossed her mind, and her panic resumed.

A loud zap echoed in the small room, making the chains rattle. Luka's body seized, and then he bellowed in pain, struggling to get out of his chains before abruptly stilling.

He turned his head toward her, and through his dark brown tangled hair she saw his eyes focus on her. His pupils were so dilated that she could only make out the faintest hint of icy-blue iris. As she watched, both the whites of his eyes and the iris were enveloped in black.

26

His nostrils flared, and he tried to turn his body more fully toward her. The deep black of his eyes and the wildness of his appearance made him look like something out of a horror film. Alice's throat constricted. She swung her focus to the ground, unable to hold his unnatural gaze.

"That m-means you r-recognize me, right?" Her voice shook with fear even as she tried to keep calm.

Glancing up, she found he'd tilted his head at her like an animal.

She inhaled as deeply as she could, but she couldn't seem to catch her breath.

He started to tug at his hands, rattling the chain. When she scooted farther away, tears blurring her vision, he snarled and began to struggle harder. His muscles strained with the effort, and he never took his eyes off her.

An ominous groan from the metal base the chain was attached to had her tucking her body into a ball. She threw her hands around her head and began to rock.

No, no, no. He was going to break free, and if he had the strength to break free, he'd surely rip her apart, whether he meant to or not.

Tears dripped onto her denim-clad thighs as she waited for the sound of snapping metal, but it never came. With her head still tucked protectively against her hands, she raised her eyes a few inches to see what had happened to Luka.

He was breathing heavily and straining against his chains, but he'd stopped trying to break free. When he saw her face, his brows drew together. He blinked and shook his head like he was attempting to clear it.

Through the curtain of tangled hair, he peered at her again. His eyes were still black, but they looked more aware than they had a moment ago.

"Are you still in there, Luka?" she asked quietly.

His lids narrowed, but he didn't answer.

He could've broken free just then; they both knew it. He'd stopped, though, controlled himself. "Thank you for stopping."

Luka seemed to relax incrementally when she spoke, so between her short breaths, she kept talking.

"How long have you been here? Were you captured, or is holding people hostage normal on this planet?" Unsurprisingly, he didn't answer, but she found talking to him had a calming effect on her too. Her heartbeat slowed to a normal rate, and her breaths grew even.

Judging from the dark matted hair that hung in front of his face, he'd been here a while. She found herself longing to push his hair back and look at him more fully.

Since it appeared to calm him and definitely calmed her, she continued speaking out loud. "Are you not answering because you can't understand me, or because the drug in your system is messing with your mind?" Alice scooted an inch toward him.

For as long as she could remember, Alice had always held a soft spot for injured and broken things. Her mother, along with her friends at work and school, had constantly chided her for being too nice. When she was a child, she remembered walking around their house, looking for bugs to catch and release into the wild. Her mother hated bugs and killed them on sight.

As she got older, and rescuing bugs had turned into rehabilitating small injured animals, Alice had decided she wanted to become a veterinarian. At present, she was putting herself through college by working at a sleazy bar.

If there was ever a creature in more need of help and tenderness than Luka, she couldn't imagine it. She studied him, her heart breaking more as each new injury was revealed.

Even dirtied and bruised, she could tell he was handsome. His shoulders and chest were broad and chiseled. The pearlescent markings she'd seen on Mr. Yellow-Eyes, Sal, and Helas also ran over Luka, but in a different pattern. They were vine-like and curved over his body, delicate against his overall powerful physique. Her eyes followed one particularly beautiful marking as it trailed down his six pack and disappeared beneath his pant line.

Alice gasped, and her gaze darted to the ceiling, her cheeks heating, when she noticed the outline of a huge erection could be seen through his thin pants. Whatever drug they'd given him must really be working.

"Come, female," a deep, rough voice said, startling her.

Goosebumps spread over her skin at his rumbled command, and for a moment, she had the inexplicable urge to do as he said. "Uh, no thanks. I'm good right here," she said, with an awkward chuckle.

"Come!" he commanded, giving his chains a hard, fast tug.

When she still didn't move, he began pulling on his chains with more force. Alice couldn't decide if it was a good thing or bad thing that he seemed to know what he was doing. On the one hand, he was threatening her by showing he'd break his chains if she didn't get closer. On the other, it meant he wasn't completely lost to whatever drug coursed through his system. Luka was still making decisions, and she hoped that meant he had more control over himself than she'd been led to believe.

When the metal gave another low groan, she blurted, "Okay!"

Slowly, she scooted toward him, ready to bolt at any second. When she was within a few feet, she stopped.

He growled low in his throat. "Closer."

Heartbeat pounding furiously, she moved until they were separated by only a foot and waited.

Why did he want her to come to him? So far, he wasn't trying to do anything to her. He just looked her over. His gaze traveled up and down her body, lingering where all men's gazes lingered. She chuckled to herself. *I guess boobs are universally appealing.*

When his stare returned to her face, he attempted to shake the strands of hair out of his eyes fruitlessly.

Without thinking, she reached up and smoothed the dark brown mass back, making sure she didn't pull at any tangles.

The bone structure she uncovered was gorgeous. Dark, heavy brows framed his black eyes. A small white tattoo wound its way from his forehead to his high cheekbone. When she started to pull her hand away, he leaned his cheek into her palm and closed his eyes.

He looked like he was deeply savoring this simple touch, and it made Alice's heart squeeze painfully in her chest. After being locked up for so long, Luka probably needed a little gentleness. Surprise, followed by warmth, spread through her when she heard a rumbling purr emanate from his chest.

"You're just a big, scary cat, aren't you," she whispered.

Eyes flashing open, he turned his mouth toward her hand and gave her lower palm a hot, wet kiss. A jolt of pleasure shot to her core. She pulled her hand away, clutching it to her chest.

He gave a weak growl and leaned toward her as far as he could.

She held up what she hoped was a stern finger. "Nope!" Her breath was shaky as she spoke, and his eyes focused on her waggling finger. "We aren't going to be doing any of that. You're not in the right state of mind, and I don't even know you."

His eyes narrowed at her words, but he did sit back.

She let out a relieved sigh. "Good boy, tiger."

This could work, she thought hopefully.

Luka didn't seem to be able to understand most of what she said, but he could speak a little and backed off when she told him to. Maybe coming in here every day and talking with him wouldn't be so bad.

Oddly, out of the few aliens she'd met so far, Luka made her feel the safest. He was turned on and could get out of his chains at any minute, but he hadn't. Apart from the scalding kiss to her palm, which she could still feel and had liked way too much for her own good, he hadn't done anything too bad to her.

If he thought he was her mate, would he even be protective of her? It'd make sense. On Earth, male animals protected the females. It was instinct. Maybe it was in her best interest to get those marks to show up after all.

Helas had said Luka's mating marks would appear on his hands and wrists. She craned her neck, trying to peek behind him, but his hands were bound too tightly. She'd have to crawl around him in order to get a good look, and she didn't trust him enough to do that yet.

"My name is Alice. Your name is Luka," she said, motioning first to herself, then to him.

He tilted his head again but didn't respond.

"It's okay." She tried to make her voice reassuring, "I can just talk for both of us. I'm good at that."

A low grinding from the door sounded, smothering the calmness she'd been feeling. Alice dashed into the corner when the door to the cell opened, revealing a pleased Helas and Sal.

Luka snarled and began pulling on his chains, struggling toward her.

"Secure him!" Helas barked.

Sal ran forward and attempted to zap Luka with a long metallic stick, but Luka rammed his shoulder into the man's belly. The force of the blow caused his chains to break. Keeping his eyes on Helas and Sal, Luka backed up into the corner in front of Alice.

Is he shielding me?

Finally, back on his feet, Sal retrieved the metal stick from the floor and limped to Luka, his gaze flashing toward Alice momentarily. Had that been fear for her illuminated in his eyes? *Can't be.*

Helas removed a slim silver weapon of his own and began stalking toward them. Luka crouched further, ready to pounce.

"Luka, stop! They're gonna hurt you!" Alice cried from behind him.

When the men were within arm's reach, Luka lunged, using his body weight and legs to land blows on each man. Alice couldn't help but marvel at the strength and skill he was able to access even with his arms tied behind his back.

As he shot his leg out behind him, connecting solidly with Sal's chest, Helas shoved the metal stick into Luka's bruised ribs, making him roar in pain and convulse. Before he could get his bearings, Sal had joined Helas and was shocking him from the other side.

Excruciating seconds passed, then Luka fell to his knees, his eyes glued to Alice's.

"You're going to kill him! Stop!" she screamed, tears running down her cheeks.

When he was lying on the floor, unable to hold himself up, Helas took a small cylinder out of his pocket and sprayed a fine mist in Luka's face. Almost instantly, his body went limp.

"Get her to her cell," Helas said, letting loose a savage kick to Luka's ribs.

As Sal passed him to retrieve her, he looked down at Luka with a sneer.

Alice ran forward, dodging Sal, and pulled at Helas' arm, trying to put distance between him and the motionless Luka, but it was no use. Everyone here was so much stronger than her. She'd always been content with being gangly and just a little too thin, but right now, she detested her slight frame, how weak she was. They could beat him to death, and all she'd be able to do was watch.

Her measly efforts seemed to have some effect, because Helas shrugged her off and turned to exit through the open door. Sal followed, grabbing her roughly by the arm. With a grimace, he dragged her out of the room, down the hall, and to her cell, ignoring her pleas to make sure Luka was alright.

He pushed her through her open cell door, but before releasing her, hissed, "Stop!" Darting a glance over his shoulder, he continued, "You need to be worried about yourself. Follow the rules." He held her stare, inhaling deeply. Before closing the door in her face, he whispered, "You can't help him."

Once alone, Alice's gaze whizzed around unseeing, and salty tears poured down her cheeks. She was furious they'd injured Luka and miserable that she couldn't do anything about it. She felt so helpless…*was* so helpless.

Alice forced herself to ponder Sal's parting words. Was he right?

She began pacing around her room, absently rubbing her palm on her hip. Under the circumstances, Luka had been incredibly controlled, but as soon as he'd gotten free, he'd lost that control. He'd fought without thinking, maybe out of some instinct to protect her, but it'd been stupid. There was no way he could've won in his drugged state. How many more impulsive things would he do? As she thought, her gaze kept slipping toward the wall in the direction of Luka's cell.

Don't think about him! Already she could feel herself caring more about his safety than her own, and in a place like this, that was stupid. She inwardly cursed. She'd jumped into the fray today. How idiotic had that been? There was a difference between standing up for someone and putting yourself in the line of fire. Helas had only flung her away this time, but what if he got angry with her next time and hurt her? She wouldn't put it past him.

If she didn't watch out for herself, both physically and mentally, she wouldn't survive. What would happen to her sanity if she got too attached to Luka, became too invested in his well-being, just to have Helas decide he didn't need Luka anymore?

Sal's words from earlier replayed in her mind: "You should stop caring about things like that."

Nothing was certain here. Not time, not Luka, and not her future. She needed to start doing what she was rarely able to do. She had to try and put herself first, even if it meant being cold and uncaring.

Her head bowed. "Luka doesn't deserve that." Steeling herself and clenching her fists, she attempted to lock down her emotions. "It doesn't matter what he deserves. None of us deserve this. I need to look out for myself, like Mom said." She began pacing and biting her nails. "He probably isn't even a good guy. He protected me, but I'm just an object to him. He doesn't care about what I want."

She knew her words were lies the moment she uttered them. An unwelcome whisper snaked through her mind. *He did care.*

Taking a few deep breaths, she attempted to calm her warring emotions.

She looked down at the palm he'd kissed and felt the telltale flutter of butterflies in her stomach.

Crap.

3

"We were really getting somewhere yesterday." Helas grinned.

Alice frowned at him, then averted her gaze, staring down at her hands resting in her lap. She'd spent another restless night in her cell and was in no mood for Helas' pretentious smiles or chipper attitude.

"If he hadn't been close to breaking his chains, I would've left you alone." Helas raised his hands in mock exasperation. "But I couldn't have him damage you, now could I?"

Damage me? As if she were property. "He didn't hurt me," she said quietly.

The more Alice thought about the events of yesterday, the more conflicted she felt. It'd be better if she turned off her emotions and stopped caring about Luka, but she couldn't seem to do it.

Helas nodded in agreement. "And as long as you do as I say, I won't let him hurt you." He leaned back in his seat and clasped his hands together. "Don't worry, we have upgraded his restraints. They lock and unlock with a fingerprint. He won't be able to break free again."

Alice leveled her gaze on Helas. Disgust roiled within her. "Why Luka? You said you hated mixed species. Is that all there is to it?"

The way Luka had fought off the two men yesterday had been impressive. If he could do that while drugged and bound, she couldn't imagine how difficult it would've been to capture him. Why would they have gone to the trouble if there were other people with mixed heritage around?

Helas' fake smile faded. "You did what I asked yesterday, so I'll answer one question. Is that really the one question you'd like to ask?"

Alice had a million questions. What time was it? Was this what the whole planet was like? How long had it been since she'd been taken? Why couldn't she remember anything after being taken from her work?

Although all of these questions and more burned within her, she couldn't fight the urge to learn more about Luka. "I'd like to know what kind of man he is." Hopefully, Helas would tell her about all the people Luka had killed or little old ladies he'd stolen from. It'd be a hundred times easier not to care if Luka was a terrible person.

Helas wrinkled his bulbous nose. "He used to work with me as a research scientist. We were trying to discover a cure for our species' infertility. He was very motivated, but after finding out about our experiments down here, it seems he was not motivated enough. I had no choice but to lock him up. He was planning on betraying me."

She inwardly groaned. Her gut feeling had been correct. Luka was a victim, and if Helas' story was true, then she also believed Luka must be a good man.

The reason Luka had been taken and locked up was now clear to her. The beatings and forced drug use, on the other hand, told her something different about Helas. The pain that'd been inflicted was unnecessary and had been done from a vindictive, angry place. Helas hadn't taken Luka's betrayal well.

"Curing infertility using a race descended from Clecanians is my organization's primary goal. You humans haven't ventured into space or interbred with any other species. Earth is a perfectly preserved, undiluted, living record of ancestral Clecanian DNA. It's unfortunate that someone with tainted blood happened to be the one to recognize you, but I have to put my distaste aside for the greater good."

"Why do you have to physically beat him and electrocute him? Don't you have a sedative or something that'd work instead?"

"Mixing different drugs with the ones already in his system may cause unwanted reactions or possibly contaminate his samples. I try to use sedatives only when absolutely necessary." He stood and moved to the door, waiting for Alice to follow. "It's time. I'd like you to touch him more today."

Alice rose, gaze fixed on the ground to hide her eagerness. "If you bring me some medical supplies, I'll touch him. He has lots of bruises and cuts that need to be tended to."

He let out a humorless chuckle and turned to face her again. "You aren't in a position to make demands." A wicked grin curved his lips. "He will not be healed. You *will* touch him. If you don't, I'll send a shock through his cuffs. Any pain or suffering he experiences today will be on your head, not mine."

Tears welled behind her eyes again. She focused on controlling her breathing to keep him from seeing how his words affected her.

He stepped through the door, and Alice followed him quietly, walking with her head hung low all the way to Luka's room. She couldn't bear to see Helas' triumphant expression. It was stupid for her to have mentioned healing Luka. Now Helas knew she cared whether the man was hurt or not. She'd shown a weakness to him, and he'd use it to control her.

This is exactly why I should try not to care! I've just made it worse for us both.

His gaze followed her as she moved through the open door of the cell. "Remember, I'll be watching."

Alice shuffled into the dim room, and her eyes locked on Luka's. He was still kneeling and chained, but now instead of his hands being bound behind him, his arms were spread wide. The shackle at each wrist was resting, as if glued, on a new metal plate on the stone wall.

"His chains allowed him to have some freedom, but after yesterday's episode, we decided restricting his movement would be wise." Helas met her disdainful stare. "Magnetic cuffs are less comfortable, but he won't be able to break out of them."

She frowned at the back of his retreating head. *He talks about chaining a man like he's doing him a favor.*

As the door closed behind Helas, she returned her attention to Luka. He tugged on the cuffs weakly and let out a pained groan. Dark, ugly bruises covered his torso, making Alice wince in sympathy. She knelt on the ground in front of him. His eyes weren't black the way they'd been the last time she'd seen them. His pupils were still dilated, but he looked slightly more aware than he had yesterday. He let his gaze roam over her hungrily.

His head snapped up when a loud voice boomed from somewhere in the ceiling. "Touch him, Alice!"

She glanced back to Luka. His whole body had tensed at the sound, and his eyes were wild.

Before she could react to the sudden command, a bolt of electricity shot through Luka's chains, causing him to double over and roar in pain.

Alice cried out and moved toward him. As much as she wanted to disobey Helas, she couldn't allow Luka to suffer. She waited until the electric buzz had faded, then, when she was sure she wouldn't be shocked, she reached out and tentatively placed her hand on his shoulder. Immediately, he leaned into her touch.

Luka glanced up at her, the pain evident on his face. How hard had Helas kicked him yesterday? If his ribs were broken, then seizing up like that must be excruciating.

Alice raised her other hand as well and caressed her fingertips over his bunched shoulders. His hard muscles relaxed under her touch, and he began purring. She smiled and whispered, "I've never heard a man purr before."

As she rubbed his shoulders more firmly, her musings from the night before came back to her. Luka was very strong. Stronger than any man she'd ever met. What if she was able to get these shackles off him? He'd already proven to be protective of her. He could help them escape.

Smoothing back his hair, she looked into his eyes. "I'm so sorry they're hurting you. Maybe we can get out of here together."

I need a plan.

Alice allowed her hands to gently run over Luka's arm until she reached his wrist. With her back to the camera, she hid his shackle from view and examined it. She'd never picked a lock before, but maybe she could learn.

"Shit," she whispered under her breath. The thick metal circling his wrist didn't have a keyhole, or any opening for that matter. *Fingerprint. I forgot.*

She was just about to move away to examine the metal plate itself when he snagged her hand with his own restrained one. She glanced at him, startled, but saw his eyes were focused on their interlaced fingers. He gently flexed and relaxed his fingers, running them against hers. His eyes slid closed, and his purring intensified.

Butterflies began flapping around in her stomach, and she attempted to tug her hand away. Luka's eyes shot open, and he looked at her with brows drawn. He squeezed her hand softly then released it.

Even drugged, he was being more of a gentleman than a lot of guys she knew. He wanted to touch her, that much was obvious, but he also released her when she asked him to.

Moving to kneel in front of him again, she reached up and wound her arms around his neck, embracing him in a hug. Luka's body tightened, and he pulled at the metal around his wrists, trying to get closer to her.

He nuzzled his head against her neck, giving her goosebumps.

Focus, Alice! she scolded.

This closeness was probably giving him the wrong idea, but she needed to talk to him without the guards hearing. In his ear, she whispered, "Can you understand me?"

He said nothing, but stilled when she spoke, so she continued, keeping her voice low in case Helas could hear her as well as see her. "I need your help to break out of here. Can you understand me?"

Again, he said nothing but instead began running his hot mouth over the sensitive flesh just below her ear.

Her plan to whisper to him and work out an escape together had failed, but Luka's soft touches were helping to melt away her stress, so she hesitated a moment too long before pulling away. Heat flooded her core when his head dipped to press a hot kiss to the junction of her neck and shoulder.

Alice felt his chest expand with his inhale, and a low, rumbling growl escaped him. She jerked away from him and found his eyes were black again. He strained toward her.

Even after everything she'd been through, Alice still found herself drawn to this man, and a fleeting urge to kiss him overwhelmed her.

Embarrassment and shame made her flush, and she quickly scooted away from him. He was restrained and loaded up with drugs to make him horny. Of course he wouldn't want her to kiss him. He probably didn't truly want to kiss her either and was only touching her that way because he couldn't help himself.

"I'm sorry," she said, hugging her knees to her chest.

Luka glanced at his manacled wrist, then back to her. He released a frustrated breath and closed his eyes in concentration. In a broken voice, he grated, "Come back...Alice."

Hope soared in her. Alice quickly scooted toward Luka and placed a hand on his knee. "You remembered my name! Can you understand me?"

He said nothing. Frustration overwhelmed her. *Still,* she thought, *if he's aware enough to remember my name, then maybe he's fighting off whatever these meds are doing.*

Helas had told her he was a scientist. If that was true, it meant Luka had to be at least a little smart. If he could break out of this haze, then maybe he'd have a clear enough mind to think of a way out of here.

A new plan formed in her mind. Distancing herself from him had caused him to talk, so now it was time for some positive reinforcement.

She removed her hand from his leg, earning a low growl from him, then pointed to him. "Luka."

He stared at the hand she'd just removed from his knee.

Alice waved a hand in front of his face to get his attention. She pointed to her mouth and said, "Luka," then to his mouth and said, "Luka," and finally, she hovered her hand over his knee.

He followed her movements with his eyes. She pointed to his mouth again and waited.

He blinked a few times but finally repeated, "Luka."

She cheered quietly, balling her fist in success before placing her hand on his knee again.

Luka purred quietly, and his gaze shot from her face to her hand. He raised his eyes to the ceiling in thought, then looked at her again and said, "Luka."

She laughed lightly. "You are a smart guy." She placed her left palm on his other knee.

Shifting in his seat, he chanted, "Luka, Luka, Luka."

Alice actually laughed out loud. "Okay, tiger, but we need to get you to say some new words." She placed her hand in front of his face. "Hand."

He looked at it for a moment and rattled his hands securely locked in place and repeated, "Hand."

Alice eyed Luka, wondering where to touch him as a reward. An odd combination of guilt and arousal assailed her as she examined his half-naked body. Even beaten and bruised, he was still magnificent. His broad, hard chest was covered in tanned, smooth skin. The small white tattoos that ran over his body begged for her to trace them with her finger.

"Hand," he repeated firmly.

She reached out and traced a small curving tattoo that ran along his chiseled abs. Luka began purring again, and the tightly corded muscles of his stomach flexed under her touch.

As she followed the tattoo with her finger lower and lower, she heard a groan escape him. When she reached his pant line, she gasped and pulled her hand back. A massive erection was clearly visible through his thin pants. She looked up at him and found his eyes were black again.

In a low, rumbling voice, he growled, "Hand."

She let out a nervous, high-pitched laugh. "Yeah, maybe if you come up with an escape plan, I'll give you a *hand*."

Alice swallowed and forced her gaze to remain fixed anywhere but his lap. It must be torture to feel constantly aroused and have no way of relieving yourself.

She looked up at him miserably, hoping he could understand the position she was in. "I'm sorry, Luka. If you weren't drugged and you asked me to fool around with you, I would without a second thought, believe me."

A booming, gravelly voice echoed from the ceiling again. "Resume touching him."

Alice reached out quickly, worried Luka would be shocked again if she didn't. "Also, they're watching." She began massaging his arms and shoulders, shooting a glare at the camera. "Having your arms stretched like this must hurt a lot."

Luka's eyes closed, and he groaned as she rubbed his sore muscles.

Alice thought back to the voice that'd just commanded her to touch him. It hadn't been Helas' voice. Had he left? Where did he go if he wasn't always here?

4

Everything was a haze. Disorganized thoughts came to him in bits and pieces, but he couldn't hold on to any of them. Every time he tried, an overwhelming lust blanketed his mind, leaving a dull, painful ache in his body.

Soft hands running over his burning skin was his only respite. He could sense her. Hear her. His mate.

While she was near him, he found he could focus. When she spoke, her voice felt like cool honey dripping down his aching body.

He couldn't understand her words, but when he spoke, she touched him, so he focused all of his energy on pushing back the dark cloud of lust that wiped away his senses and identifying the items she indicated. *Hand. Door. Alice.*

She was touching his shoulders now. Running her soft palms over his back. He tried to remember where he was, how he'd gotten here, but every time he did, his mind would devolve until a single thought remained. *Take her. Take your mate.*

He focused on her hands and her soft words. *Concentrate on her.*

She was his lifeline. The only thing connecting him to his unclouded mind.

He felt cold metal circling his wrists. Although he couldn't remember how they'd gotten there or why he was restrained, he was thankful. If his hands were free, he wasn't sure he'd be able to control himself.

5

∞

Alice had been keeping track of her days the only way she could without a clock, by counting her visits with Luka. Assuming she'd been brought to him every day, she'd counted two weeks in this place.

She looked forward to those visits more than she could say. Luka not only offered her comfort, with his deep voice and familiar icy-blue eyes, but he also made her feel like she wasn't alone. Whenever nightmares plagued her or when her anxiety rebounded out of nowhere, Alice knew she could wrap her arms around his neck the next day and he'd soothe her. She'd cried into his shoulder a handful of times now, becoming less and less embarrassed about it the more it happened. He'd nuzzle her neck as she wept and lightly purr, somehow knowing, even through his haze, how to make her feel better.

After her visits, Sal, Gishen, or Helas would bring her back to her cell, where food would be waiting. If Helas brought her back, as he had today, he'd speak to her about the day's progress and occasionally, depending on his mood, answer some of her questions.

Today, Helas sat quietly in the corner, arms crossed, watching Alice as she ate. His normally unreadable mask of innocent charm was gone. Instead, his lips were thinned, and his brow was furrowed in thought. Something had happened to cause this change in his controlled demeanor, but she had no idea what.

Alice ate her food slowly, forcing herself to swallow the bland mush she'd been given every day. Either people on this planet only ate once per day, or they were only feeding her once per day.

"He doesn't have his marks yet," Helas said, more to the room at large than her.

Unsure what to say, she blinked.

"Do you have any thoughts on this?" he asked with narrowed eyes.

Taken aback, she sat up a little straighter. He'd never asked for her opinion about anything before. *Asshole must really be at a loss.*

The same question had run through her mind every night. Why *hadn't* Luka's marks appeared? The most logical conclusion was that she wasn't his mate.

Anxiety took hold every time she pondered this. The possibility she could be Luka's mate was the one valuable thing about her and was, consequently, the only thing protecting her right now. If Helas came to this conclusion as well, her visits with Luka would likely change dramatically.

Although she fought with herself constantly to not become attached to Luka, to not care for him, the simple truth was, she did. She was just too weak to keep her heart locked away from someone who'd done nothing wrong. He was her rock, and although they could barely speak to each other, she'd grown to feel a connection to him that she'd never felt with anybody else.

"Well," she began, trying to think of a good answer, "maybe it would help if he could speak to me. He doesn't seem to always understand me. Also, I'm always touching him, right? Maybe if his hands were free and he could touch me a little, it'd work."

"You'd be fine with him touching you? The smell of your fear may be detrimental," Helas replied, eyeing Alice.

The smell of my fear? She pondered his words but decided not to question them. "As long as I have space to get away if I need to." She tried to make her voice casual, but the thought of Luka wrapping his strong arms around her and hugging her back made her heart pick up speed.

"He can't understand you because we haven't updated his translator. Your translator has been programmed with our language, but his has not been programmed with yours."

"I have a translator?" Alice blurted. She'd wondered why she could converse with Helas, Gishen, and Sal, but she'd just assumed they'd learned English.

Helas cocked his head at her like she was child who'd said something funny. "What did you think? We all spoke your language on *our* planet?"

Alice flushed, feeling stupid for not coming to this conclusion earlier.

Helas waved a hand dismissively. "Mating is instinctual. There's no need for you to speak with him, and while drugged, I doubt he'd be much of a conversationalist anyway."

"Then maybe you should stop giving him drugs." She could guess what his response to this idea would be. Helas' main goal may be to gauge whether she and Luka could procreate, but his sick side project of purifying Luka's genes seemed like something of an obsession.

"No, I think we can do better than that." He leaned toward her. "He will be unclothed tomorrow. You will touch all of him."

Alice jerked her head back as though slapped.

Her outrage at touching a drugged, chained man had weakened with each passing day. While it once had felt intrusive to run her hands over his chest, she now knew the contact helped them both stay grounded. Even so, she argued with herself endlessly that what she was doing was okay because of their circumstances and because he wanted her to. She remained unconvinced.

Now that he knew a few words, he would often string simple sentences together. *"Alice hand arm."* But there were boundaries. It may seem like he wanted her, but unless they were out of this place and he was no longer intoxicated, she couldn't assume anything.

Touching him…down there…would be wrong, and being told to do it by Helas turned her stomach. There had to be an alternative. "I think it might be better to sleep in there or in here with him."

Instead of yelling at her and threatening Luka as he normally did when she openly disagreed, he considered her offer.

"You said proximity might do it. I'm only with him a few hours per day. If you brought him in here and let him stay, they might appear," she quickly added, hoping he'd agree with her reasoning.

Helas nodded slowly, staring at the ceiling of her room. "We'll need to make alterations to your room so chains can be attached."

Alice let herself relax a fraction.

"Let me be honest with you, Alice." He glared at her with unmasked impatience. "One of my colleagues messed up recently. The same ship you were transported on was carrying another female. She escaped six months ago and was found by citizens who don't share our opinions. Luckily, she didn't know who took her, but her sudden appearance caused quite a stir. The situation was resolved, and all personnel who had information about this location were killed, but we're running out of time here. Powerful people are aware of our existence and every day my colleagues grow more nervous about using these facilities. I need for these experiments to work."

Another female? Six months ago? Alice's heartbeat picked up speed. That nagging feeling that she was missing time wasn't just in her head. But how? If they'd been transported on the same ship, why couldn't she remember whole months of time? She didn't know how long she'd been down here for certain, but she knew it hadn't been months. A ringing sounded in her ears.

"What happened to me during those six months?" The only thing that kept her narrowing vision from fading completely was the knowledge that her body had appeared untouched when she'd examined it upon arrival. Surely she'd know if something was done to her. Right?

As usual Helas ignored her question. "I'll allow you to try out your idea for two days." Helas' stare hardened. "If they haven't appeared by then, I'll strip you bare, double his medication, and throw him in this room with you unchained."

Fear sliced through her at his words. Luka had been mostly in control of himself, but there were still rare moments when his eyes turned black and his muscles bulged that frightened her. In those moments, she was reminded she didn't really know him or how much control he had.

Oddly enough, she was almost thankful. Those glimpses of darkness allowed her to keep part of her heart locked away from Luka. Alice knew how it felt to be betrayed by someone you thought you could trust implicitly.

"If I were you, I'd do everything in my power to make his marks appear before then." Helas held her terrified stare for long moments before finally rising. "You'll need to come with me so they can alter your room," he said casually, as if his previous threats weren't hanging in the air.

Hate was something Alice didn't have much experience with. She always tried to find the good in people, even those who were seemingly awful.

Everyone has a past. Something that's shaped who they are, she'd tell herself whenever she met an unlikeable person. She even felt a twinge of sympathy for Sal and Gishen. What had happened in their lives to make them so heartless?

There was no excuse for Helas, however. He had a rotten, black soul, and Alice was able to say with certainty that she hated the man. She hated his small, cold eyes and his fake charming smile. She even hated the faint scent of rubbing alcohol that clung to him like a sterile mist.

"How many women have you taken from Earth? How many mixed Clecanians have you kept drugged down here? And why can't I remember six months of my life?" she asked, simmering with indignant rage.

In an instant, Helas' passive coolness transformed into anger. He'd crossed the room and roughly grabbed her by the nape before she had time to react. Her hands latched onto his, trying to pry them away.

Through gritted teeth, he said, "Why don't we go see the other test subjects right now?"

He dragged her out of the room, his cold fingers gripping the back of her neck. She let out a pained cry as he pushed her down the hall ahead of him.

A roar erupted from Luka's room.

Helas wrenched her head close to his own. "Looks like your friend can smell your fear."

She tried to keep quiet, knowing Luka was likely struggling to break out of his cuffs.

Helas guided her through a network of identical-looking hallways until they finally reached a large brass door. He raised his palm and placed it on the metal surface. A buzz sounded, and then the heavy door swung open, revealing a control room of sorts.

Both Gishen and Sal turned in their chairs, but neither looked surprised. She noticed Sal's fingers momentarily clench the arms of his chair.

In front of her were dozens of holographic screens displaying video from different parts of the facility. A wave of hopelessness ran through her. She'd done what she'd thought was solid recon a few days ago, counting all the cameras she'd seen between her room and Luka's, but looking at the screens before her, she realized she'd underestimated the security of this place. Her stomach turned when she saw a group of video images showing women, all alone in rooms similar to hers.

"Sal, I need you to come with me." He released his painful hold on her neck, and she scrambled away. "Gishen, stay here and watch her. We need to make some changes to her room."

The winged man, Gishen, nodded solemnly and stood. After Sal and Helas departed, he grabbed her by the arm and plopped her into the vacant seat. "Stay here," he rasped.

Too mesmerized by the multitude of images in front of her, she didn't respond. At least five human women were visible. Some were meandering around their rooms. A couple of them were sitting quietly, and one was huddled on her bed, head in her hands, crying.

As she examined the small woman, Alice felt like she was having an out-of-body experience. It was as though she were watching herself on that screen. She ground her teeth together and balled her fists. She was tired of feeling like that woman. Vulnerable and scared. These monsters needed to be stopped.

Alice scanned the other displays, looking for Luka. Interestingly, most of the hallways and small rooms on the screens were vacant and bare. In fact, other than Sal, Helas, and the women, she didn't see any other people. Were these three captors the only ones standing between her and freedom?

At last she found Luka, and a weight settled in her stomach. He was pulling at his wrists savagely, trying to break free. Blood trickled down his forearms from where the shackles cut into his flesh. She needed to get to him, to calm him down.

"Gishen, can I use the speaker to calm Luka down? He's going to hurt himself," she pleaded.

Gishen glanced at her with his ugly red eyes and sneered. "Sure."

He reached for a button amid hundreds on a panel in front of him, and she leaned forward uncertainly, readying to speak.

When he pressed on the button, she saw Luka's body convulse as electricity zapped him. Gishen laughed cruelly. "Oops. Wrong button."

Alice felt the tears she so hated beginning to well once again. "You're an asshole."

"I've never heard that term, but it didn't sound like a compliment," he said, shoving his thumb onto the button and holding it down.

Luka was already limp and hanging from his wrists when the electricity coursed through him again, causing him to seize violently. Alice dashed out of her seat and attempted to pull Gishen's large form away from the panel.

Her efforts intensified his laughing, and he flung her to the floor, seeming to draw pleasure from her screams of protest.

Alice swung her gaze around, trying to find anything she could use to stop him. Out of the corner of her eye, she saw the glint of metal. Crawling quickly over to Sal's chair, she found his abandoned prod.

Pressing the button at the base as she'd seen Helas and Sal do, she shoved the electrified poker into the juncture of Gishen's wings.

He released a high-pitched shriek. His wings jerked as though trying to flap and dislodge the poker, but the electricity restricted his movements, allowing Alice's firm hold on the weapon to stay in place until he finally fell limp.

Shit! Shit! Shit!

She needed to act quickly before he woke up. She searched the room, finding a pair of magnetic cuffs. She opened and closed them experimentally, but they wouldn't latch closed.

They need a fingerprint. Her eyes darted to the still form of Gishen.

A metallic cabinet, which she prayed was as heavy as it looked, sat against a wall a few feet from Gishen, slumped and unmoving in his chair. From that position, his wrist wouldn't quite reach the cabinet, and she needed to attach the cuff to metal.

Knowing she'd never be able to drag his heavy form, she inched toward him, holding the poker at the ready.

Using all her strength in one quick motion, she pushed on his chest, causing the chair he was sitting in to tip backward. Gishen tumbled to the floor near the wall and groaned.

Alice dashed to his sprawled form, wrapped one of his large palms around the cuff, and manipulated his limp hand into cuffing his wrist. She did the same with his opposite wrist, then raised both his arms to the metal cabinet behind him. An electronic buzz sounded.

When she stepped away, his cuffs stayed glued to the wall. She let out a triumphant laugh, and quickly stepped out of reach. Once he woke, he'd be very mad, and although he no longer had use of his hands, she was sure his legs and wings would be just as deadly.

Adrenaline still pumping through her, she stepped to the control area and searched for the screen showing Luka's room. Her heart beat wildly in her chest when she saw his body was still limp.

A groan behind her told her Gishen was rousing.

Alice turned to face him, holding the zapping rod in her hand. *I can do this. I can do this.*

In order for her escape attempt to work, she needed Luka free. Somewhere on that control panel was a button that could free him, but she had no idea which one would do it. If she pressed the wrong one, she might end up electrocuting him again, and who knew how much more he could take before his heart gave out.

Alice needed Gishen to tell her what to do, and she knew he wouldn't do it willingly. Her grip tightened on her weapon. He'd need some motivation. As Gishen slowly began to rouse, she fought back nausea.

Even after everything these beings had done to her, she still felt apprehension about causing them pain. When she'd electrocuted him before, she'd done it to stop him from hurting Luka. Now, he was tied up and helpless. What she did next wouldn't be in self-defense or in immediate defense of another. It'd be straight-up torture, and she didn't know if she could go through with it.

Gishen let out a sharp cry of pain while attempting to sit up, and her grip loosened. Her breaths grew erratic while she tried to contain her pathetic tears.

"You miserable piece of Earth trash!" Gishen barked, pulling at his restrained wrists and flaring his wings. The cabinet shook with his struggle but stayed in position.

"I'm sorry," she squeaked, jumping back when he swept his long, talon-tipped wing across the floor, almost hitting her legs. "I n-n-need you to tell me how to release Luka and the other prisoners."

Gishen stilled, then his whole body began to shake. A cackle erupted out of him. "Absolutely! Let me get right on that!"

Heat rose on her neck. She was standing over a chained man wielding an electric poker, and even *he* knew she was weak. "Don't make me use this," she said softly, holding up the poker to illustrate her point.

"Go ahead!" he challenged, leaning back against the cold metal casually. "I'll never release that disgusting traitor or those Earth breeders."

Breeders?

She stiffened and glanced back to the video of the small woman who was still crying silently on her bed. Alice felt a part of her being shift. Rage like she'd never known overpowered her.

Those women had been taken from their homes. They'd been taken from their partners, and possibly their children, and this asshole had the nerve to refer to them as breeders? She straightened and turned her cold stare to Gishen. To her delight, she noticed the smallest flash of concern cross his face.

All of the hesitation and worry she'd been feeling dissolved. The only thing standing in the way of those women's freedom and enslavement was her, and she'd die before she failed them.

The strong, sure voice that poured out of her as she spoke was unfamiliar even to herself. "You'll tell me how to free them, or I'll shove this poker into your crotch so hard that you'll never *breed* again."

Gishen hesitated for a moment but paled when she gently placed the rod between his thighs and let her finger hover over the on button.

She made sure to enunciate each word as she said, "Which button releases his cuffs?"

***

The smell of burnt hair and flesh floated up to his nostrils, rousing him. Luka tried to rise on his knees to support his body. His shoulders ached from carrying the weight of his unconscious form.

Panic made him shoot upright, all of the pain suddenly a distant memory. Something was wrong, but his damned clouded mind couldn't remember what it was. Dread knotted itself in his gut as he renewed his struggle against the immovable magnetic cuffs.

The memory of a sharp scream played in his mind.

My mate! Someone had hurt his female. He'd gone mad with fury when the bitter scent of her fear had reached him.

Although still feeling like he was wading through deep, murky water to sort his thoughts, his goals became clearer. He needed to get free, to get to her.

He glanced desperately at his cuffs. How long had he been unconscious? Where had she gone? He couldn't scent her anymore.

Just as he reared back, readying to break his thumb by wrenching it through the metal, the cuffs opened and his arms dropped. He stared in bewilderment at his wrists for a moment. His skin was burned and blistered, but he could make out the faint outline of blue bands circling his wrists. Somewhere deep down he recognized the marks for what they were.

He stood, feeling his strength return to him tenfold.

Just then, a feminine voice echoed from the ceiling, making his shaft go hard. He couldn't understand most of her words, but he recognized his mate's voice. Two words she'd recited stood out: "Luka" and "door."

He stumbled toward the door, staring fixedly at the ceiling, and felt his focus waver. Hearing her voice caused every nerve within him to tingle.

Once again, he tried to break through his blocked mind and find the rational, logical part of himself that'd allow him to find her.

An electric buzz at the door drew his attention. He tested the handle, finding it unlocked. When he stepped into the hallway, he could still scent the faint trace of her fear from earlier.

Possessiveness and fury roared through his senses, overtaking him until all he wanted to do was kill, fuck, and protect.

6

Alice ran down yet another white hallway, glancing at the messy directions she'd scrawled on her palm, the electric prod clutched in her other hand.

Before freeing Luka, she'd made sure that Helas and Sal weren't wandering the halls. Fortunately for her, they'd both been in her room, attaching Luka's new chains to her ceiling. When she'd learned she could remotely lock and unlock doors, Alice had taken the opportunity to seal them in her cell.

In addition to freeing Luka, she'd spoken to each of the Earth women. They'd been yelling questions to the camera, but she couldn't hear them, so she'd tried to explain their situation quickly and told them she'd be unlocking their doors and then attempting to find them.

Alice had brought up a map of the facility and directed the women on how to get to a meeting place. Gishen hadn't initially been very forthcoming with the map, explaining that none existed and he could give her directions instead. After a few quick electric zaps to his balls, he'd changed his tune.

Luckily, Alice was able to use the map to see that most of the women were being held in cells near each other. Hope swelled in her even more when she saw they were all located on the same floor.

She ran through a large set of doors and then down an enormous spiral staircase.

All she had to do now was find the women on the floor below her and then follow the route she'd memorized to freedom. Or at least the possibility of freedom. She still had no idea what they would do once they made it outside. Run in a random direction? Wait for Luka's drugs to wear off and hope he could help?

She paused, glancing up the stairs. *Where is he?*

Alice was a reasonable woman and she knew there was no way for Luka to know where she was, but she didn't have time to look for him. If it was a competition between him and the abducted women, she had to choose the women.

An unchained Luka had at least a fighting chance against their captors, but the women wouldn't. Still, her heart ached thinking she might escape and leave him trapped here.

If I get out and you don't, I'll find help. I swear it.

She turned, running down the stairs once again. She needed to hang onto her newfound strength and not worry about her confused, drugged alien.

Bolting through the lower level doors, she looked around in a panic. *Where are they?*

The women were supposed to meet her here. Had something happened to them? Had they gotten lost?

Just as Alice began moving in the direction of their cells, she heard quick footsteps down a hall to her right.

Peeking around the corner, her heart leapt when she saw a small group of frightened-looking women running toward her.

A beautiful raven-haired woman near the front of the group greeted her. "Alice?"

"Yeah." Alice panted, overwhelmed with joy at the sight of other humans.

"Sorry for the holdup. I'm Vanessa." She pointed behind her toward the small woman Alice had seen crying. "We don't think she speaks English, and she didn't understand what you were saying. We had to practically drag her here."

Alice nodded. "Thanks for making sure she came with you." Moving back to the door, she said, "We have to get going. I've only seen three men who work here, but there might be more. The exit is on the top floor."

Vanessa, along with a few others, nodded, moving to follow Alice toward the spiral staircase.

On their dash up the stairs, she only allowed herself a swift glance at the door leading to the floor with her and Luka's cells.

When they finally reached the top floor, she glanced around the deserted hallway nervously. Seeing no sign of life, she waved her hand behind her, motioning for the women to follow toward the large, silver door at the end of the hallway.

According to the map, this was the way out. She had no idea what she'd find beyond that door, but its proximity made confidence at their escape flourish.

Ice ran through her veins when Helas and Sal stepped from the shadows and blocked the door.

Alice skidded to a halt, causing some women to collide into her.

Helas gave a cruel, humorless laugh when they turned back in the direction of the staircase, only to find Gishen blocking their path.

How the hell did they all get free?

"Did you really think you could escape?" Helas taunted with a sneer. "A group of weak females?"

A loud, familiar roar sounded nearby, and a wicked grin spread over her face. "Not just a group of females."

The women behind Alice cried out when Luka's enraged yell sounded from near the top of the stairway. Alice looked over her shoulder to see a marvelous and terrifying sight. Luka was standing at the end of the hallway, eyes pitch-black. His naked chest rose and fell rapidly, and his gaze was fixed on her.

Without looking away, he grabbed a cowering Gishen by his throat and threw him into the wall like a ragdoll.

From in front of her, she heard Sal whisper, "He has his markings. We need to get out of here!"

Alice glanced down to his wrists in surprise and saw that there were, in fact, blue markings she hadn't noticed before around his bloody wrists and fingers, and new black markings stretching along his forearms.

She turned to Helas, hoping to see the same fear he'd been instilling in her light up his eyes. Instead, she witnessed his cowardice.

Using an electric prod, he stunned Sal and then bolted out of the main door. She turned to Luka, hoping she could make him understand. "Luka! Get Helas!" She pointed to the still-open doorway Helas had just run through. He couldn't get away with this. Even if they all managed to break free and get to safety, it'd be a hollow victory if Helas wasn't punished.

Luka looked toward her finger, then the door, and curled his lip. He sprinted, running faster than anyone she'd ever seen, and caught the handle before the door fully closed.

Seemingly the bravest of the group, Vanessa leaned toward Alice. "Geez, he's fast. Do you know him? Is he a white hat or black hat?"

"It's a long story, but I think we can trust him. They drugged him, so he might be a little out of it right now," Alice quickly explained before motioning for the women to follow her to the door.

Vanessa gave a derisive snort from behind her. "Yeah, well, it seems like you have him whipped, drugged and all."

Alice scowled, feeling heat spread over her cheeks, but chose not to think about how true that statement might be. If his marks had appeared, that meant Luka thought of her as his mate. Assuming what she'd learned about mates from Helas was true, she'd have to deal with a drugged, newly mated male very soon. She could only hope he'd remain "whipped" after the threat of danger finally passed.

Alice held the electric prod in front of her when they reached the exit, where a crumpled, unmoving Sal still laid.

Keeping one eye on him, she pulled at the door handle. *Locked!*

Alice felt like an idiot for not thinking of this before. *Of course it'd be locked! It's a top-secret facility—why would they leave the front door open?*

"What now?" an older woman with flowing white hair asked from behind her.

Alice's mind raced. She tried to think through how they unlocked her door, but most of the time she was inside her cell when they locked and unlocked it, and Luka's room had always been open when they'd brought her to him. She didn't remember seeing any keys.

"The control room," she muttered.

"What?" said Vanessa.

"Sorry, I've gotten used to talking to myself these days. Help me move this guy and put his hand on the door."

A few of the women eyed the man warily and didn't move. Others rushed over to help.

As they hoisted Sal's heavy weight, Alice explained, "When they took me to the control room today, that guy Helas put his palm on the door to open it. Like a scan."

Sweat beaded Alice's forehead as they tried to keep the man's hand in place on the door while hefting his upper body awkwardly.

The women cheered when the door buzzed and unlocked. A sudden groan from Sal made the women drop him and jump away. His head hit the tiled floor with a loud crack. Vanessa and Alice looked at each other with matching guilty grimaces before Vanessa finally shrugged. "Well, he was a bad guy anyway, right?"

Alice nodded, still feeling a twinge of guilt, and held the door open so the women could pass through in front of her.

When the last woman was out and only Alice remained, she took one final look at the pristine white hallway. The world that awaited her beyond these doors would be alien and probably terrifying, but at least she'd never have to see these hallways again.

On the opposite side of the doors, Alice found a set of stairs leading up to an opened hatch. Moonlight poured in, illuminating the steps as she climbed.

Taking her first deep breath of alien air, she stepped into the night.

The women were gathered together, looking around their surroundings, the wonder evident on their faces. Some gazed into the black sky, heavily littered with stars and unfamiliar galaxies. Others craned their necks to take in the jagged mountains behind them.

The hatch they'd just emerged from was in a small clearing. The air out here was damp and slightly warm, much like a rainforest. Behind them, sharp mountains rose diagonally. Their peaks sliced through wispy translucent clouds and stood out starkly against two large rising moons, one of which had a faint ring around it.

To their left, the ground sloped and transformed into a dense forest. To their right, the ground inclined and carved a trail through the rocky mountain pass. Immediately in front of them, the land stretched out flat and bare as far as the eye could see.

Alice squinted, trying to make out any signs of civilization.

A short, young woman with perfectly highlighted hair said, "Well, Toto, I've a feeling—"

"If you say that line right now, I swear to God..." interrupted a tall, slim woman with a surly expression.

The shorter woman held up her hands and tipped her head in mock surrender.

The sound of shuffling to their left made them all jump then tense. From the corner of her eye, Alice glimpsed the small woman with salon-quality hair crouched in a fighting stance. *At least one of us knows what we're doing.*

Alice stood still, her breath trapped in her throat as they waited to see the cause of the noise.

Luka appeared from around the base of the mountain, an unconscious Helas in tow.

Alice clapped her hand over her mouth when she took in the swollen, bloody state of Helas' face. Her worry ebbed slightly after seeing the shallow rise and fall of the unconscious man's chest.

Luka dragged the pitiful-looking man to Alice and placed him at her feet, then stared fixedly at her.

Vanessa chimed in from behind her, "Well, I guess he knows how to fetch."

A few of the women snickered, but Alice shot her a glare.

Vanessa walked forward and spoke to Luka directly. "Hey, big guy." She waved in front of him, trying to shift his focus off Alice. "Do you know how to get out of here?"

Luka didn't so much as glance at the gorgeous woman addressing him. His gaze stayed solidly on Alice, and she felt herself wilt under his intense stare.

"Is there something wrong with—Hey!" Vanessa yelled as Luka suddenly hoisted Alice over his shoulder.

Before Alice had regained a breath to argue, Luka was running back toward the base of the mountain he'd emerged from. He was so fast that the few women who tried to chase after them fell behind almost immediately.

After a few minutes of pounding on his back and demanding to be returned to the group, Luka stopped.

Rather than set her down quickly, he angled her so that she slid down his front, rubbing every inch of him as she went until she was on her feet, still firmly tucked against his body.

Oh, shit.

Her knees wobbled. Luka was free, he thought she was his mate, and the drugs must still be in his system, because she could feel his massive erection prodding her stomach.

She pushed away from him, glancing around. Behind her, a smooth rock wall stretched up, forming the base of the mountain. A trickle of water wound its way down the surface of the rock and pooled in a glittering pond to her left.

Luka moved toward her again, a purr starting in his chest. When she took another step back, he furrowed his brows in confusion.

Alice felt a moment's relief. He'd brought her to a romantic spot away from everyone else, and it was clear what he wanted. During all of their other encounters, she'd been the one in charge. Luka had been chained and at her mercy. Now that he was free, she wondered what he'd do. Her heartbeat increased, and her fingers tingled as though electrified. Was it fear or anticipation making her breath hitch?

She allowed her gaze to run down his body. With him standing at his full height before her, she marveled at just how big he was. She took another step back, and this time, instead of looking confused, a seductive, predatory grin spread over his face, sending shivers down her spine.

He hunched slightly, as though preparing to run.

Heat flooded her core at the thought of him chasing her down, but she tried to ignore it. "Luka, this isn't a game. Stop, okay?" Her voice was shaky as she continued to back away.

He stalked closer. His nostrils flared, and a small growl escaped him. Her breasts felt heavy and sensitive under her thin T-shirt.

She thought back to Helas' earlier comment about scenting her fear. Luka had smelled her before, and she realized he could probably scent more than just her fear.

Alice threw her hands up in the air. "I know what you smell, but I can't control that, dammit!"

For weeks she'd craved Luka's touch. She'd told herself that if circumstances were different, she'd have jumped his bones on day one, but she couldn't get past his state of mind. She wanted him, badly, but she needed to know that he actually desired her. Not because he was drugged or because of his mating marks, but because of who she was.

She looked around, trying to figure out how to escape, but he'd boxed her in. On one side of her was the curve of the mountain; on the other was the pond.

Maybe if I jump in there, he won't be able to smell me.

Before she could decide what to do, she felt her back hit the smooth, warm rock face.

Luka's smile widened, and the sight made her sigh in appreciation. She hadn't seen his smile before. He'd never had a reason to. But the vision of Luka happy was almost enough to make her stop fighting.

He closed the last few feet between them before she could blink. Instinctively, she put her hands on his chest, intending to push him away.

Luka laid his palms on top of her hands and gripped her wrists, guiding them up to rest on his shoulders. A loud purr rumbled through him, and she found herself frozen in place.

Slowly, he traced his hands down her arms, seeming to savor every inch of her skin.

Her breaths came in short pants. She wanted to pull away, knew she should, but just couldn't bring herself to do it.

When his hands continued roaming down over her waist, he leaned in and began softly kissing her neck.

Goosebumps broke out over her skin when she felt his tongue glide over her collar bone. "Luka, we...we really... You shouldn't..." Alice found she had trouble holding on to her thoughts as his hands traveled further down her body.

He grazed her hips, then slid his hands behind her to rest on her ass.

This was going too far. Alice needed to put a stop to it.

Just as she was beginning to pull back, Luka firmly kneaded her ass, shoving her lower body tightly against his. He nipped at her neck with his vibrating mouth, and Alice's eyes slid shut. She let out a wanton moan, feeling heat pool between her thighs.

Luka gripped her ass, lifting her until she wrapped her legs around his waist. She leaned forward for a kiss, but he jerked away.

Raising a hand to her chin, he moved her face until she was looking directly into his eyes. He groaned and rocked his hips against her core, tearing a moan from her throat.

His wrist caught her eye before he lowered his hand. Angry red burns and charred skin circled the flesh where his shackles had been. His light, shining marks had turned black near his wrist and faded to gray then back to white as they traveled up his muscular forearm. Seeing his injuries reminded her of what they'd just escaped and stirred her from the aroused fog she was in.

"Luka, I don't want it to be like this." She pushed away from him again, squirming to be let down.

At first, he made no move to drop her, but then his whole body stiffened, and he set her on her feet. Turning away, he snarled viciously.

Alice craned her neck to see what had upset him and shrieked to find a large man pointing what looked like a gun at Luka.

Luka advanced, running toward the man at full speed. The click of a trigger was followed by the faint sound of a whizzing object.

Alice looked on in horror as Luka slumped to the ground, mere feet from his attacker.

When he was sure Luka was no longer moving, the man straightened, lowering his weapon. "Sorry about that. Didn't mean to scare you," he said with a lopsided grin. "The females down the hill told me Luka had been drugged, and he carried you off, so I thought he may need to be sedated."

Alice couldn't seem to find her words. Why was this man here? Was he going to drag her back to the underground facility?

"I can see you're starting to panic," he said, holding up his hands. "But I'm part of the rescue team. I'm Izzo." He gave a small kick to Luka's shin. "And this idiot is my brother."

7

∾

"Brother?" Alice glanced between the two men, not sure whether to scream or relax. He was large like Luka, and some of their features were similar. The man standing before her could be related to Luka, but that didn't mean she should trust him.

Izzo began hefting his brother's limp body onto his shoulders with impressive ease.

"Wait!" she yelled, not knowing what to do but not sure she should be allowing this stranger to take Luka away.

Izzo froze, brows raised in question.

She took a few involuntary steps forward. The sight of Luka lying there motionless made her thoughts tangle together and her heart pound furiously. "How did you find us?" If this was his brother, why hadn't he come to rescue him earlier?

"He implanted a tracker on himself somewhere, but I guess it didn't work underground. When you guys escaped, it lit up, so we came to find him."

It was a reasonable explanation, but she still couldn't decide whether to believe him. Her gut told her he was telling the truth, but she'd learned the hard way that her gut was a lying bitch who couldn't be believed. "How did you get here so fast?"

"They must have had some kind of scrambler or jammer set up in the cruiser when they brought him here because his signal cut out about 20 miles away. We've been searching around that area in shifts for weeks. When the tracker started pinging again, we were already close."

Alice narrowed her eyes. "How do I know I can trust you?"

Izzo shifted the dead weight on his shoulders and scrunched his face in thought.

His eyes lit up. "Pizz-za!"

"Pizz-za? You mean pizza?" Alice repeated dumbly, trying to understand how this alien knew what pizza was and why the mention of it would make him trustworthy.

Izzo nodded happily, displaying perfect white teeth. "I know another Earth female, and she told me one of the things she misses the most from Earth is pizza. She also said pickles and ice cream, and…most of the things she's mentioned are food, come to think of it."

Alice focused her gaze on Luka and nibbled on her thumbnail. His back rose and fell with his breathing.

He looks fine, and no bad guy would stand around waiting for me to give the all-clear, right?

It was very unlikely that any woman being held against their will would've mentioned something as inane as pizza to an alien unless they really were comfortable with them.

"Okay, let's go." She nodded, relaxing slightly when he began to walk away, his focus no longer on her.

He moved down the winding path, and as she followed him, she thought about the woman who'd told Izzo about Earth food. "Izzo, the woman you mentioned," Alice panted, trying to keep up with his long strides. "Is she pregnant?"

Izzo spun toward her, Luka's dangling arm flying wide and almost hitting her in the face. "How did... No... Uh...what makes you think that?"

Alice shrugged, wondering what the fuss was about. "Those aren't really normal foods to miss, but some pregnant women crave things like that. Except for pizza, I guess. You can always crave pizza," she amended.

Izzo ground his jaw and grimaced. "Oh, I didn't know that." He lifted the corner of his mouth in an uncomfortable smile. "Mind not telling anyone about that? She's keeping it quiet for now."

Given the events of the last few weeks, hearing about a secret pregnancy of an Earth woman made Alice uncomfortable. She nodded in agreement anyway and resumed biting her nails.

They rounded the corner, and Alice saw the group of women waiting near the now-closed hatch. One man stood still and watched the uneasy women, while another carried a struggling Helas to a pair of silver floating ovals a few feet away.

Her steps faltered, and she studied the objects with wide eyes. A panel slid open on one, revealing seating. *Must be their version of a car.*

How were things so large and seemingly heavy floating like that? She clicked her tongue. *Why am I surprised? They can literally fly through space, or float in space, or whatever you do in space. Hovercars are probably nothing to write home about.*

A trill of excitement rang through her. For the last few weeks, her life had been so bleak. The fact that she was on an alien planet had been lamentable because of the circumstances, but now, hopefully, she was going to see another side of this world. The wondrous side. The side that had flying cars. Her enthusiasm faded when her eyes focused on Luka being loaded into the second floating vehicle.

Many people would kill for the chance to explore an alien planet, yet all she really wanted to see was the light blue of Luka's eyes, clear and aware.

Movement out of the corner of her eye caught her attention. Vanessa urgently motioned for her to join the other women. Alice hurried over, keeping one eye on Luka.

She slowed as she neared the group, noticing a few women were gone. Only three of the five remained. "Where did the other two go?" she whispered.

Vanessa glanced around, making sure they weren't being overheard. "They left before these dudes got here. When that guy carried you off, they got freaked out and decided to take their chances in the woods instead."

Alice glanced at the tree line of the dense forest.

Who in their right mind would choose a black alien forest? Are they trying to be eaten by the Predator? She stifled the judgmental thought and reminded herself that she had no idea where they were coming from. For all she knew, those women had suffered much worse than she had.

"Should we tell the men?" Alice glanced at the remaining women, trying to recall who was missing. The ill-tempered woman and the small one who'd snapped into a fighter's stance at the first sign of danger were both gone. Alice found it odd they'd decided to go off together, considering their short-tempered exchange earlier.

The older woman with long, flowing white hair spoke in a slow, smooth voice. "They've had so many choices taken away from them. If they want to leave, they should be allowed. It's their choice."

Alice found that she agreed with the woman. Personally, she thought it was stupid to run out into the dark forest of an alien planet, but it wasn't her choice. It was theirs. Still, she couldn't stand the thought of them alone out there. "What if we learn more about this place and the people before deciding anything? If we all agree those girls would be safer with us than in the woods, we tell someone."

Vanessa and the silky-voiced woman nodded, but the small woman Alice had watched cry in her room only darted glances between the three. Alice recalled Vanessa saying she hadn't thought the woman spoke English. She only knew a little Spanish and French. Maybe the girl would know one of those languages.

"¿Hablas español? Parlez-vous français?" she said, doing her best with her accent.

The small woman knitted her brows and stepped toward Alice. She pointed over to Izzo, standing near the floating vehicle that was apparently being used to transport Sal, Gishen, and Helas. In perfect English, she said, "What's going on? Can we trust them?" Her voice was loud, as if she was unable to monitor her volume.

Alice quickly raised and lowered her hands and mouthed, *"Too loud."*

The small woman clapped a hand over her mouth, tears making her amber eyes glassy, and shot a fearful glance toward Izzo. He stood watching her with his head tilted. When a tear slid down her cheek, his brows drew together.

Vanessa scooted next to her and began to run her hands up and down the terrified woman's bare arms. Her forehead crinkled in concern as she looked between Alice and the silver-haired woman. "She must not be able to hear us."

Alice caught the girl's attention and, making sure to exaggerate her mouth movements, she slowly said, "What's your name?"

"Daisy," she whispered, almost too quietly for Alice to hear. "The things that took me hurt my ears. I haven't been able to hear anything for a few days now."

Alice nodded and patted Daisy on the hand, then turned her attention to the last unnamed member of the group. It was clear this woman was older than the rest of the group, but she'd aged so gracefully. Her tanned face and laugh lines told stories of being happy and being in the sun.

"Rita," she intoned with a warm smile.

They all straightened when they saw Izzo walking over to them.

"We're ready to head out now." He addressed the group, but his eyes kept flashing toward Daisy.

"Where are we going?" Vanessa asked, stepping in front of Daisy, who was clearly uncomfortable with his lingering gaze.

Izzo frowned. "Gishen, Sal, and Helas will be taken to prison, and you'll be escorted to The Pearl Temple."

"What about Luka?" Alice asked a little too urgently.

Vanessa smirked at her then turned back to Izzo, waiting for an answer.

He looked confused by her question but said, "He'll ride with us, and then I'll bring him back home. We need to get the drug out of his system and figure out what happened." He pointed to the second floating vehicle. "We'll take that cruiser with him, but don't worry, he won't wake up."

"But—" she started, intending to explain that she wasn't afraid of Luka, but Izzo was already heading away.

The women in the group didn't move but instead looked to her. She flushed.

Are they waiting to see what I do?

Alice had never been a leader before, but it seemed as though her show of bravery earlier had earned her the respect of these women.

Chin lifted, she walked over to the floating machine and found Izzo already seated inside, Luka slumped in a corner to his left. Alice frowned as she sat across from Luka rather than next to him.

Daisy sat next to her, keeping her head down and her gaze averted from Izzo, who continued to stare at her. The man was so enthralled with the quiet girl that he hadn't even seemed to notice Luka's mating marks. Or maybe he had noticed and didn't care. It was possible Helas had lied about how rare they were.

When all of the women were loaded into the vehicle, the door slid closed. Everyone except Izzo tensed.

He glanced around with a nervous smile. Attempting to lighten the mood, he held out his hand to Alice, palm up. "I was told this is a polite greeting for Earthlings."

Alice glanced at his upturned palm and tried to figure out what he meant. With a chuckle, she realized what the human woman he'd mentioned before must've told him. Tentatively, she took his large palm and turned it to the side, then grasped it with her own and shook his hand.

Izzo's cheeks reddened. "Oops."

Both Vanessa and Rita shook his outstretched hand when he offered it. When he held it out to Daisy, Alice could see him hold his breath.

"It's nice to meet you," Izzo murmured.

Daisy's eyes were still trained in her lap, and when she made no move to shake his hand, he looked to Alice in confusion.

When did I become the human-alien mediator?

"Her hearing's been damaged. I'm not sure how," Alice explained while softly nudging Daisy. "She can't hear you."

Daisy looked up to her then toward Izzo's outstretched hand.

Alice reached over and squeezed her arm with an encouraging nod. She couldn't imagine how much more difficult and terrifying this whole situation would be if she couldn't hear. At least she'd been able to speak to Helas and understand that she was on an alien planet. How much did Daisy understand about what had happened to her?

The fear shone on her face, but Daisy lifted her hand to Izzo's anyway. Their eyes locked as he clasped her hand in his much-larger one and shook slowly.

Everyone's eyes widened as a low purr sounded from Izzo.

Vanessa and Rita began to giggle. Daisy glanced at the laughing women and then quickly snatched her hand back, blushing profusely.

"You can freakin' purr?" Vanessa blurted between restrained laughter.

Izzo let his hand fall to his side but looked unashamed while he dreamily muttered, "Sorry."

Listening to Rita and Vanessa laugh made warmth spread through her and her eyes glaze with tears. The cab of the cruiser was filled with a lightness she never thought she'd experience again. Vanessa let out a small snort, which only made her and Rita laugh harder. Even Daisy was now looking around the cab with a smile, though she continued to avoid Izzo's avid stare.

During the rest of the ride, Izzo spoke endlessly of their city and the place they were going to now, called The Pearl Temple, but she'd only been half listening. Her eyes and thoughts kept straying to Luka, still unconscious in the corner. Would he be as chatty as his brother was when the drugs finally wore off?

Her gaze traveled down to the bloody, burned skin around his wrists, and her fingers twitched. Having been able to touch and console him at her leisure for the past few weeks, she wasn't surprised to feel the ache to hold his hand and whisper comforting words in his ear.

Was it wrong for her not to want to bring up his marks to Izzo yet? If she brought them up, she'd have to describe the events leading to his marks appearing, and she wanted to hang on to the happiness she felt just a little while longer before reliving that nightmare. Keeping it to herself also made her feel more connected to Luka. As if they shared something special and private.

She felt subtle anxiety start to creep around the periphery of her thoughts. Although she'd done her best not to become too attached to Luka, she knew she was. Even now, the idea of being separated from him made her skin tingle with panic.

A knot tightened in her stomach, then another, and another as thought after thought ran through her mind.

What if he wakes up and is angry with me for making his marks appear? What if he never wants to see me again? Worse yet, what if he doesn't turn out to be the person I think he is?

Alice had been in a lot of bad relationships in the past. Not just romantic ones, either. People seemed to think that because she was a nice person, they could walk all over her. And the sad truth was, she let them. Last year, after her piece-of-shit boyfriend, Jeff, cheated on her for the third time, she'd yelled and cried, but his response had reduced her to ash. The words replayed in her mind now: *"Why don't you leave me, then?"*

Why hadn't she left him after the first time she'd caught him cheating? Because she had a bleeding heart, that's why. His tearful apologies, excuses, and promises had pulled at her heartstrings.

It was ridiculous, but she already felt closer to Luka than she ever had to Jeff. What if Luka turned out to be just as bad or worse? She couldn't imagine he was, but what did she really know? They'd never even had a real conversation.

Stop it! You're spiraling. She blinked away her unshed tears and tried to focus on something positive. These were all what-ifs, and there was no point being upset about them now.

A thought popped into her mind. "Izzo. Do you know what time it is?"

He glanced away from Vanessa, who'd been grilling him endlessly for the past five minutes. "Uh, yeah." Reaching over, he touched an innocuous part of the cruiser wall. A display full of alien symbols popped up. "It's six before prime."

Alice sighed a pent-up breath and slumped in her seat. She crossed one arm over her stomach and began biting her nails again. *Of course it is.*

8

From the name "The Pearl Temple," Alice had been expecting to be taken to a white marble-columned building on a hill, where they'd sequester her with other unwed women. Looking at the scene before her made it clear she hadn't been listening to Izzo at all.

The word *temple* must just be an odd translation of this place because, to her eyes, she could see nothing resembling a temple.

After walking through a towering arched gateway and seeing their new home for the first time, the women had all stopped in their tracks. A shallow body of water, thousands of feet wide in every direction, sprawled out before them. Although expansive, the lake somehow looked quaint, like a koi pond in a giant's garden.

The two moons, now closer to each other in the night sky, illuminated hundreds of floating blossoms on the water. Some of the pale pink and yellow floating flowers were small enough to fit in the palm of Alice's hand. Others were as large as a car. But they all seemed to angle themselves toward the soft moonlight.

They must be where that wonderful smell comes from. The delicate scent of sweet flowers hung in the heavy air even without a breeze. Though not as humid as the mountain had been, the air here was still thick and warm.

Glowing creatures in various shades of blue and green were visible just under the surface of the water, swimming lazily and illuminating the thick stems of the watery plants. Their long, eel-like bodies twisted and curved as they swam, delicate ribbons of light trailing behind them.

Hypnotized, Alice followed the progress of one creature as it moved, but it disappeared near the center of the lake where a large, domed building stood. *The water must be deeper there.*

The round building rose from the middle of the lake like the center of a giant lotus with smaller buildings jutting from its sides like petals. Scattered over the rest of the large lake, hundreds of small, pale homes sat floating on the water. The white sides of the structures shone with a faintly iridescent shimmer, similar to that of a pearl.

Is that where the name comes from?

"Why is this place called The Pearl Temple, Izzo? On Earth, 'temple' means a place for worship, not housing." When he didn't answer, Alice glanced over and found Izzo watching Daisy take in her surroundings with a contented smile. She stifled a grin. "Izzo?"

With raised brows, he focused on Alice, seeming surprised to find her there. "Oh, uh…" He cleared his throat. "Centuries ago, this lake was used for spiritual purposes. People would come here to pray or meditate or think. The bilom," he said, pointing at a glowing creature swimming nearby, "are the guardians of Pearl Lake, so when they built here, they named it The Pearl Temple. The bilom are electric and sting anyone who gets in the water."

Rita leaned over, watching a bilom flit back and forth. "But why Pearl? They don't look like pearls."

Izzo shrugged. "I don't know what pearls are on your planet. Our translators do what they can, but they aren't always perfect. The bilom produce little stones instead of eggs on occasion. We call them pearls."

"That's pretty close to what Earth pearls are, I guess. Not the same kind of animal, but hey—" Vanessa smiled, propping her hand on her hip "—who's to say one animal's trash isn't as good as another animal's trash when it comes to making jewelry? Do you guys gather the pearls?"

"There's another lake deep in mountains where the majority of bilom live that some people harvest pearls from, but it's difficult to do without disturbing their environment too much." A grin spread over Izzo's face. "It used to be if a person wanted to court someone, they'd try and prove their love by diving into the water and retrieving a pearl. If they weren't stung, it was meant to be."

An image of Luka slowly emerging from the lake in a sopping-wet white shirt, with a satchel of pearls in hand, popped into her mind. *Well, hello, Mr. Darcy.*

"Do people ever do that anymore?" Alice asked.

Izzo laughed and shook his head. "Males do sometimes. On a dare, if they're foolish or young. But they all get stung nowadays. Usually, they're carted off to the medbay without so much as a pebble."

"That's interesting and all..." Vanessa squinted, scanning the water. "But how are we supposed to get around? Is there a boat?"

"You need a pass. Oh, look," he said, pointing across the water, "there she is now. Metli will give you passes and escort you over."

A woman wearing a bright purple coat emerged from the central building and walked to the edge of the floating green platform that surrounded the structure. Then, she stepped off. As one, Alice, Vanessa, Rita, and Daisy took a step forward, eyes straining to see what the woman was walking on. From this distance, it appeared as if she were stepping on the water itself. But that couldn't be right.

Each foot closer Metli came, the more certain Alice was that there was a platform under her feet, but it seemed to be clear.

"I have to take Luka home now." Izzo's eyes lingered on Daisy. Motioning to Metli, only a short distance away now, he added, "She'll take you to meet the Queen."

"What Queen?"

"Is the whole world ruled by a queen?"

"What's Metli's job?"

Rita and Vanessa shot questions at Izzo while Daisy glanced between them all with raised brows, but all Alice could concentrate on was the fact that the only thing in this world that made her feel safe was about to be taken away from her.

"Maybe I should go with you, in case Luka wakes up." She glanced past Izzo to the open door of the vehicle, visible through the archway.

Izzo glanced between her and Luka, slumped in the cab, finally noticing her interest in his brother. "I assumed you wouldn't want to see him after…after the way I found you two together. Did you spend a lot of time with him in the facility?"

Alice decided it wouldn't do any harm to answer honestly. "Yes. Helas was trying to get him to recognize me as his mate."

Izzo's jaw slackened, and his posture straightened even more. He squinted toward Luka, then did a double-take. He mouthed a few unintelligible words then finally focused back to Alice. "He recognized you? His marks appeared?"

She nodded, hoping he'd decide to bring her along.

The woman finally appeared next to them. She was shorter than Alice by a foot at least, but somehow still appeared willowy. It was as if someone had placed a model's limbs on a petite woman's body. She wore a magenta coat that ballooned out around her neck and shoulders, then cinched at her small waist and ended mid-thigh. On her legs, she wore one piece of matte-black material that acted as both her shoes and pants.

Although odd, the whole ensemble worked. Metli's strange frame and coiffed gray-blue hair, along with the stiff geometric clothing, made her look like she'd stepped out of a high fashion spread from a science fiction magazine.

"Hello, human females. My name is Metli. Please take a token and two of these pads." She raised her arms, hands outstretched, and Alice flinched. Metli's long arms extended toward them just a little too far, and the subtle alien difference in anatomy scratched at Alice's senses as if she'd just recalled the sound of nails on a chalkboard.

In one hand, Metli held four small purple tokens. In the other was a small stack of long, oval translucent pads.

Alice peered at the unfamiliar alien woman, then turned pleading eyes toward Izzo.

He crinkled his forehead and shook his head slowly. "It'd be dangerous for him to wake up in this state with you around. It makes sense now that he tried to attack me earlier. I thought it was just because he was drugged, but if he's newly mated, he'll be a little more vicious than normal. Stronger too. It'd be better if you stayed away."

Alice had the urge to sprint to the cruiser and barricade herself inside like a stubborn child, but what Izzo said made sense. Her shoulders slumped, and she nodded. There was no way to be sure how much he'd remember anyway. A sharp pain clenched in her gut. He may not even want her there.

Izzo walked over to Metli, who was waiting patiently. "Please let the Queen know Luka's mating marks have appeared."

Metli raised her delicate smoky-blue brows in surprise and followed Izzo's nod toward Alice.

His eyes lingered on Daisy when he said, "I'll see you all again very soon. Have a good night."

Alice watched as Izzo walked away and disappeared into the cruiser. Blue markings on a battered wrist was her last glimpse of Luka before the cruiser door slid closed.

Vanessa approached and handed her a thin metallic purple token and a pair of squishy oval pads. "You're going to have to tell me more about that later," she whispered, glancing up at her knowingly.

"The token will register you in the Temple system and allow you to traverse the lake. Place it on your wrist." Metli displayed her inner wrist, on which the token seemed to be stuck. "Then place the pads on the soles of your feet." She lifted her foot, which was longer than it should've been, considering her frame, and pointed to her own translucent green pad. "Then follow me. Our Queen is very anxious to speak with you."

Alice placed the ovals on the soles of her feet, the solid gel-like substance somehow sticking easily to her Converse, and then experimentally shifted her weight around. Vanessa and Rita both did the same, then Rita helped Daisy to attach hers.

Alice frowned as she watched Daisy; the dark-haired girl's intelligent eyes were flashing around, taking in everything.

Apart from a few tears, Daisy hadn't complained or raged or anything. She'd taken her sudden hearing loss in stride and had adapted so well that Alice had almost forgotten she couldn't hear. If she were in Daisy's shoes, she'd have pulled someone aside and asked them to mouth every single thing being said.

Damn, that girl is a trooper!

Once all four women had attached their shoe pads, they examined the token, likely thinking the same thing as Alice. It was one thing to stick something to your shoe, but quite another to willingly attach a piece of alien tech to your skin.

They all peered at her expectantly. A million thoughts of what could happen ran through her mind, but instead of showing the others her anxiety, she decided to be brave and take a leap of faith.

Closing her eyes and clenching her jaw, she held the token against her wrist. The metal was warm against her delicate skin, but the jab of pain or searing burn she expected never came. She started to pull back the token, ready to explain to Metli that hers was defective, but it didn't move. She pulled a little harder, stretching her skin until finally it released with a pop. Pushing it back again, she felt the familiar warmth, and when she let go, it stayed in place.

Alice gave a thumbs up and puffed her chest with a sense of pride as the three other women attached their tokens to their arms. She'd never been the one people turned to for leadership. They constantly came to her with their problems, that was for sure, but there was always a lack of respect. When she had a group project due, she'd always be the one to do the work but was never the group's leader. At Molly's, she often went above and beyond to make sure the tables were cleaned and bussed, even though she was also a bartender. Yet it was Trent, her coworker who sat on a barstool most of the time, who'd been promoted to manager.

"Follow me, please." Metli turned and began walking on the water again, heading toward the domed central building.

Alice, Vanessa, Rita, and Daisy stood perched on the edge of the lake, not sure how they were supposed to cross the water.

When they didn't follow, Metli paused and turned back.

"How are you walking on water?" Alice asked.

"Oh, I am so sorry. I didn't think to explain," she said, quickly returning to meet them at the shoreline. "If you're holding that coin, a platform will appear under your feet as you walk, see?"

Now that Metli was near and they could examine the water more closely, they could see that a clear flat platform rose to just above the surface of the water under wherever Metli hovered her foot.

"How does that work?" Vanessa asked, stepping onto her own platform in awe.

"I'm not sure." Metli shrugged, eyes flashing back toward the building anxiously.

I guess it's not good to keep the Queen waiting.

One by one, they stepped onto the water and slowly trailed behind Metli, the gel on their shoes gripping the smooth material of the platform. Alice could see Metli's barely contained annoyance shining in her eyes whenever she had to stop and wait for them to slowly catch up.

Although the walkway was probably as ordinary as an Earth sidewalk, Alice and the others walked on it as though traversing black ice. She chuckled as she imagined what they must look like to observers, walking on tiptoes with their arms outstretched like the solid surface was a tightrope.

When they finally reached the speckled green platform circling the domed building and its offshoot buildings, they released a collective sigh.

Moving more quickly and with more agitation than before, Metli ushered them through the large curved sliding doors of the largest building, down a curved hallway, and into an interior room.

About a dozen women of various shapes, sizes, and ethnicities, were milling around the large room. Some were talking to each other quietly, and others were sprawled on low couches or plush chairs. As Alice's group entered, all faces turned to them. Some of the women broke out in smiles and walked over to greet them.

Humans. Alice couldn't be sure, because so many of the aliens she'd met looked similar to her, but she had a primal feeling in her bones that these women were human.

Dazed, she accepted hugs and handshakes from a few of them and nodded politely as they told her their names, which she promptly forgot.

After a few minutes of greetings went by, a regal-looking woman with a deeply lined face who hadn't yet moved to meet them rose from her seat.

She wore a high-collared, long, plain purple dress that complemented her pale lavender eyes. Although simple, especially in comparison to Metli's garb, her clothing was tailored to perfection and exuded an air of no-nonsense sophistication. The woman looked old in the same way a pyramid or castle might. She was strong and powerful and the sign of age only enhanced that aura.

"Please have a seat." She motioned to the many chairs and couches surrounding her. When she spoke, her words seem to dominate the room, even though her voice wasn't raised. *This must be the Queen.*

Alice looked around at the faces of the new women near her. They all seemed content. Not happy, but not unhappy, either. It gave Alice hope that perhaps this place wouldn't be that bad.

After the women were all seated, the Queen spoke again. "I am Queen of this city, Tremanta. Located on the planet of Clecania."

So, there were other kings or queens in different cities? Why hadn't the woman given her name? Was she just supposed to call her Queen?

Vanessa began to speak, but the Queen held up her hand, silencing her. Vanessa clamped her mouth shut and crossed her legs in annoyance.

"We have very sensitive matters to discuss." She looked to Metli. "You may secure the room now."

A cheerful blonde next to her leaned in and said, "Oh, I love this part. It's so cool."

Alice had only a moment to ponder what the woman was referring to when the whole room began to move.

She glanced out of the windows lining the right side of the room and saw they were beginning to sink. Her initial shock and fear were squashed when she peered around to the calm faces of the other women. It was obvious they'd done this before without drowning.

As the building continued to sink lower into the water, Alice saw Daisy rise and cross to a large curved window, placing her hand on the glass.

It was as if they were in a submarine, looking out into the ocean, but here they were gazing upon a whole new kind of underwater world. Neon bilom swam around smaller, gently glowing creatures that resembled flowing golden balls of ribbon, illuminating the various underwater plants and the pale ground.

The room finally settled on the lake floor, and the Queen spoke again. "I'm sure you are all very tired. You have been through so much, and I can't imagine that you could take much more, but I would like you to try and listen." The Queen's eyes strayed to Daisy, still staring out the window.

Alice got up and guided Daisy back to their seats. Unsure how to address an alien Queen, Alice said, "Ma'am, this is Daisy. Something happened when she was taken that damaged her hearing."

The Queen nodded, appearing unfazed by the new information. "We will make sure to repair her hearing tomorrow. I will meet with her again privately to convey the information from today."

Alice glanced from the Queen to Daisy, and her heart swelled for the girl. If it were true...

She tried to mime and mouth the information that they might be able to return her ability to hear soon, but Daisy just looked confused.

Alice sat and decided she'd find a piece of paper and write it down for her later.

"All of the females in this room, save myself and Metli, are humans who were illegally taken from Earth," the Queen began once Alice's attention had returned to her. "All but the four of you—" she pointed at Alice, Vanessa, Rita, and Daisy "—were rescued a little more than five months ago when one of the Insurgents' locations was discovered."

"Insurgents?" Rita interjected.

The Queens eyes rested on Rita. "Although they haven't formally named their organization, we have begun calling the group who took you Insurgents." She scanned the room again. "A month prior to that, a human female named Jade was found. She had escaped her abductor and made it to our city of Tremanta. At the time, I had my suspicions about the possibility that a group, rather than an individual, had been illegally kidnapping females in the hopes of finding a cure for our procreation problem."

"What kind of problem?" Vanessa questioned.

Metli glared at the woman briefly, and Alice wondered whether the Queen was normally interrupted or questioned. Perhaps she was being lenient with them because they were alien and unfamiliar with the customs here. Metli did not look as forgiving.

Alice decided to answer Vanessa. "Apparently the men outnumber the women twenty to one, and they are slowly going extinct. Helas' group...I mean, the Insurgents...were trying to find a race descended from Clecanians to see if they could get us pregnant and solve the problem."

After she was done explaining, both Rita and Vanessa's faces were pale.

Vanessa spoke first. "We're... Humans are Clecanian?"

"I guess so. Didn't Helas explain why you were taken?" Alice questioned, recalling her many conversations with him over the weeks.

The women shook their heads slowly, confusion clear in their expressions.

"If they wanted women for reproduction, why would they have taken me? I'm not exactly a spring chicken," Rita said, the normally velvet quality of her voice altered. "I'd only been down there for a few days before we escaped."

Vanessa nodded, as did Daisy, who'd been focused on their mouths, likely attempting to read lips.

"Us too. We were brought in at the same time, only a few days ago," said Vanessa.

The Queen spoke then, drawing Alice's attention. "How did you come to learn this? Did Helas speak with you openly?"

Alice shrugged. "Not completely openly, no, but he was attempting to make Luka recognize me as his mate, so he did talk to me sometimes. I think he was trying to make sure I cooperated."

The bubbly blonde sitting next to Alice spoke excitedly. "Did he recognize you? Oh, it's so romantic, don't you think? The idea of mates." She caught the eye of a brunette with startling gray eyes nearby and smiled knowingly. "I'm definitely going to participate in the ceremony next time it happens." Looking back to Alice, she added, "The guys here are sooo hot."

Vanessa now huffed out an annoyed breath and spoke directly to the Queen, causing Metli to bristle. "Mates? Ceremony? Can you please explain?"

"In Tremanta, females who wish to find a male to marry for three months participate in the ceremony. When Jade first arrived, I required her to participate, as well. Initially, she was averse to the idea, but she came to care for her husband. He recognized her as his mate, and they have chosen to remain together."

The Queen paused, taking a seat. "When a Clecanian finds their true mate, they will want to be with them until death. It is a physical, mental, and instinctual event that has been lost to us for some time. There has not been news of a newly mated pair for centuries. However, it seems that human females are awakening our people's mating instincts once again."

Helas had explained mates to Alice, but she hadn't grasped the weight of matehood until now. Did that mean Luka would want to be with her forever? Her heart leapt into her throat at the idea.

The Queen's face became serious. "The news of Theo and now Luka recognizing their true mates must be kept secret until we decide how to proceed. Jade and Theo have been in hiding for months now, claiming their absence is a traditional Earthling custom." She looked into each of the women's eyes, willing them to take her words to heart. "If word got out that humans can be recognized as mates, I feel your world, Earth, would be in danger. Clecanians of all genders would flock to your planet, hoping to find their mate, and unless the laws change very rapidly, they would be doing so illegally."

A flash of weariness crossed the Queen's face. "Most of our people are good, law-abiding citizens, but I worry the allure of a mate may cause some to ignore our laws and take humans by force."

It was curious that the Queen wasn't mentioning the incredible news that Jade was pregnant. The fact that Earth women could become pregnant and possibly solve their extinction issue was even more reason for the Clecanians to venture to Earth looking for partners, but the Queen hadn't made this point. Did she not know? Or was she keeping it to herself? Izzo had said that Jade wanted to keep it secret.

Rising, the Queen pinned Alice with her stare. "Metli will be available to answer any more questions you have. I have other business I must get to. Alice, would you please join me?"

Alice blinked for a moment, then realized the Queen had, in fact, been addressing her. Vanessa's curious gaze met hers before Alice rose to join the Queen, who'd retreated through a door on the far side of the room.

She rushed over to Rita and Vanessa and leaned in. "Make sure to ask about how we get Daisy's hearing fixed, and also I'd appreciate it if they have a spare watch or something that I could have. My head is all messed up from being underground."

Vanessa nodded. "I'll get to that, but first I need to figure out when we're going to be able to get out of here. Hopefully, the next ship to Earth is soon."

Alice hurried away, averting her gaze from a glaring Metli.

Go back to Earth?

It sounded so obvious when Vanessa said it. They'd been taken against their will; it made sense that they'd be returned. But was that what she wanted? There were so many possibilities here. Alice felt like she'd finally grown into who she was supposed to be. Brave, respected, and confident— mostly confident, anyway. On Earth, she was just a quiet, older-than-her-peers college student with mountains of debt, no family, and a crappy job. Here, she was the woman who'd just broken seven people out of a secret facility and was about to have a meeting with a Queen. And one other problem— Luka was here.

The room the Queen led her into was dark and almost windowless. A round section of glass in the ceiling allowed a beam of refracted light to dimly illuminate two comfortable chairs in the middle of the small room.

The Queen sat in one and waited patiently as Alice sat in the other.

Without pretense, the Queen said, "I need you to tell me everything you remember since your abduction."

Alice considered the powerful woman before her. Mere weeks ago, she'd have wilted under the intense, confident gaze of a person like this, but not anymore. She refused. "I'll tell you everything I know if you agree to answer my questions."

Her chin rose, and she stared down at Alice for long moments, but her gaze was more curious and assessing than angry. Alice waited until finally the Queen gave a tight nod. Mini fireworks erupted in Alice's mind, and she silently patted herself on the back.

As she recounted everything she could remember from the previous weeks, the Queen listened silently, never interrupting or asking questions. When she tried to delicately describe her interactions with Luka, she felt her face flush.

"And then that's when Izzo brought us here," she finished.

The Queen looked skyward for a moment, her eyes darting back and forth, working through all of the information Alice had provided. "You said Helas believed they were running out of time."

Alice nodded. "Yes, he said when they...you found Jade, they had to make progress more quickly."

"That is quite distressing," the Queen said with pursed lips.

Alice thought all of Helas' actions were distressing. Why was this one so bad?

Before she could ask, the Queen explained, "If what we have learned from your escape along with Jade's escape, is true, then there are many Insurgent facilities all over our world, all working toward similar goals." The Queen spoke to Alice but seemed to look through her. "To find a descendant species to procreate with and to eliminate hybrids entirely.

"Izzo informed me you discovered Jade's secret."

She already knows about Jade's pregnancy.

"We have been keeping the discovery of human females and the pregnancy of Jade very quiet, but..." The Queen's eyes flashed with concern, the first real glimpse of emotion Alice had seen from the woman. "What will the Insurgents do to the countless humans they are currently holding when they discover their theory has proved successful, and what will they attempt to do to all the Clecanians with mixed ancestry?"

Alice's jaw slackened as she realized what the Queen was getting at. If the Insurgents were attempting to find a descended race that could successfully procreate, then their work was done. Her blood ran cold. They'd no longer need to hold the human women captive, but that didn't mean they'd release them.

What would they do to all of the illegally obtained humans, and God knows what other species, being held in those facilities?

"I can see from your expression you understand the gravity of this situation."

Alice could only manage to shoot the Queen a pained look.

"In the coming days, I would like to meet with a select few humans and Clecanians to come up with a plan. Would you be willing to join us?"

"Me?" Alice said, taken aback. Yes, she had gained some confidence recently, but did the Queen really want her to be included in a discussion of this magnitude?

"Your insights thus far have been valuable, but I understand if you would prefer not to see Luka, considering what Helas forced you to do."

Alice flushed again. The truth was that she desperately wanted to see Luka again.

"It would also be good for you to be part of the discussion concerning our next steps with humans."

"Next steps?" Alice asked, roused from her thoughts of Luka.

"Yes. When there was only one human, Jade, the decision to make her a bride seemed the most logical. Now, we know that humans are compatible with Clecanians in more ways than one. Once more of our population know that humans can be mated, there will be calls for action. It is likely I will meet with leaders from across our world and vote on our course of action. I would like to consult human ambassadors and hear your opinions on the matter before deciding how I will vote."

All in all, Alice had to say the Queen was being very reasonable. She wasn't only taking her own people's needs into account, but the needs of humans as well.

If I want to be a leader, then I need to act like one.

"I'd like to be a part of that group," Alice announced, earning her an approving head tilt.

"Very well. I will make sure Metli notifies you of our schedule. I need to be on my way. Ask your questions."

Alice blew out a slow breath. "Helas said I was taken at the same time as Jade, but I can't remember anything from before a few weeks ago. Why?"

"Do you recall feeling weak upon waking, but otherwise untouched?"

"Yes," Alice exclaimed, leaning forward in her chair.

"It is likely you were placed in a stasis pod. Most of the other humans reported a similar experience. Our doctor will be able to tell you for sure when he checks you and gives you an off-worlder health clearance."

Stasis. Alice relaxed in her chair. A wave of relief built at the back of her mind, but she pushed it away. She needed confirmation from the doctor.

"Is there anything else?"

Suddenly, everything Alice had been intending to ask was gone. Scrambling to find a question for the expectant Queen, she blurted, "Do you have a name? I mean, is Queen your name or your title or both?"

The Queen arched an eyebrow. "In Tremanta, when the people choose a Queen, she accepts the position by abandoning her name and forfeiting mate rights."

Alice leaned forward, interested. "You mean you can't have a mate."

"When I became Queen, I painted my hands." She held her hands out in front of her, and Alice saw that up to her wrists, the skin was a slightly different shade than the rest. It looked like she had very well-made form-fitting gloves that were nearly invisible. "Even if I recognized a mate, I wouldn't know for certain until a new Queen was chosen and my paint was removed."

Alice continued to stare at her hands until she delicately set them back in her lap. The mention of mating marks drew her mind back to Luka. "Would it be possible for me to leave The Pearl Temple?"

The Queen's eyes grew unfocused, and she remained silent for a moment. "That is a very difficult question, Alice. You, in particular, may leave, but I will ask you to do so sparingly so as not to upset the other females. None of the other humans are allowed to leave the Temple right now. I can't risk them walking in the markets and accidentally triggering a mating response from a male before we have decided what to do." She focused back on Alice. "If you'd like to leave, you need to speak with a guard or Metli about arranging transportation and accompanying you until you learn your way around."

Alice nodded. She could sense that it was special to be allowed to ask the Queen any question she wanted. This was a once-in-a-lifetime opportunity. So why could she concentrate on nothing except returning to Luka at that very moment?

The Queen stared at her, waiting.

"Do you know of any mates who didn't want to be together?" How would he feel about her when the drugs finally wore off?

Misunderstanding her, the Queen answered, "You will not be forced to stay with Luka, if that is what you're worried about. Because humans do not experience matehood in the same way we do, you will not be held to our laws of matehood."

"It's not that," Alice started, feeling heat creep into her cheeks. "I'm worried he might not... The whole time we were together, he was..."

Alice felt herself shrink under the woman's perplexed gaze. *She's the Queen, for God's sake. You don't talk to the Queen of an alien city about your boy problems!*

"Never mind. I can't think of my other questions for some reason," Alice said, failing to meet her eyes.

112

"You've had a long day. Many long days, in fact. Think on what you'd like to ask me. I'll reserve time after our next meeting to speak with you again."

"Thank you." Alice sighed, overwhelmed and grateful for her understanding.

The Queen leaned toward her and rested a hand on one of Alice's. "You have been so brave and resilient these past weeks. Now that I have met you, I can see you are also very forgiving, kind, and compassionate. I am sure Luka would be infatuated with you in any state of mind."

Alice peered up at the woman, a small smile curving her lips. "I hope you're right."

9

Large blue eyes stared up at him pleadingly. Her soft moans echoed in his ear as he tasted her sweet skin. He needed her more than he could say, but she pushed him away.

He reached out to clutch her to him more firmly, but his fingers only grasped at air. Panic made his whole body tense. He spun, looking for her, calling her name. The tranquil mountain setting faded, and hard gray walls rose around him, caging him.

A shadowy figure loomed over him, laughing evilly. Hatred burning in him, Luka lunged at the man, intending to rip his throat out.

As his hands shot forward, an invisible force wrenched them back. He began to struggle though his arms were weak. He needed to get to her. "Where is she?"

The shadowy figure only laughed harder, his loud voice booming and echoing off the walls.

"Luka, wake up!" a distant voice called.

Luka's eyes shot open. Cold sweat beaded on his skin, and his breaths came in quick, ragged gasps. He was in his room, on his bed, but he couldn't move his arms or legs. Figures loomed over him. Needing to be free, he began to thrash in his bindings.

A familiar voice thundered over him, "Luka, you need to calm, or I'll have to sedate you again."

Luka stilled. *Maxu?*

His vision was improving with each second, and as it did, the hulking figure of his brother Maxu came into focus.

"Thank the Goddess. I thought we were going to have to knock you out again."

Luka turned his head toward the voice coming from his other side and found his youngest brother Izor grinning back at him. He studied his brothers' faces and noticed the dark circles under their eyes and their strained expressions.

"What happened? Why am I tied down?"

Luka tried to recall the last thing he remembered, but a nagging panic and anxiety kept pulling at his thoughts. There was something he was supposed to be doing, somewhere he needed to be, but for the life of him he couldn't recall what it was.

His brothers looked at each other, the concern showing clearly on their faces. "What do you remember?"

Frustration welled in him. "Let me up! I can't think tied down like this."

Izor pulled the corner of his mouth back in a grimace. "You punched Zed pretty hard last time we let you go. Don't you remember trying to run out of here?"

Maxu said nothing but began loosening Luka's restraints.

Luka furrowed his brows, trying to recall attacking his older brother Auzed, but it was as if he were examining his memories through thick ice. Hints of images appeared before him, but he couldn't make out anything clearly.

Suddenly a vision of deep-blue eyes flashed in his mind, startling him and making his scalp tingle.

Soft, unintelligible words floated through his awareness. His cock twitched in response.

What the fuck is happening to me? He absently massaged his now free, aching wrists.

The beautiful, haunting eyes slowly faded, and he felt his gut clench painfully at the loss. Who did those eyes belong to? Were they even real or just a dream?

"What happened?" he said to Maxu more forcefully, feeling an overwhelming urge to leave his home and run…somewhere.

"We have only learned some of the details recently, but from our understanding, you have been working undercover to investigate Helas."

He stiffened and rose from the bed. His brothers shouldn't know that.

Luka had been suspicious of Helas for quite some time now. Since starting his role on Helas' research team, Luka had suspected he may have been doing experiments on his own.

116

His misgiving intensified six months ago when Helas started missing work without a clear explanation, then reappearing with controversial ideas for their research that he'd come upon seemingly out of nowhere.

When Helas had started casually joking that the Alliance laws were holding back their research, Luka had finally broken down and approached the Queen directly with his concerns. His instincts had always warned that Helas was less harmless than he seemed to be, and he'd recognized a grain of truth in the man's repeated joking.

He'd fully expected to be shut down and punished for accusing a superior. But to his surprise, the Queen had agreed and confided in him that there were rumors of an underground organization bent on saving their species no matter the cost.

The Queen had requested his assistance in bringing this organization to light, and Luka had agreed. He'd convinced Helas to join him and a few colleagues on an extended research trip in the isolated Skuzio Valley. Initially, Helas had declined but a few weeks after their arrival, he'd shown up, claiming his plans had changed. For the last five months Luka had huddled around fires and tromped through marshes, all while attempting to grow close to Helas and learn his secrets. There was no way his brothers should have known about Helas, unless...

Luka's eyes widened as the memory of a stark white hallway and a set of monitors came back to him.

"Helas found out, didn't he?" As he looked between his brothers' tight expressions, bits of memory came rushing back. He began pacing around the room, the heels of his palms grinding against his temples, and tried to follow his thoughts as they returned to him.

Izor and Maxu eyed his movements but stayed quiet, possibly sensing the tenuous grip he had on his memory at the moment.

Luka remembered attempting to infiltrate Helas' group. He'd slowly earned the man's trust by laughing and agreeing to his comments about the Alliance laws. He'd then started voicing opinions of his own to Helas concerning their research and how it'd never amount to much at their current pace.

Luka had spent months in the lab and then in the wilderness, carefully convincing Helas' he was an intelligent, likeminded male, set on saving their species at the expense of others. During the last week of their trip, Helas had finally offered to show Luka a "project" he'd been working on in his free time.

In preparation, Luka had contacted the Queen and implanted an antiquated tracking device into his calf.

"What happened? How were you found out?" Izor asked quietly.

He turned to face Izor, his head pounding from the onslaught of recalled memories. "I remember him bringing me to an underground facility," he began. "He took me to a room with viewing screens and showed me some live feeds, explaining they were from other outposts."

Luka blanched as he recalled what he'd seen on those screens. He looked to his brothers. They knew too. Their somber expressions gave them away. "There were females being held captive," he croaked.

Guilt washed over him as he recalled losing his temper and exposing himself to Helas. What had happened to the females from the screens? He could've saved them if he'd kept up the ruse, but instead, he'd broken character and had allowed Helas to see his outrage.

The last thing he could remember before his thoughts became too muddled was Helas' two henchmen knocking him out.

"I'm not sure which females you saw, but we've found several from two separate locations, and Helas is in custody," Maxu said quietly, resting his hand on Luka's shoulder.

A momentary wave of relief washed over Luka, but then the familiar anxiety set back in. There was something they still weren't telling him. When had he moved so close to the door? And why did he still feel the urgent need to leave? Luka stared at his bedroom door and twitched, suppressing the urge to bolt.

Maxu silently stepped in his path and crossed his arms over his chest.

Luka narrowed his eyes and looked back to Izor, who was staring fixedly at the ceiling and rocking back and forth on his heels. "Izzo, what aren't you telling me?" Luka asked through gritted teeth.

Izor's eyes flashed to meet Maxu's, and they exchanged telling glances.

"You were captured one month ago, and we don't know everything that happened to you in that time, but one of the females rescued was able to fill us in on the events of the last few weeks," Maxu said slowly. His eyes were fixed on Luka's face, never straying. It was as though he were purposefully forcing himself not to look anywhere else.

How would a female know what happened to me?

"Apparently," Maxu continued, "they were testing a drug on you that allowed them to collect your seed more easily."

Bile rose in his throat. He felt violated and sick over the fact that he couldn't recall the last month of his life or what had been done to him against his will.

He dropped to his knees when he thought about the female who'd known the purpose of his drugging. How and why had she known he'd been drugged for this reason? What had Helas forced *her* to do?

A tangible feeling of mind-blanking lust came back to him, and he paled further. *What had I forced her to do?*

"The female—" he began. "Is she...? Did I...?"

Izor knelt down before him, his eyes flashing down to his wrists before settling back on his face. "She's okay. I only spoke to her briefly, but from what she said, I don't think you did anything to her. She was actually more concerned about you than anything else."

120

"Why was she concerned for me?" Luka rasped, not sure he could handle any more revelations right now.

Izor inhaled deeply and gave Luka a lopsided forced smile before continuing, "Well, I'm not sure exactly how it happened, but you guys fought your way out. When your tracker suddenly started working again, we came to retrieve you." Izor glanced at Maxu and then down to Luka's lap again. "I sort of had to tranq you when I found you, because you were trying to..."

Izor didn't have to finish his sentence. Somewhere in the back of his mind, Luka could recall the feel of soft flesh under his palms and warm skin on his tongue.

He hung his head in shame. It didn't matter that he'd been drugged. It didn't matter that he hadn't been in his right mind, or that the female seemed to be incredibly understanding. He'd be sent to prison, and he knew deep down that he deserved it.

Was the panic he was experiencing an impulse to run? To avoid punishment?

"We should go to the Queen now so she can decide my punishment," he said, standing.

Izor stepped in front of Luka, halting his progress toward the door. "The Queen has already decided there will be no punishment. The female agreed."

Luka swung his confused gaze to Maxu. "How can there be no punishment? I tried to force myself on a female! Drugged or not, it doesn't matter."

Maxu, who'd always been the most reserved of his brothers, stared at him oddly but said nothing.

"I would say it was more like heavy petting, not forcing, and because of your circumstances, and the female's acknowledgment of your innocence, the law is on your side," Izor said brightly.

Luka stared at him slack-jawed. There was no law that would protect him from harming a female.

Maxu finally spoke. "The laws of matehood are on your side," he clarified.

Again, the image of blue eyes flashed through his mind, and his stomach clenched painfully. Luka blinked at him, not understanding. Why would the laws of matehood protect him?

A wave of dizziness came over him as he recalled the feeling of supple hands sliding over his body.

Alice, his mind hissed.

Maxu finally allowed his unwavering gaze to slide down Luka's body, settling at his wrists.

Luka followed the fixed direction of Maxu's stare and had to take a step back. Blue mating marks circled his wrists.

10

Alice lay on a warmed wooden patio, chin resting on her overlapping hands. Her eyes traced the path of a small glowing bilom as it swam in circles around a floating blossom while she thought about Luka for the millionth time.

It'd been a week since she and the other women had been rescued and brought here, and she missed Luka deeply. At the facility, he'd been her only company. She missed his large, warm body close to hers and hearing his deep voice repeat her words. The anticipation of really meeting him for the first time was excruciating, like the slow climb to the peak of a roller coaster drop.

Alice didn't know what to think. They'd never had a conversation, and yet, she felt so connected to him. Was that connection only born out of trauma, or was there more to it? There was only one way to know for sure.

Why hasn't he come to see me? she thought miserably, reaching down to hover her fingertips over the path of the flowing blue creature.

Whenever she'd asked to see him, she'd been told he was still recovering.

A part of her wanted to believe his recovery was indeed the reason he hadn't visited, but an evil, nagging part of her mind whispered differently.

He finally woke up and found out what I did to him. He's disgusted.

Just because Luka had been her rock in that place hadn't meant she'd been his. It must be a lot of pressure to wake up and find out you have a mate. Did he remember anything? If he saw her again, would he be disappointed, disgusted even, because she was human?

A deep sigh escaped her. *Think of something else!*

Lifting her right hand, she pressed the pad of her forefinger and thumb together, then huffed in frustration at the black alien symbols that appeared on the back of her hand.

After her meeting with the Queen, all of the new human women had been taken to the medbay to be checked and healed. While waiting for the long cylindrical healing tube to work its magic on Daisy's ears, Alice had noticed bright red symbols kept appearing on the friendly doctor's hand.

When she asked about them, he'd explained it was an implanted watch, called a hand clock. He'd been taken aback when Alice had practically fallen to her knees and begged for him to give her one as well. Although he'd eventually given in, Alice still hadn't managed to memorize enough of the symbols or understand how time was marked in order to read the watch, and no one seemed too interested in teaching her. Apparently, keeping time wasn't a major concern for most Clecanians.

The doctor, Flen, had explained while some things, like schools and the government, were expected to run on a strict schedule, most things in Tremanta operated with little regard for the time. Implanted watches were only utilized by a few people, and Alice's insistence that she be one of the few had surprised the doctor.

Luckily, his interactions with the first wave of rescued humans had prepared him for odd requests. At the insistence of some of the other women, he'd begrudgingly offered a variety of birth control methods during their visit.

Meg, a chatty human woman who seemed more excited than anyone else to be there, confided in Alice that she'd been the one to argue with the doctor until he finally relented. Meg had babbled endlessly about how she wanted to make sure she was protected, just in case, because as soon as she could, she was going to travel and see the new world. Something she'd never been able to do on Earth.

It wasn't only the offer of birth control on a planet nearing extinction that had surprised Alice, but the variety. For one, there were options for both men and women. After she'd learned the thick underwear every woman wore did double duty as a scent blocker and a period panty, Alice had opted for birth control that would allow her to skip her menstrual cycle.

Although the doctor was able to confirm that she had in fact been in stasis for about five months, worry still plagued her. Doctor Flen had explained that she was untouched but had been asleep for much longer than any other woman he'd inspected. *Why?*

The only way she'd be able to find out for sure would be to ask Helas directly. The fact that acid rose in her gut every time she thought of the man, made it clear she wouldn't be ready to do that for quite some time.

She activated her hand clock again and tried to focus on something else. "Okay, squiggly line with a T and two dots means…four? No, fourteen? Is that even a number, or is that the time of day?"

The faint sound of a branch snapping made her raise her head. She squinted, trying to see through the overlapping foliage. The hairs on the back of her neck rose, and a tingling sensation crept over her.

Is something watching me?

She held perfectly still, scanning the trees for movement, but couldn't see anything out of the ordinary.

A sound behind her caused her to yelp and roll to her back. Misjudging the space to her left, she rolled too far and fell off the patio. A gasp of surprise was all she managed before she hit a solid floating platform a few inches below.

Daisy looked down at her and grinned. "Careful. Remember Metli said those glowing things in the water sting."

Alice let out a relieved breath and slowly raised herself back to a standing position on the platform. Luckily, she'd slept with her token stuck to her arm. "I know you're used to being really quiet, but now that you have your hearing back, maybe you could make more noise when you come over here."

Alice grinned and embraced the small woman, accidentally inhaling a mouthful of her curly brown hair. Although still very quiet and shy, since being healed Daisy could always be seen with a smile plastered on her face.

"If I made more noise, I wouldn't be able to see you do fun things like that, though." Daisy grinned, gesturing to the water. "I was hanging out at Vanessa's, and a guard came by."

"Izzo?" Alice teased, nudging Daisy in the ribs.

Daisy blushed furiously but said, "No, some other guy." Quietly, she added, "I haven't seen Izzo since that first day."

All of the women had noticed Izzo's infatuation with Daisy, and when Daisy had casually brought up his name in conversation, they'd started to tease her. After recounting everything that had happened since their rescue to Daisy, who'd heard none of it, Daisy's only question had been in regard to diving for pearls. "So, if they aren't stung, it's meant to be?"

She'd promptly quieted after Alice had casually suggested she ask Izzo to retrieve a pearl for her.

"This other guy told me to come get you. I guess there's a meeting or something going on in a little bit that you're supposed to go to."

Alice's eyes shot to the front door. *Finally!*

She'd been eagerly awaiting this meeting ever since the Queen had asked her to be a part of it. Each day she'd asked Metli when the meeting would happen, and each day Metli's annoyance had grown as she'd told her the meeting was postponed until all parties could be in attendance.

Metli hadn't gone into specifics, but Alice guessed the "party" Metli was referring to was Luka.

Her heart picked up speed, and that empty feeling of excitement and fear washed over her. *I'm finally going to see him again.*

She glanced down at her casual lounge outfit in distress. "Help me figure out what to wear, okay?" Alice said as she dashed inside to a large wardrobe near her bed.

"Trying to look nice for Luka, are we?" Daisy teased.

Alice poked her head out. "Yeah, maybe you could ask Izzo what style his brother likes," she countered with raised brows.

Daisy rolled her eyes and slumped on the long, deep maroon couch.

After leaving the doctor's office, feeling brand new again having received something called the "elixir," Alice, Rita, Daisy, and Vanessa had been led by Metli to a group of small floating houses. Metli had been confused when the women had decided to all sleep in one house for the first few nights. She'd told them they were safe and no unauthorized person could traverse the lake, but Alice and the others had clung together regardless.

Yesterday, when Alice could take no more of Vanessa's aversion to cleaning, or of Rita's morning and evening Tai Chi sessions that seemed to take up half the living room, she'd wandered over to the house that jutted the farthest into the lake and explored her new home.

She'd found the interior of her small floating house was very similar to the one she'd been living in with the other women. Each of the houses reminded Alice of upscale overwater bungalows. Back on Earth, she could never have dreamed of making enough money to stay in one of the trendy structures.

Silver lining number one, awesome house.

The living room, kitchen, and bedroom all occupied the same space, but the furniture could be programmed to sink into a panel on the floor when not in use. If she pressed the right symbols on the control panel near her door, a large, soft bed would rise to a location of her choosing. In the morning, she could lower the bed back into the floor panel and program her long couch and coffee table to occupy the room instead.

Alice had spent a long time arguing with Rita, Daisy, and Vanessa about how the magic furniture worked. In her opinion, all of it was housed in a basement-like space in the water below the house, but Daisy had claimed the furniture was actually being teleported to a giant warehouse somewhere and waited to be recalled.

After their fourth bottle of mott, a strong alcoholic beverage, they'd decided the most logical way to figure it out would be to draw straws. Whoever drew the short straw would sit on a piece of furniture, be lowered into the floor, and see where they ended up. The morning after, they'd all groggily agreed that asking someone would be the much more logical answer.

The constantly changing furniture had bothered Alice, and after arriving in her home yesterday, she'd programmed all of the furniture to occupy the room at the same time.

The house was a little cramped, but nowhere near as crowded as Vanessa's house had been. After having lived in one house with three other women for the last week, and sleeping on a lumpy cot in a cell for the two weeks before that, sleeping in a bed of her own, in a house of her own, had felt like heaven.

The only other room in the house was a bathroom that contained a cleansing unit, a toilet, and a large glass tub sunken into the floor. The depths of the lake could be seen through the transparent sides of the tub.

It must be very surreal to take a bath in there.

Alice had stared at the tub for a long time when she'd first seen it, musing that, to the creatures living in the lake, the glass tub would look like a large fish tank containing the body of a very odd-looking naked fish.

"Make sure you pick something that shows off your legs," Daisy said, frowning at a long black dress Alice had tossed to her.

Her legs were her best feature. Not being able to afford a car and riding a bike everywhere had sculpted and toned her once-skinny legs to perfection.

A soft sky-blue garment caught her eye. It was similar to a romper but was made of fabric that felt like silk and breathed like cotton. Perfect for a hot summer day like today.

Alice didn't think it was the most appropriate piece of clothing for a top-secret meeting with the Queen, but she found she only cared whether Luka liked it or not.

"Hey there, lady friends!" Vanessa entered without knocking and dove onto the couch, her legs resting across Daisy's lap. "Fashion show?"

Daisy waggled her brows. "Alice is trying to figure out what to wear to a meeting Luka might be at." She glanced back toward the front door. "Where's Rita?"

Vanessa rolled her eyes. "Rearranging the furniture *again.*"

"Do you think this is too revealing for a meeting?" Alice asked after changing into the romper.

"Maybe on Earth, but it doesn't seem like they care about that stuff here," Daisy said.

She was right. Of all the alien women she'd seen, there seemed to be no one style or standard. Some women like Metli wore high-fashioned structured garments while eating breakfast. Others wore baggy, shapeless clothing, and a few confidently strutted in pieces that were little more than modest bikinis.

Alice activated the hidden mirror on the wall and gave herself a once-over, fluffing her shining, chocolate brown hair, which only a few days ago had been brittle and damaged. A short romper might not be entirely appropriate, but it did show off her perfect, unblemished skin and new golden tan. Since learning that this planet had protected its ozone layer much more effectively than Earth, she'd lounged joyously in the sun, allowing her tan to deepen every day.

No more worrying about skin cancer and sun damage!

"How do I look?" Alice asked, spinning toward Daisy and Vanessa.

Daisy's smile widened. "You look great, but I'd recommend bringing a sweater or something."

I want to take off clothes with Luka, not put them on! "Why?"

Vanessa spoke. "We all know you want to show Luka your headlights, but maybe whoever else you're meeting doesn't want to see them."

Alice blinked at her for a moment. "Headlights?"

Daisy pointed to her chest, and Alice looked down to see her nipples were jutting slightly through the thin material.

She threw her hands in the air. "Well, what am I supposed to do if they don't provide bras?"

Alice moved back to her wardrobe, intending to change but finding nothing better. Each woman had been allowed to purchase clothing, but they'd felt guilty about spending money that wasn't theirs and only picked out a few items each.

"So, Lucy might have a lead for me," Vanessa called, drawing Alice's buried head out of the wardrobe.

Ever since Metli had explained to Vanessa that she wasn't allowed to return to Earth, Vanessa had been determined to do just that.

"That's awesome! Let me know what she says." Secretly, Alice had been relieved to learn that going back to Earth wasn't an option.

"You really should get a move on. That guard is waiting for you," Vanessa said, walking over and rifling through Alice's clothing. She pushed a soft sweater into her hands. "Just wear this."

"But—" Alice started.

Vanessa began herding Alice toward the door. "Luka was obsessed with you when you were smelly, dirty, and living in a cell. I really don't think he's going to have a problem with a sweater over a dress. You're overthinking." When Alice continued to argue, Vanessa pushed her through the doorway. "Or don't wear the sweater. If these aliens don't believe in bras, then they're probably used to nipples anyway."

Daisy dashed forward and lingered in the doorway. "Remember to ask about the girls again. I asked a few days ago if they'd been found, but still no luck."

Alice nodded and felt a small prick of guilt. The day after they'd arrived at the Temple, they'd decided it'd be best to tell someone about the two women who'd run off into the woods. A search party had been formed to find the women, but to their disappointment, the two humans had seemed to vanish without a trace. At this point, Daisy was the only one still holding out hope they'd be found.

Alice lowered her eyes and solemnly agreed. "I will."

A tall guard appeared next to her, startling her and forcing her to haphazardly shove the sweater over her head.

"Let's go," was all he said before walking ahead of her.

Alice waved goodbye to her friends and followed, examining the man. He was tall and handsome and looked eerily familiar. She'd seen him patrolling around The Pearl Temple, along with a handful of other guards. He was quiet but had always acted very professionally in front of them, unlike some of the guards who she'd caught openly staring at her and the other women on several occasions.

She increased her pace, attempting to keep up with him. "What's your name?"

He glanced at her sidelong. "Auzed."

"Hi, Auzed. I'm Alice. Um, do you have an update on the two missing humans from where I was rescued? Have they been found? Is there any sign of them?"

His lips thinned and he picked up speed. "There hasn't been any sign of them, but we're still looking."

Poor girls.

His long strides made it difficult for Alice to keep up without running. The soft material of the sweater felt stifling in the sun, and she cursed herself for not choosing a more appropriate outfit to begin with. "Auzed," she panted, "Would you mind slowing down? I didn't run on Earth, and I don't intend to run here."

He stopped and turned to face her, taking in her sweat-glistened forehead. Suddenly, his eyes darted behind her toward the tree line, and his large shoulders stiffened.

The feeling of being watched settled back over Alice, and she spun, attempting to scan the tree line as well. Silently, Auzed stepped in front of her, eyes still trained ahead, and rested a hand on a thin weapon strapped to his broad chest.

Fear worked its way up Alice's spine. Had one of Helas' lackeys come back for her?

His shoulders relaxed, but his eyes remained hard.

"What's out there?" Alice whispered.

Auzed stepped back, his gaze flashing between her and the trees. "It was likely just an animal."

"An animal?" She didn't know enough about this planet, or its wildlife, to know whether that made sense, but Auzed's clenched jaw and angry eyes told her he didn't believe what he'd just said.

"Don't worry," he said in a falsely reassuring tone. "No one can walk to The Pearl Temple without authorization. They'd fall into the lake and be stung repeatedly."

Alice pursed her lips. "Don't you mean, *nothing* can walk to The Pearl Temple without authorization?"

Auzed gave a sharp nod, avoiding her eyes. "We need to keep going. The Queen is waiting."

He reached out to touch her shoulder in an attempt to guide her forward, but at the last moment his eyes shot to the trees once more. The hand he was hovering over her shoulder dropped. "Let's go," he repeated.

Slowing his pace, he walked ahead of her. Alice followed but kept glancing back to the trees. Something was still watching her, and Auzed knew more about it than he was letting on.

When they drew close to the rounded central building the humans had started calling The Dome, Alice's suspicion was replaced with anxiety and apprehension. She absently smoothed her hair and clothing while running her gaze around the perimeter of the building, looking for Luka.

Where is he?

Auzed held open a door to the building and motioned for her to enter, remaining outside when she did. Before leaving him, she urged her voice to sound forceful and authoritative as she said, "Thanks, Auzed, but don't think I didn't notice how shifty you got back there. After this meeting is over, we're going to have a discussion about what you saw in the woods."

Auzed tilted his head, the corner of his mouth lifted in a curious smile. "You can call me Zed."

The fact that her tone hadn't had the effect she'd wanted was frustrating, but the friendly gifting of his nickname was flattering. Not knowing which reaction to focus on, she awkwardly said, "Fine. Zed," and sped inside.

The meeting room looked almost the same as the room she'd been taken to her first night here, except in this room, one large round table dominated the space. Already seated at the table was Lucy, a sociable blonde human Alice had never really spoken to, a handsome blue-green-skinned man, and…a demon?

Alice stood frozen, staring at the terrifying giant. He was larger than any man she'd ever seen before and had razor-sharp purple horns extending from his temples and curling toward the back of his head. His skin was deeply tanned and tinted almost red. Upon first glance, his curling hair was black, but upon closer inspection, she saw it had a deep purple sheen to it.

He turned to glance at her, and Alice was startled to find his light gray eyes were warm when they caught her stare.

She couldn't bring herself to look away from the horned man even as she inwardly cursed her brain to do so. Her heartbeat began to slow when she saw the demon shift in his seat. Alice must be crazy, but she could swear he looked self-conscious.

A woman's annoyed, out-of-breath voice sounded from behind her. "I'm fine! Would you relax!"

The pretty redhead, who looked far too pregnant to be walking easily, was waddling into the room. A large, angry man with thick, black tattoos covering all of his exposed skin walked behind her. The open doorway from which they'd emerged revealed the interior of a cruiser. They must have guided the cruiser over the lake and directly here in order to keep her hidden from view.

His focus was firmly on the woman as she walked. Every so often, he'd reach out to grab her hand or arm, trying to help her, but she'd just shoo his hands and continue forward unassisted.

The woman's eyes lit up when they landed on Alice. "Oh, hey! Alice, right?" As quickly as she could, which wasn't very quick at all, the woman changed course and began making her way to Alice.

The man anxiously walking behind her glanced to the chairs, and then back to the woman. In a deep, rumbling voice, he said, "Jade, you need to go sit down."

Jade continued toward Alice but rolled her eyes. "Once you have grown a person in your uterus, you are more than welcome to weigh in on what I *need*. Until then, I'll be the judge."

The man stopped and shot a furious glare at the back of her head. In a low growl, he said, "Jade, you will go and sit now, or I'll carry you home."

Jade stopped and inhaled deeply. She turned and batted her lashes at the man, who was now towering over her. If she were Jade, Alice would've been terrified. The tattooed man was very handsome but in a severe, dangerous way, and right now, he looked close to murder.

Jade reached up and grabbed his neck, tugging him down to whisper in his ear. Alice had no idea what she said to the guy to get him to relax, but she deserved a goddamned medal. Alice watched as the man's tension and anger slowly faded until he stood with his cheek against her hair, smiling faintly.

Jade planted a swift kiss on his lips and resumed her trek toward Alice. The man followed, and although he looked annoyed, the ghost of a smile clung to his lips.

Alice quickly walked toward the pair. If she waited for Jade to get to her, it'd take all day.

Jade pulled her in for a firm hug then released her. "So, you're Luka's mate! That's so exciting! This grump behind me is Theo. One of Luka's brothers." Jade hiked her thumb toward the man, who was now peering at Alice curiously.

"Izzo is your brother too?" she asked. *How many siblings does Luka have?*

"Yes," he said simply.

One brother is a Chatty Cathy, and the other is quiet and broody. She searched the room again. Who would Luka be more similar to?

Theo continued to stare at her, but Alice didn't know what else to say. She motioned to his arm. "Um...I like your tattoos."

Jade let out a loud bark of laughter and then beamed at Theo's surprised face. She grabbed his hand, and a purr resonated in his chest. "Told you so."

Alice wasn't sure what they were talking about, but she sighed longingly at their exchange. Theo purred and gazed at Jade like she was the sun itself.

She hoped one day Luka might look at her that way. If he and Theo were brothers, then maybe he wouldn't find the relationship between humans and Clecanians unappealing.

"Let me introduce you to everyone," Jade said happily, waddling to the table and tugging a besotted Theo behind her.

As they approached ahead of Alice, the large demon stood and greeted the couple warmly.

Must only look scary. Alice tried to combat her knee-jerk response of fear.

Jade turned to her. "This is Rhaego. He's a really great guy and one of Theo and Luka's good friends."

Alice smiled as the demon gave her a low formal bow. "It's an honor to meet another human female."

Well, he may look like a demon, but he has the manners of a prince.

He glanced nervously between her and Jade. "I'm sorry if my appearance is startling to you."

Alice felt a pang of guilt for her earlier reaction. "No, it's my fault. I'm still not used to seeing aliens who look...alien," she finished dumbly.

Theo made his way to the vacant seat next to Rhaego. The two men sat and began speaking casually.

Jade awkwardly sank into her chair. "I tried to explain what a demon is on our planet in order to prepare him for other humans' reactions, but I feel like he got offended," she whispered, glancing back toward Rhaego. She smiled. "He's the biggest softy ever, and his dream is to find a mate. I think the fact that most of us are pretty terrified of him when we first see him has dashed his hopes a bit."

Alice looked back to Rhaego and felt sympathy bloom in her chest. Sure, at first he'd looked like something out of a nightmare, but now that she'd met him, she found he was

140

very handsome in his own way. If she wasn't so infatuated with Luka, she was sure she could get on board the sexy demon train. Alice decided she'd try and talk him up to Vanessa.

11

∞

Luka watched from the trees as Alice sunned herself on her floating patio. The orange light danced off her shining brown locks, and he could just make out lighter shades of gold streaking the hair around her oval face.

Loose shorts and a sleeveless shirt covered her well enough but did nothing to keep his mind from guessing at the soft curves beneath. She was like something out of a fever dream. In his case, she actually was something out of Luka's dreams.

The glowing bilom swimming in the lake, reflected on her face, obscuring the true color of her eyes, and he found himself cursing the beautiful creatures. No matter how mesmerizing the bilom were, the deep blue eyes he'd been dreaming about were a hundred times more so.

After he'd awoken in his bed and his brothers had explained what'd happened to him, he'd been a wreck. Helas' violation of him was a trauma he could overcome in time, but if he'd found a true mate only to lose her because of what Helas had done…well, he didn't know if he could come back from that.

As far back as he could remember, he'd yearned for a mate and a family. His own mother had died before his mind had been mature enough to properly remember her. In the wake of her death, his father had done the best he could to divide his attention evenly among his five children, but when Luka looked back on his childhood, he couldn't help but remember feeling neglected.

He'd always wished he could have a female all to himself. Someone whose attention wasn't divided among many. A female he could shower with affection and who'd hopefully return the sentiment. A permanent mate he could share his life with.

But in a world under strain, where loyalty to saving their species outweighed loyalty to any single person, seeking a wife who'd be willing to stay with one husband was nearly impossible.

To the Clecanian's knowledge, only three compatible species have existed. The Dyasque, who live on an overly populated planet galaxies away and whose females kill their partners upon successfully mating. The Ryg, who were peaceful and timid, but who'd gone extinct after their planet had been demolished by a rogue asteroid decades ago. The Traxians, from whom Luka and his siblings were descended.

Neither the Traxians or the Dyasque had any interest in migrating to Clecania no matter how many times the government had attempted to persuade them. Female options for a heterosexual Clecanian male were limited to say the least.

As a young male, Luka had understood that finding a female to call his own, who'd lower her guard and openly love him the way his mother had with his father, could only happen if their species was safe from extinction. Either the ratio of males to females had to become more equal, or matehood needed to suddenly return after being lost for so long.

Ever the realist, he'd chosen to enter into the field of research most likely to result in the salvation of his species. He'd decided the science behind procreation, infertility, and animal mating would be his area of expertise.

Many of his colleagues devoted their time and effort to researching matehood, rather than fertility, feeling as though that was the answer to their problems. Luka, however, had always been one to think to the future. Without sufficient evidence to the contrary, he'd concluded their species must've evolved past matehood. Mating should be viewed as an immovable thing of the past, so as not to muddle the progressive science of today.

Yet, there she was. His mate, *Alice*.

Beyond all reason, the universe had given her to him, and what had he done? Based on Izzo's retelling, he'd captured her, taken her away, and ravished her. His neck heated with shame just thinking about it.

He crept forward through the brush to get a better view. A few days ago, when he could no longer stand the nagging pull that'd been present in him since he'd woken up, and while his brothers had been preoccupied, he'd allowed his mating instinct to direct him to these woods, the closest he could get to her without crossing Pearl Lake.

He'd scarcely blinked when he'd first seen her, laughing with the other women in their shared home, worried if he took his eyes off her for even a second, she'd be gone. The home she'd been living in at first was far away from the shore, and he could only see the patio and part of the kitchen, but yesterday, as if drawn closer to him by an unknown force, she'd moved to the house that jutted closest to where he sat every day. Had it been the bond or dumb luck that'd made her pick that house?

He felt a perverse pleasure watching her like this. Whenever a sense of satisfaction at being near her came over him, guilt immediately followed. Opposing feelings weren't something new to Luka. From stories his brothers had told him, he knew they felt the same.

His mother, a full Traxian female, had shamed her clan and family by seeking aid from the Clecanians and marrying a Lignas male. Often Luka and his brothers felt their more primal Traxian sides battling to be acknowledged. While their Lignas half guided their reasoning and social skills, their Traxian half burned in them like small fires waiting for fuel.

His sister, Asivva, seemed to be unaffected by her Traxian blood, but he and his brothers had struggled their whole lives to contain and repress that side of themselves. That side called for blood whenever there was a simple argument, or wanted to fuck when they should be making love. The brutality and possessiveness that was a biological trait of his people had always caused his family nothing but trouble in the civilized city of Tremanta.

Now, the Clecanian part of him urged him to leave. He knew watching her while she was unaware was wrong, but the Traxian side of him whispered reassurances that stalking his mate was acceptable because she was *his*. How else could he ensure her safety?

Even now, the urge to not simply dive into the bilom-infested waters and swim through their painful stinging to get to her was a battle.

Luka squatted down, ripping at the soft moss covering the ground. He'd tried to learn as much as possible about her since waking, but his brothers had been pretty useless. Since Izzo was the only one she'd spoken to, Luka had made him recount his interaction with her a multitude of times.

Observing her had told him more than any of his other research had. He'd seen that she was kind and caring toward the females she'd lived with. The ones she'd rescued that night. Pride swelled in him. His mate was brave. She'd saved them all that night.

Compassion was another virtue he'd witnessed from his dark hiding place. On a few occasions, he'd seen her console a dark-haired female with a tenderness most Clecanians kept hidden.

And she was intelligent, often approaching the unknown with a scientific curiosity that called to his own. As far as he knew, no one had shown them how to use the technology in their home. While it irked him to think of the ineffectual way in which they were settling new humans into their world, he marveled at how easily she was able to figure out things he assumed must be brand new to her.

Watching her discover the food synthesizer, for one, had been a treat. She'd examined the small machine with her eyes and hands before finally testing a few controls. She must've tried and failed fifty times before finally working out how to use the machine. But she'd never given up, and the smile that had lit up her face when she'd successfully prepared her first dish had made his breath catch in his throat. He'd kill for her to smile at him like that.

Every day, he wracked his brain, trying to remember their time together, but very little of what he recalled made sense to him. She was the clearest in his dreams, yet he couldn't accept those as real memories. They were too good to be true.

The one he'd had last night had him groaning awake, taking his shaft in hand, and finding release with only a few swift strokes. In the dream, she'd run her hands all over his arms and chest, massaging him before finally pressing her body to his in an embrace and whispering unrecognizable words into his ear.

He knew the dream had to be a fantasy because no female in that situation would ever touch a crazed, aroused male so tenderly.

He watched as she activated her hand clock and squinted at the numerals. It was odd for a person who didn't need a clock to have one implanted. The earnestness in which she stared at the time made it clear that it was important to her.

Frustration made his shoulders bunch. It was obvious from her pretty pout and scrunched brows that she couldn't read the clock. He'd need to remedy that soon. If there was anything he could do to make her happy, whether it be imparting knowledge or commissioning the most beautiful clock she'd ever seen that displayed Earthling symbols, he needed to do it.

Luka pulled at a large clump of moss, snapping an attached twig as he did so. The sound echoed over the water, and he froze, watching to see if she'd heard. Sure enough, her head snapped in his direction, and her eyes scanned the area near where he was hiding. How would she react if she found him here?

A figure lurking in the darkness of her house had Luka's protective instincts firing, forcing him to rise and dash toward the lake. He was only a few feet from the edge of the tree line, about to reveal himself, when the figure emerged into the light. He skidded to a halt and retreated into the shadows, recognizing the small girl named Daisy whom Izzo would not shut up about.

When the two females retreated into the darkened house, Luka began to pace. In a few minutes, he'd be attending a vital meeting. There were many reasons this gathering would be important, but the one that weighed the most heavily on him was that he'd have the opportunity to speak with Alice for the first time. He'd gone back and forth in his mind endlessly about whether he should request a meeting with her alone or wait. Ultimately, he decided it'd be better if she were around other people. That way, if she didn't wish to speak to him, she wouldn't feel cornered.

Outside of the terrible conditions in which they'd met, they hadn't had any interactions. What would she think of him? Did she hate him? Would she want to be anywhere near him?

Insecurity was a new feeling for Luka. Whenever he set out to do something new, he made sure he was prepared, that he did all of the necessary research to be successful. But now, there were so many unknown variables.

He couldn't begin to hypothesize about what her feelings would be or how she'd act around him. Even with the information he'd learned, she was still a human. There was a whole lifetime of experiences from a different world that would shape her personality and reactions, and he could only begin to guess at what those might be.

The fact that she didn't have a mating bond of her own was also problematic. If she did, she'd understand his need to be near her. To make sure she was protected and safe.

The distance that separated them now felt like hundreds of miles. If she was within his reach, he didn't know if he'd be able to stop himself from simply grabbing her.

Nodding, he decided that taking control of this mating instinct was of paramount importance. If he could do enough research about mates, maybe he could figure out how to suppress his instinct long enough to charm her properly. In his present condition, where most coherent thoughts were interrupted with daydreams of ripping off her clothes and devouring her golden flesh, civilized seduction would be impossible.

Looking down, he found he'd worn a path through the moss with his pacing. Movement near Alice's house drew his attention again. Auzed, his brother, was striding toward her home. His mind argued Zed was likely escorting her to the meeting, but his instincts urged him to throw his brother in the lake and escort her himself. Clenching and unclenching his fists, he stood simmering.

He watched as Alice emerged from her home and followed Zed. Luka dashed along the tree line, needing to move quickly to keep them in view as they weaved around floating houses. Unable to tear his gaze away, he continued to trip over fallen branches. Slippery moss and pebbles seemed to place themselves underfoot. Luka couldn't recall the last time he'd tripped. He wasn't a clumsy person, but her outfit and the fact that she was walking with another male made it impossible to focus.

The clothing she'd picked had her bare legs on full display. Shapely, tanned legs. He could just imagine running his hands up her thighs until they disappeared under the hem. The wind whipped, fluttering the light fabric higher and causing his mind to blank.

A large rock hidden by moss made him slip yet again. His ankle rolled unnaturally, followed by a sickening crack. He cursed, falling to a knee. When he peered up again, both Alice and Zed were staring at the tree line.

The pain in his ankle shot up his shin, but he attempted to freeze.

I have to control this!

He had to figure out a way to dampen his attraction, or he'd make an utter fool of himself when he finally talked to her.

In order to replace the image of a crazed, chained, horny male she'd grown accustomed to, he needed to be charming when they spoke. Delicate. How was he supposed to sweep her off her feet if he was sporting a bum foot and an ever-present erection?

Out of his four brothers, Luka had always been the one to keep a level head. When Theo and Zed would lose their temper and get into bloody fist fights, he'd been the one to have arguments using reason and logic. That wasn't to say his brothers had responded in kind. He'd had to learn how to defend himself from an early age, and he supposed he should be grateful for that. Protecting his mate would be much more difficult if he didn't know how to fight.

He rose, favoring his good ankle. From this distance and from the research he'd done on humans, he knew Alice wouldn't be able to see him, but Zed, with his perfect eyesight and extensive guard training, would.

Luka saw the moment Zed spotted him. His scowl remained in place but became annoyed rather than alert. He turned and almost touched Alice before lowering his hand again.

Luka let out a relieved breath. At least his brother was aware of the effect the mating bond was having on him.

A spark of urgency and embarrassment tugged at him as he hobbled along the shoreline. He couldn't show up like this. He'd look weak in front of her. She couldn't see him like that.

Luka waited until Alice had been escorted into the building then made himself visible to Zed, who was glaring in his direction.

Zed began to jog toward him, the clear platforms rising to meet his feet with each long stride. He wished he had the clearance to call those platforms to the surface. Then he could go see Alice in her home whenever he wanted.

No, stop! No more stalking her! he scolded, even as he ached to snatch the small token giving Zed access to the lake.

"What the fuck are you doing, Luka? Is this where you've been disappearing to?" Zed barked. Glancing over his shoulder, he lowered his voice. "Do you know what would happen if you were to be caught here? I'm head guard, for Goddess' sake! I should be—"

Ignoring his brother's lecturing, he asked, "Do you have a healer on you? I hurt my ankle."

Zed slammed his mouth shut, a muscle ticking in his jaw. "No," he said through gritted teeth.

"Where is the closest one?" He glanced around Zed, eyes drawn back to the meeting house, even knowing he wouldn't be able to see inside.

"You'll just have to suck it up. You're late as it is."

Luka's eyes flashed to meet his brother's amused smirk. *He knows where a healer is, but he's not telling me. Punishing me for my behavior.*

Zed turned and began walking along the shore, forcing Luka to limp behind him. "I can't go in there like this."

Zed shrugged. "You don't have a choice. They're going to be submerging as soon as the Queen is ready. That'll barely give you enough time to get there and get settled."

"If you escort me across the lake, I'd have time," Luka argued through clenched teeth.

Zed rounded on him, annoyance splashed across his face. "You need to be escorted by Metli, like all of the other attendees."

Luka reached out to smack his brother, but even with his mated-enhanced speed, his ankle slowed him down. Zed stepped back until he was standing on a platform in the water, just out of reach. Zed lifted his hand, displaying his hand clock for Luka to see.

Being late to something like this wasn't an option. The Queen always did things on time, and if he arrived too late, they'd submerge without him, and he'd lose his chance to speak with Alice in a non-threatening group setting. Luka cursed and began hobbling the long way around the lake toward the main entrance.

When he reached a waiting Metli, precious minutes later, he was covered in sweat, and a sharp pain stabbed through his ankle with every step. Already foul, his mood darkened further when he thought about the first impression he'd be making on his new mate.

"What happened to you?" Metli asked, eyeing him up and down with a quirked brow. "And where is your paint? The Queen made it very clear that both you and Theo need to cover your marks when in public."

I don't have time for this. "Can you please escort me to the meeting, Metli?" His words were polite, but his tone was biting.

Pursing her lips, Metli shoved a large ball into his hands, then hurried off over the water without a word.

Luka groaned, taking a few quick breaths to prepare himself for the pain, then staggered after her. He'd need to apologize to her later.

Peering at the red ball in his hands, he wondered if he could somehow take it with him. The object was chosen as a guest pass, allowing visitors to cross the water, because it was unlikely to be stolen. Bright red and large, it'd be difficult to smuggle unnoticed.

When he reached the other side of the lake, he found Metli waiting with arms outstretched. Lips pursed in a tight line and eyes aimed upward, she tapped her foot impatiently.

The females of this world were not used to being spoken to so curtly. Metli, a respected employee of the Queen, was especially not used to it.

"I'm sorry, Metli. Would you mind if I kept this with me so I can visit the medbay after the meeting?" He lifted the leg of his pants, exposing his swollen ankle. Angry red bruises were already beginning to spread over the engorged skin.

She crinkled her nose, grimacing. "Fine, but only because Flen is already aware of your matehood. Keep your hands in your pockets and talk to no one else." Eyeing him then the pass with suspicion, she added, "If you keep it for too long, I'll have it deactivated." Without another word, she walked into the dim room.

The door to the meeting space was only a few feet in front of him, but it may as well have been a mile. Once inside, he'd be able to sit, but until then, he had to make a good impression. Metli had just reminded him that females didn't take kindly to weakness.

He needed to stride in and be seen as a strong, attractive male Alice might be proud to call her own, while also keeping his distance. Already, it was difficult to concentrate on anything other than the pain. Carrying on a conversation would be impossible.

It was unfortunate he wouldn't be able to talk to her, but he decided that going to see the doctor before speaking to her would be the best course of action. Some females even found patience and aloofness attractive, so this may work out in his favor. He took an experimental step and choked. Maybe this wasn't a good idea.

Just as he was starting to feel that a visit to the doctor was more urgent than the meeting, his enhanced senses picked up her scent. Like a slap across the face.

I have to see her, he thought desperately.

Holding his head high, he limped the few feet to the door and then willed a mask of indifference to overtake his features. Inhaling deeply, he opened the door and stepped through, evenly distributing his weight. Searing pain shot through his ankle with his movements. Nausea roiled within him, but he kept his face stoic and scanned the crowd, eager to spot an open chair but more eager to spot Alice.

When his eyes landed on her, he almost forgot the searing pain. She was so lovely, sitting there, smiling. All of his dreams of her had been accurate. His unconscious mind hadn't played tricks on him by enhancing the beauty of her eyes or the wicked curves of her body. She was real and perfect. A true, unguarded smile flashed over her face, and she laughed at something the male next to her, Rhaego, said.

Wait. Rhaego? The hazy spell cast by her visage dissolved. She was talking and laughing with Rhaego.

He took a step toward her, his intentions dark, but halted, feeling as if someone had stabbed him in the ankle with a burning metal poker. The pain was worsening, and the cold sweat that broke out over his skin told him he needed to get off his bad leg soon, or he'd make a joke of himself by fainting in front of his mate.

This is a mistake. I have to get out of here. She hasn't seen me yet.

Without warning, the room began to sink. His gaze whirled toward the control panel and found Metli. She picked at a spot on her floor-length navy vest, unaware of his lethal glare.

He scanned the room again, looking for a chair. All he could do now was wait it out. The free seat that was closest to him was on the opposite side of the table from Alice.

He walked slowly to the seat, trying to look nonchalant and casual but more likely looking insane. A bead of sweat trailed across his temple, and he promptly wiped it away. He clumsily plopped into the soft chair, drawing glances from the attendees nearest him.

She hasn't even noticed I've arrived!

He ground his jaw when he realized his bold attempts to ignore his injury had been in vain. He could've crawled to his chair, and she would've still been engrossed in conversation with Rhaego and…Verakko!

Verakko, a green-skinned male from Swadaeth ancestry, spoke to her with a small grin pulling at his lips. In return, she smiled brightly back at him, laughing at whatever presumably inane thing he'd said. Luka crossed his arms over his chest and attempted to shoot mental daggers at the male with his eyes.

The Swadaeth Clecanians, from the arid western deserts, were a very solitary culture and had evolved in relative isolation from other Clecanians. They tended to prefer the privacy and simplicity of the desert oasis in which they lived.

Because of their self-imposed seclusion, most Swadaeth were known to be antisocial and uninterested in most personal interactions. There'd be no reason for Verakko to want to speak with Alice unless he found her attractive and was trying to charm her. Luka had spoken with the male a few times before and had never seen even the hint of a smile on his face.

So help the male if he is attempting to sway her. Glancing down to his marked wrists, Luka's temper relaxed a fraction. Verakko knew she was someone's mate. Even he would respect that.

Luka rested his crossed arms on the table in front of him, scowling in their direction. He needed to calm down. When she finally did notice his arrival, it would put her off to see him looking so angry.

He allowed his eyes to close briefly, inhaling through his nose to calm himself. Her scent hit him again like a bag of rocks. The sweet, feminine aroma called to him, making him want to rub his head in the crook of her neck.

Jealousy raged through him; he knew the two males near her were able to smell her divine scent as well. His gaze flashed back to where they sat at precisely the wrong moment. From the corner of her eye, she spotted him and did a double-take. The wide smile she'd been sporting only a moment ago faded as she took in his aggressive demeanor.

Way to fucking go, Luka.

As his heart climbed into his throat, another jab of sickening pain sliced through his ankle.

12

∞

There he is. Finally.

Alice was momentarily stunned into silence. The last time she'd seen him, he'd been dirty and wild-looking. Now, his bruises were healed, and his skin had changed from a pale, scratched mess to a healthy bronzed tan. His hair, now clean, hung around his ears in dark brown waves she wanted to run her fingers through. Roaming her gaze down his body, she marveled at the bulging muscles of his crossed arms. It shouldn't have been possible, but since being rescued, he'd somehow filled out even more.

The vision before her was perfection, except for one small thing. He appeared to be seething. His beautiful pale-blue eyes glared at her, and it looked as though every muscle in his body was on high alert. The tension radiating off him was so palpable that the occupants of the chairs near him subtly leaned away.

Her initial heart-pounding joy at both seeing him and beholding his downright gorgeous face was snuffed out. She inhaled shakily. All of her worst fears were being confirmed. He was angry with her. Probably hated her for what she'd done to him in that cell. She'd been stupid to think they might be able to have a relationship after all that. The fact his mating marks had appeared for her must drive him crazy.

She felt herself shrinking under his hard gaze and looked away. Turning to her left, she attempted to engage Verakko in conversation once again. Anything to distract herself from Luka's accusatory stare. "What were you saying about the lake platforms?"

In any other circumstance, the muscular man speaking to her now should've captivated her. The skin near his forehead was a soothing shade of teal, but as it continued down toward his chin and neck, it faded into a vibrant green. His hair was cut short on either side and left long on top, allowing his pointed, pierced ears to be prominently displayed. Streaks of sea-green, aqua, and gray ran through his thick charcoal hair and matched the color of his heavy brows.

Verakko was gorgeous but deadly looking the way a snake might be. When they'd first started speaking, his dry sarcasm and pessimistic disposition had added to his serpentine aura.

She noted the quiet intelligence that radiated off him as he described the platforms in a deep, silky voice, the tone almost melodic. Alice wouldn't have been surprised to learn Verakko's ancestors used their unique timbre to lure prey. Yes, this man in front of her, who looked at her with glowing green eyes, should've been more than enough to keep her attention, but she couldn't keep her gaze and thoughts from straying to the sour-looking man across the table.

"And… You're not listening to me, are you?"

Oh, crap. He must've realized she wasn't paying one lick of attention to his descriptions of the technology employed by The Pearl Temple.

"I'm so sorry. That was rude," she said, forcing her gaze to remain locked on Verakko.

He looked between her and Luka and gave her a wry smile, exposing overly sharp canines. "So that's your mate, huh? I've met Luka a few times, but he's never appeared quite so…angry."

Great, so it's just me, then. "Yeah, I think he's angry I'm his mate."

Verakko snorted. "Then he's an idiot."

Alice shot him a sad smile. What would happen now? Were there any cases of mates becoming unmated? From everything she'd learned, it seemed like mating was for life, but that didn't mean he had to like her.

"He's right to hate me. I forced the marks to appear. I didn't want to do what Helas said, but I didn't have a choice, and now I'm Luka's mate forever, and he hates me and…" Alice's voice grew tight as she rambled on.

"Hey, uh, no need to be upset," he said without conviction. Verakko's gaze shifted around the room; he was clearly uncomfortable with her show of emotion. He leaned in, continuing in a lower tone. "Look, I don't know what happened to you in that place, and I don't know what Helas told you, but you can't force mating marks to appear. They appear or they don't, no matter the circumstances. They may show themselves at different times for different people, but there isn't anything anybody can do to draw them out."

Alice glanced at Luka again, her eyes stinging with unshed tears. Being consoled had always made her cry more, rather than less. Luka still looked furious, but now his hard stare was turned on Verakko. He began to stand but then sat back down quickly, his face paling.

"Look at me, Alice," Verakko commanded. His tone was velvety, and she could feel his words ringing through her mind.

She shook her head to clear it and noticed Verakko's eyes had darted away. Could he actually use his voice to entrance? She peered at him with raised brows.

He cleared his throat and mumbled a quick "sorry" before returning his gaze to hers. He continued without any further explanation. "You're his mate. He isn't yours. If he doesn't have enough sense to see how lucky he is to have found you, that's not your problem. He needs you. You don't need him." He shot a glare toward Luka, then leaned in to whisper, "You tell me if he acts like a pishot, and I'll make sure to hack into his home's programming and make his life a living hell."

"Thanks." Alice chuckled, wiping at her eyes with the sleeve of her sweater. "What's a pishot?"

"No translation for that, huh? It's what you call someone who's acting like an idiot or is a very unlikeable person. How to describe the actual meaning..." He narrowed his eyes, squinting toward the ceiling, and ran the tip of his pointed tongue over his sharp canine. "I believe it originated in the mountains where the Pesque live. I think it means 'One who spits into the wind.'"

She laughed again, drawing out a small smile from Verakko.

He has a point. If Luka wanted to be mad at her, then that was his right, but she needed to remember she didn't really know him. Sure, they'd spent many weeks together, but that hadn't been the real him.

In that place where she had nothing and no one, she'd at least had him. A strong male who'd tried to protect her as best he could. Alice realized she'd been clinging to that version of him, the protector, while forgetting he was also a real man. Scratch that. She'd kept forgetting he was an alien. One she didn't know and might not want to know.

Verakko was also right about Luka needing her. It would hurt to cut ties with him, seeing as she'd grown so attached, but she'd be able to move on if she had to. She was infatuated and attracted, but she wasn't in love, and even if she was, people got over heartbreak all the time. If he was truly interested in being with her, he'd have to work for it too.

She stared up into his tumultuous blue eyes once more. She'd give him a chance, but she needed to hold on to her newfound strength. If he blew it, that would be the end. No second chances. No seeing the good in someone that just didn't exist. No attempting to fix him. Alien or not, he could either win her over or live his life as a mated man without his mate.

One thing was clear—she and Luka needed to sit down and talk it out. She rose, taking a moment to prepare herself for the backlash she might get.

When she approached him, he stood, his eyes trained on her. Whenever she'd entered his cell in the facility, his body would relax, like he'd been waiting all day just to have a glimpse of her. Now, tension rolled off him in waves, and he clenched the back of his chair as though he might crush it at any second.

"Hello, Luka," she said quietly.

He inclined his head a fraction. "Alice."

Over their weeks together, her attraction to him had wormed its way deep into her very marrow. He'd only spoken one word, but his familiar, deep rumbling voice made a bolt of electricity shoot up her spine.

They stared at each other for long moments. This was the first time they'd really spoken since...ever. When she glanced around, she saw everyone's attention had turned to them.

She felt heat rising on her cheeks. "After the meeting, could we talk outside?"

"No," he said swiftly. The knuckles of the hand still gripping his chair were white.

She nibbled her lip, unsure how to reply to the blatant refusal. He opened his mouth, but then closed it again. Was it just her, or did he look pale?

"We should really talk. I want to apologize for what happened down there," she urged, wondering if she was causing his sickly reaction. "I know you may not remember me or what happened, but I—"

"I don't wish to talk to you right now, Alice," he said through gritted teeth, then sat back down, not meeting her eyes.

Alice bit the inside of her cheek and continued to stare at the side of his face. Shame and embarrassment washed over her. She could feel everyone's eyes on her. Taking in the uncomfortable exchange.

As she shuffled back to her seat and plopped down, she could just imagine the vivid shade of red her face had turned. A small part of her relaxed when she noticed most of the eyes in the room remained angrily fixed on Luka.

A deep scowl was clear on Verakko's face, the most emotion she'd seen from him yet, and even Rhaego, who'd been nothing but kind and sweet to everyone he'd spoken to, sneered in Luka's direction.

It's not his fault. He has every right to be upset with me. If I were in his shoes, I wouldn't want to see me, either.

Luka kept his gaze trained on his interlaced fingers in front of him, ignoring the silent berating directed toward him.

He could've handled it better, though. That was very rude. Alice's chest puffed a little, indignation mixing with her embarrassment and sympathy. A part of her reasoned she didn't know enough about the alien culture to assume Luka's actions were rude, but the reaction of everyone else, paired with the kind, respectful treatment she'd been given from all of the other men, told her differently.

The Queen emerged from a door to the right along with a tall, elegant woman. The new woman's eyes met Alice's, and she gave a courteous nod before moving to sit next to Jade and Theo.

The Queen now stood near an empty seat at the table. She turned to Metli. "Is everyone accounted for?"

Metli nodded.

Alice told herself she needed to concentrate on this meeting. Make sure the Queen didn't regret inviting her. But no matter how hard she tried to keep her mind focused, her thoughts and eyes strayed back to Luka.

She couldn't decide if she should be heartened or wary of the fact that he kept glancing at her too. Whenever her gaze wandered to him, she'd catch him watching her before quickly looking away. His bitchy attitude with her must've made him feel better at least, because he no longer looked like he wanted to throttle her.

Great! Yet another person who feels better after taking it out on me. Just what I need.

Willing her mind to forget about Luka for a few minutes, she looked around the room, eyes landing briefly on each of the attendees. They all sat at a large round table with a hollow center. Verakko and Rhaego sat on either side of her. Next to Rhaego sat Theo, then Jade, then the graceful woman who'd been speaking with the Queen. Next to her, and directly across from Alice, sat the brooding Luka.

166

A pale woman with a platinum-blonde pixie cut and sour expression sat on his other side, her lips pursed. She didn't look too different from a human, but the barely visible white markings running along her neck and bare shoulders were enough to tell Alice she was a Clecanian. Next to her sat Lucy, the only person in attendance who looked excited to be here. The Queen sat on Lucy's other side, then Metli, and finally Verakko. Eleven in all.

Alice focused her attention back on the Queen and waited.

"Thank you all for attending this meeting. I am grateful to each and every one of you for your discretion," the Queen said, sweeping her eyes around the room. "We are here today to discuss three things. One: the immediate threat of the Insurgents. Two: the revelation that humans are a compatible species and are able to not only bear Clecanian children but also to call forth our long-dormant mating instinct. And finally, three: to decide the best way to move forward with the rescued human females and how to proceed, now knowing what we know."

The Queen stayed silent a moment longer, allowing for her words to sink in. "I'd like Luka to begin by recounting everything he has learned about the Insurgents from his investigation before being taken and anything he can remember after. Any piece of information might be enough for us to learn where their other locations are."

Luka nodded, eyes flashing to Alice before settling on his tightly clasped hands once more. "Well, to start, they don't have an official name. They have a code, sort of like a motto they use to identify each other. Before my…detainment, Helas taught me the code. They clasp forearms and say, 'Purity. Reform. Integrity. Clecania.' And I learned Helas was in contact with many other facilities. Outposts, he called them."

Lucy began to snicker, and quickly covered her mouth. Everyone's eyes focused on her, and she held up a hand. "Sorry. Sorry. It's just…" She gave another small chuckle. "They call themselves PRIC?"

Jade and Alice began to laugh, but the aliens remained silent, seeming confused.

"On Earth, 'prick' is a slang insult. It means small penis," Jade said, her shoulders shaking with repressed laughter.

Rhaego quickly stifled his deep laugh in a cough, and even the Queen's mouth twitched in amusement. Luka's lips stayed thinned, his jaw still clenched.

"How fitting," the Queen began. "Metli, could you please make a note about the change of nomenclature? Moving forward, it seems only right that we use the name they've chosen. They'll be referred to as PRICs or Insurgents." She gave another brief nod toward Luka and said, "Please continue."

"I wasn't able to learn much before he figured out what I was doing, but he did show me five to six monitors with live feeds of incarcerated beings, held in other outposts. Mostly human females, but some Clecanian males and females as well." Luka cleared his throat before continuing, "He inferred they'd emptied their cells of all non-human species since they

felt they'd found what they were looking for in the humans."
His voice grew distant, and he shifted in his seat. "I don't
know what was done with the others."

Pricks, indeed.

Alice studied Luka. His emotions were mostly hidden, but
she thought she saw guilt lurking in his eyes. Even after his
harsh treatment of her a moment ago, she felt her heart go
out to him. He must know he couldn't have saved them.

Verakko chimed in from next to her. "The ability to
display other facilities' vids means the outposts were
connected. I tried to hack into the system after Jade was
rescued and then again when Alice escaped, but in both cases
the connection had been severed. They must have had a
failsafe in place."

Luka's deep voice rang through the room, making
goosebumps erupt over her skin. "From what I saw, their
technology is outdated. I'm not sure how long they've been
active, but it looked like the vast majority of their tech hasn't
been state-of-the-art for fifty years, at least. Early on, they
were even using plain metal chains to tie me down rather than
magnetic until…" His jaw clenched again, and he kept his
stare trained on his hands. "Until they broke."

"When they took me, they told me their organization had
been active for a hundred years at least," Jade confirmed.

"I'd like for you to continue looking for any trace of a
signal. Just in case we missed something," the Queen said,
addressing Verakko.

"I'll keep working on it, but even if I were to somehow gain access," Verakko began, "I still wouldn't be able to pinpoint their locations. It's likely they're frequency hopping multiple times per second. Without time, copious amounts of money, and unlimited resources, there'll be no way for me to trace the signal to a physical source. Unless they were dumb enough to label each station link with its geographic location, we'll have access but won't be able to lead a team to rescue the captives."

Another moment of silence passed, in which Alice caught Luka's gaze. There was an answer staring them in the face, so why hadn't anyone mentioned it yet? "Helas probably knows where the other outposts are." Her stomach turned sour at the mention of his name.

Luka flinched almost imperceptibly as well.

The Queen let out a long sigh. "As of this morning, he has been less than forthcoming with that information."

"I could make him talk," Theo said gruffly, gripping Jade's hand.

If Theo's admission had affected the Queen, she didn't show it. "We don't know the extent of Helas' reach. It's clear the Insurgents have many powerful people working with them to have remained undetected this long. Helas is currently being detained at an undisclosed location, but there could be Insurgent moles lurking anywhere. For all we know, they could decide to destroy the outposts and start from scratch if they think we are getting too close. Keeping things quiet is our best chance to find the outposts and free the prisoners without any fatalities. All mention of the PRICs, humans, mating, and outposts needs to be contained to this room." She turned her attention to Jade. "Does anyone else know about your pregnancy?"

The woman to Jade's right answered before Jade could. "Wasde, from The Intergalactic Alliance, and Reana, from The Galaxy Supervision Federation, were both present for the announcement of the sex. They are trusted friends of mine and have sworn to keep what they know to themselves until we've decided what to do. In the meantime, they are thinking through action plans of their own to bring to their superiors, when the time is right."

The woman turned her attention to Alice and Lucy. "My name is Asivva, by the way. I'm a member of The Intergalactic Alliance, and I wanted to make sure we were prepared for the frenzy that will ensue once it's revealed that Jade is not only pregnant but mated."

Alice smiled, grateful the woman was making it a point to explain things to them.

"That brings us to our next topic of discussion," the Queen said, interlacing her fingers in front of her. "Originally, when Jade was found, I had decided she should follow our rules and participate in the ceremony. Now, the situation is more complex. Since Jade's rescue, the twelve human females found have been kept here, at the Temple. Humans are able to become pregnant with Clecania children, and they are also able to call mating marks forward. No male humans have been rescued, but it's likely they will have the same effect as the females."

The Queen eyed Luka's wrists momentarily before continuing. "Because mating marks seem to only affect the Clecanians, it would be immoral to follow our currently outdated laws of matehood. Humans don't feel the pull of matehood, and as such, I can't force them to remain with their mates. Once we have control of the Insurgent situation, humans will be allowed to choose who they want to be with, where they would like to live, and how often, if ever, they will participate in the ceremony, whether or not they have called forth mating marks."

Luka's eyes flashed to Alice then to the Queen. "No!" he barked.

The Queen's eyebrows rose. "Would you prefer I force Alice to stay with you against her will?"

He glanced to Alice again, and she felt as though he were actually trying to judge how to answer the clearly rhetorical question. Another shiver ran through her. *Just because he doesn't want to be with me doesn't mean he's impervious to the mating bond.*

Rather than answering, he allowed composure to wash over his pinched features, answering her as a researcher interested in the topic would, void of emotion but curious and logical. "The answer to that question seems obvious, but I cannot in good conscience say one way or another. We don't know the effect that unrequited matehood could have on our people. It's been too long since a Clecanian mated pair walked our streets, and in those days, there was no question about whether the feelings would be reciprocated or not. We don't have enough evidence to know what'll happen to a mated Clecanian if they're not permitted to be with their mate. For all we know, it could cause severe illness or death." Luka fixed his gaze on his hands once again and winced. "Personally, I've already begun to experience some side effects."

What side effects? Alice pondered how she should feel about that. What if it turned out he hated her but still needed to be close to her to relieve the negative side effects of the mating bond? Even through the hurt and embarrassment of their first meeting, she found herself wanting to be close to him.

Would she be able to be intimate with Luka without her emotions getting in the way?

Not likely.

"I'd like permission to begin research in the archives so I can see if there are any ways to calm the side effects and also to understand what mated Clecanians might need to know before we decide for sure that our laws need to be changed."

The Queen nodded. "I see your point, Luka, and you will have the access you need."

"I'll also need access here," he said coolly. "I'll need to be able to visit Alice from time to time."

Luka was holding her gaze with deadly calm. The hair rose on Alice's arms. She'd learned she was safe with Luka, that even crazed he wouldn't hurt her, but looking at his dark, unreadable expression now, she wondered if it was a good idea for him to have access to her home. She didn't know this man. Didn't know how he thought. Alice had been ready to jump in with both feet if he'd shown the smallest amount of interest, but now, fear tempered her excitement.

The Queen spoke, rousing Luka from his unwavering stare. "I understand your reasoning, but the decision of when and how often you visit will be left up to Alice. If she permits you to visit, you'll be escorted. I cannot give you unfettered access to the Temple."

Alice let out a relieved breath. Luka said nothing, but she could see the whites of his knuckles, clenched on the table again.

When Luka remained silent, the Queen continued, "What will happen to the human females and the laws concerning matehood will likely change worldwide when news of their existence becomes public knowledge. I can make the laws here, but it is likely other cities will have different ways of dealing with the issue. Rhaego, forgive me if I'm wrong, but your people may not give as much choice to human females as we will."

Alice could have sworn Rhaego's purple horns darkened a shade. He nodded solemnly. "Matehood is revered in Tuva. Once word spreads, the chase will likely continue with renewed vigor, and I can only assume our citizens will become vicious and possessive of the human females if it is found they can be mated. In the minds of my fellow Tuvasta, mating is not something that can be controlled by laws. I fail to imagine King Yaskan putting any law into place that would keep a mated male from his female, and even if he did, none of our citizens would pay any attention to that law."

"Thank you for your honesty. I assumed as much." The Queen glanced around the room. "Many cities across Clecania will feel the same. The only way for human females to be protected is if there are laws put into place worldwide by The Galaxy Supervision Federation. Once we have revealed their existence and importance, we will need to have at least the beginnings of laws worked out with your contacts, Asivva. I'm afraid if we don't, and we keep the females hidden here, the other cities will rebel. They will want the chance to visit and mate the females, and some of the more aggressive cities might try and take them by force."

Rising, the Queen began to pace back and forth near her chair. "This brings me to our final issue. When the world learns of the humans' existence and what they are capable of, there will be a call for action. Most leaders will want more females brought here."

Alice was startled when the platinum-blonde sitting next to Luka finally spoke. In a cool voice, she intoned, "And why would we not bring more humans here?"

Alice eyed the pale woman. She was pretty, the way most of the Clecanians tended to be, but her dour expression lessened the effect. So far, she'd been watching the conversation with disinterest. Why had she been invited?

"For many reasons, Vila," the Queen began. "Their planet is a Class 4 planet and is therefore off limits to us. They are a sentient species and not merely a herd of cethid. We cannot land on their planet and abduct hundreds, if not thousands, of Earthlings. We would need permission to reveal ourselves to the leaders of the planet, and then, we would need to find a way to transport only willing humans. I don't know much about Earth," she said, looking at Jade, Alice, and Lucy for support, "but I can assume they wouldn't take kindly to aliens taking their citizens."

Alice couldn't even imagine the worldwide panic that would ensue if not only one group of aliens but galaxies of different alien species were revealed to exist. She inwardly snorted; maybe the leaders of Earth would finally come together for once.

"The fact that humans are Clecanian descendants and can be mated may hold the key to a cure for the people of this planet. Many believe our early interference with natural evolution may be, in part, why we are no longer fertile. Humans have not altered themselves in the same way. Studying their unique genetics could save us all. They may not take kindly to us in the beginning, but they'll adapt, just as these females have," Vila said, gesturing to Alice, Jade, and Lucy.

"I agree, but communication and peaceful exchanges are our only answer. We cannot simply take what we want because we can," the Queen said sternly.

"It'll happen regardless. You know that," Vila said quietly, holding eye contact with the Queen.

Alice decided she didn't care for that woman. She could see where she was coming from, but the way she spoke suggested she'd already made her mind up about how they should handle the humans. Would this woman, Vila, keep the information from this meeting quiet?

"Which is why I appreciate your silence," the Queen said, reading Alice's mind. "We need to come up with a plan before individuals start taking matters into their own hands."

Vila leaned back in her chair and lifted her chin. "I vow you have my silence, for now, but you need to come up with a plan quickly. Mating marks are not something you're going to be able to keep quiet for long even if the males paint their hands. And if you're able to rescue females from all of the outposts, word will spread even more quickly."

The Queen held Vila's stare. "Do any of the humans present have anything to add?"

Lucy stood, smoothing her long dress. "Hi, I'm Lucy," she said brightly, smiling around the room. "Personally, I don't mind being here, but I can say with absolute certainty that no matter how awesome this place is, people are going to freak out when they learn about aliens for the first time. You need to make sure that when you do reveal yourselves, you work on maintaining a certain image. I don't know if your goal is to bring men here too, but if you just want heterosexual females, then you need to show off the Clecanian men. Also show any happy alien-human couples a lot too. If you bring some hot, charming aliens to Earth for your first meet-and-greet and put them on social media, you're going to have ladies lining up around the block to hop on a spaceship back here." She tucked a strand of honey-blonde hair behind her ear.

Alice tilted her head and smiled at Lucy, who'd relaxed back into her seat. She had a way of making even the most daunting task seem reasonable and achievable. Her chipper attitude would cause many to believe she was shallow, but she spoke with a sort of optimistic intelligence that made it difficult to not both respect and like her. Alice wondered if she'd worked in media back on Earth. She'd have made a great reporter.

"I agree," Jade said, still sitting. "It was hard to remember why I shouldn't want to live here when I watched my hunky husband dote on me. There are plenty of Earth women who'll come voluntarily, but there are also plenty who are in loving relationships, and others who'd object to a lot of the customs here. It's going to be difficult at first, but I think if you offer up some of your knowledge of technology and space travel, without asking for anything in return, that'd help grease the wheels."

"Thank you all for your valuable insight. I'm going to think on what you have said. I am hopeful that the next time we meet, we will have a plan that is clearer." The Queen waved a hand toward Metli, who'd been silent throughout the meeting, diligently typing into a small screen in front of her. As Metli moved to bring the room back to the surface, people began rising and talking to one another.

Luka stayed seated, his hard stare back on her. Alice was readying to retreat when the Queen approached her. Now that she was close, Alice could make out faint dark circles under her eyes and the strained note in her voice as she said, "Have you recalled the questions you would like to ask me?"

Not wanting to keep the busy woman longer, she asked about something she'd pondered while sitting alone in her quiet house yesterday. "On Earth, I was studying to be a veterinarian, a doctor for animals. I started late, so I haven't gotten that far into the program, but I was wondering if I'd be able to continue that training here."

The Queen gave her a small smile. "That is a marvelous idea. It's wonderful that you feel you could stay here and make a career for yourself."

Alice looked over to find Luka watching them with narrowed eyes.

The Queen continued. "Yes, of course you can continue your studies here, although you may need to start from the beginning, seeing as our animals are different." She frowned then. "I'd ask that you hold off on this endeavor until we have revealed the presence of humans to our world. For now I can arrange for someone to teach you our language at The Pearl Temple, if you'd like?"

"That'd be wonderful," Alice exclaimed. She may be able to communicate with everyone thanks to her translator, but she couldn't yet read Clecanian writing, as evidenced by her hand clock.

"I'll teach her," Luka said loudly, startling both women.

Alice frowned. A minute ago, he'd implied he wanted unrestricted access to her, and a few minutes before that, he'd wanted nothing to do with her. Why would he want to teach her? *Make up your mind!*

"I don't want you distracted from your research, Luka. No, I'll find someone else to help Alice," the Queen said.

"No males," Luka said simply, still not bothering to rise from his seat.

Alice's annoyance and frustration finally began to outweigh her embarrassment and hurt at his earlier rejection. Before the Queen could respond, she stomped over to Luka. "You have no right to tell me who I can or cannot take lessons from. You've made it abundantly clear you have no interest in me, so I don't understand why you even care. I'm not going to keep apologizing for what happened at the outpost. I had no choice, okay?" She felt heat spread over her cheeks. Alice turned and walked away, muttering, "Why don't you just run to the archives and get to work on your research so you can figure out how to get us unmated already." When she reached the Queen, she noted her amused expression. "If you don't need me for anything else, I'd like to leave."

The Queen smirked at her and gestured to the exit.

On her way out, she heard a scuffle behind her; turning to look, she found Jade and Theo approaching a pained-looking Luka. He had risen and was now looming over the table, watching her with brows drawn, the way he used to look after Helas had hurt him.

Alice forced herself to turn her head. *Don't feel bad. Don't feel bad.* Just because he was mated didn't give him the right to be proprietary with her.

On her short walk back to her home, her thoughts were in turmoil. She wavered between anger and empathy for Luka. On the one hand, he had no right to treat her like property. Being cold to her one moment then controlling the next. On the other hand, she had no idea how the mating marks were affecting him. She knew mates felt a strong pull toward one another, but she didn't know how strong that pull was.

If he was feeling this connection to her but also anger toward her, then obviously he was bound to have conflicting emotional outbursts. It'd make sense he didn't want to talk to her but also didn't want her to talk to any other man.

She didn't know how to feel. Should she be mad, or should she give him a break? Old Alice would've given him a break, no question about it. The terrible situation in which Luka found himself would've called to her. Tugged at her heartstrings. She would've tried again and again to make him like her. Convinced herself he just needed time.

Even if she accepted that his actions were normal in this culture, and even if this was what men acted like on this planet, could she live with that?

She slammed the door as she entered her house. *Not this time,* she thought, angrier with herself than Luka. *If he wants to apologize, I'll hear him out, but I'm not going to let myself be walked on all over again. He's been nothing but rude to me since we escaped, and I don't deserve that. I was abducted and locked up too! No more thinking about Luka, that's it.*

13

Fuck, this hurts. Luka tried to stand. To chase her. To tell her he wasn't thinking clearly right now. But a searing pain shot up his leg, forcing him to fall back into his chair.

He turned to see Theo and his new mate, Jade, approaching. Today was the first day he'd seen Jade, but even with his attention divided he'd noticed Theo didn't seem uncomfortable or self-conscious when he was with her. The change in his brother was glorious and made him wonder how Alice might improve his own life. If he was able to undo the damage he'd just done, that is.

"What's wrong with you?" she said angrily, without any introduction.

"I—" he began, but she cut him off.

"Theo told me what happened to you in that outpost. That poor girl rescued you, and you treat her like that?" Luka tried to speak again, but Jade held up her hand for silence. "You couldn't have just let her down easy. If you don't like her, that's one thing, but to embarrass her like that in front of everyone? Cold. Stone cold," she finished, shaking her head disapprovingly.

Luka eyed his brother, a silent plea for help. The corner of Theo's mouth lifted in a smirk, and he stood back, allowing Luka to be scolded by his small pregnant wife.

Before she could resume her yelling, Luka spoke. "I didn't mean to treat her poorly, but I'm in a great deal of pain. Do either of you happen to have a healer on you?" he asked as politely as he could through clenched teeth.

He'd found that while sitting, he could manage the pain, but any time he stood, blackness threatened to overtake him. He hadn't meant to be so short with Alice, but he'd made the mistake of standing, as males were supposed to do when talking with a female, and at the time, pushing her away had seemed preferable to fainting on top of her.

Theo's grin faded, replaced by concern. "You're hurt?" he said, scanning Luka's body.

"I tripped on the way here. I think I may have broken my ankle. I was already running late and had no time to heal it before the meeting started, so I decided to bear it instead."

"You tripped on the way here?" he repeated with narrowed eyes. Jade settled herself into a seat next to him, and while she was preoccupied, Luka sent Theo a warning glare. A muscle ticked in Theo's jaw, but he said, "Let me find a healer for you. Stay here with Jade for a moment."

When Theo had left the room, Jade scowled at him once again. "Why didn't you just tell her you were injured and in a lot of pain instead of acting like an ass?"

Luka's eyes widened in surprise. Jade wasn't altogether wrong, but he wasn't used to a female being so unguarded with her words.

I was an ass.

"Limping in injured and weak wouldn't have been attractive," he muttered, feeling as though his plan had only worked to hurt his chances with Alice.

"So, you thought it'd be more attractive to look uncaring and possessive than weak?"

"Yes!" His shoulders slumped, and he added, "At least for a Clecanian female."

Luka didn't know what else to say. A Clecanian female wouldn't have approached a male. She would've waited for him to approach her. It hadn't factored into Luka's decision that Alice may try and initiate a conversation with him. He also knew he'd vastly underestimated both his injury and the effect seeing her with another male would have on him. He flinched. Telling her she couldn't be taught by a male had been over the line. It wasn't his place to say that to any female. At least, not in that way.

"A Clecanian female—" he began to argue before being interrupted yet again.

"Ugh, this again. Sometimes I feel like Izzo is the only one of you with any brains. At least he had the good sense to come and ask for my advice about a human girl he likes. What makes you think you know how to act around a human?" She spoke her next words slowly, making Luka wonder if he liked Jade after all. "Alice is not Clecanian. She's human, and I'm guessing by her reaction, she's utterly offended right now. As well she should be. Most human women appreciate honesty. If you wanted to appear strong, congratulations, you did it. She now thinks of you as the strongest jerk around."

The female was rude and condescending and…right. He didn't know how human females behaved or what they'd want out of a male. So far, he'd spent his time researching medical information pertaining to humans and watching her from afar, but he'd never thought to use one of the best resources he had at his disposal. A human female. His sister-in-law, no less. Luka was a proud male, but he was also a scientist. His logic had failed him, and he could admit when he was wrong.

"You're right. I thought she'd act like a Clecanian female, and now I worry I've ruined any chance I had. Can you help me?"

Jade, who'd been shifting uncomfortably on the chair, looked at him with brows drawn. Slowly a smile curved over her face. "Wow. I'm glad you aren't as stubborn as your brother. Or me, for that matter. I thought that would've been a hell of a lot harder fight. Ego being what it is." She shot him a sheepish grin. "Sorry for going off on you. Between being cooped up in the house and close to full term, my temper's out of control."

"That's an understatement." Theo entered then, carrying a healer. Jade rolled her eyes but said nothing.

Luka could sing with relief. He needed to go and see Alice. Make things right. Explain why he'd behaved so badly. But first he had to learn more about humans from Jade.

Grabbing the device out of Theo's hand, he ran it over his swollen ankle.

"You know that'll only help with the pain temporarily," Theo said. "You need to go and see a doctor right after this to fix any breaks."

Thankful the small device could give him any relief at all, he let out a sigh then looked to Jade. "What do I need to know to win a human female?"

Theo snorted from behind Jade.

Jade swatted at him then turned her attention back to Luka. "First, tell me, do you really like her, or do you just want to charm her because she's your mate?"

Luka had wondered this himself, but the more time passed and the more he watched her, small memories from the cell came back to him. "I can't lie and say the bond isn't causing me to have…intense feelings for her, but those feelings are more of a sexual and protective nature. I want her for those reasons, but they aren't all. She saved me in more ways than one at the outpost. I was drugged, nearly out of my mind, but present enough to dimly understand what they were doing to me. If my foggy memories are correct, she was kind when she didn't have to be. And brave. There aren't many people who can boast that kindness and strength. My mating instinct may

186

have drawn me to her initially, but she's the only reason I was able to survive in that place. She tied me to my sanity. Gave me a reason to keep fighting. If she never wants to see me again, I'll understand, but I'll never stop wanting her."

Jade stared at Luka, a wide grin on her face. "Just tell her that. Easy-peasy."

"What?"

"That was a great little speech." She counted off on her fingers. "You like her for who she is. You're insanely attracted to her. You'll work hard to win her over, but you won't try to force her to be with you if she doesn't want to."

"She'll be satisfied with that?" Luka asked curiously. "She won't want gifts or a demonstration of my abilities or my grades?"

Jade glanced toward Theo pleadingly. He took a seat near her, sighing. "We're going to be here all day, aren't we?"

***

As Luka left the medbay Theo had escorted him to, he reflected on what Jade had told him. If she was right, Alice wouldn't need the showmanship that normally accompanied a courtship.

Her descriptions of a human relationship were too good for Luka to believe. Constant affection? Shared bed for sleeping? Luka had never in his wildest dreams thought those things were possible, even if he found a cure for Clecanian infertility.

In order to have all that Jade had told him, though, he'd need to redeem himself to Alice.

He'd learned that his ankle, now fully healed, hadn't been broken. The slender bone directly above his ankle, however, had been. When the doctor had examined him, he'd been surprised to learn Luka had not only been dealing with the pain for over two hours, but had tried to walk on the injured limb.

Holding his guest pass ball tightly in his hands, he stared across the water at Alice's small floating house. Anxiety made his heartbeat quicken and heat crept up his collar. Luka frowned.

In his world, he excelled at almost anything he tried. If he set his mind to something, more often than not, he succeeded. Feeling anxiety wasn't something he was used to.

Whenever he'd interacted with females before, he'd been either charming, as his studies had taught him, or uninterested. He'd made it to the testing phase of the ceremony twice now, but had always refused to participate to avoid being chosen. He knew himself, and he knew what he wanted. A temporary wife was not that. Anytime he used what he'd been taught in school to charm a female, it'd always been with the direct and outspoken goal of having sex.

As Luka felt his palms grow damp with sweat, he realized it was different with Alice. He cared if she liked him. He wanted her to like him. To seek him out for conversations. He wanted to be a person worthy of her attention, and right now, he didn't feel that way.

He set off, relieved when he found the platforms appear under his feet as he walked to her home. *How soon before Metli deactivates the pass?* Being stung by bilom would only send him back to the medbay and away from Alice once again.

When he reached her door, he took a moment to compose himself, then knocked.

A small voice sounded from behind the door, "Hello? Who is it?"

"Luka."

He scowled when his reply was followed by silence. Just as he was ready to speak to her through the wood rather than in person as he'd hoped, Alice opened the door.

His breath was temporarily stolen at the sight of her and the exposed skin of her arms and shoulders. She was no longer wearing the sweater from earlier.

After holding his gaze for a moment, she stepped to the side of the doorway. "Would you like to come in?" she asked, her lips thinned.

This must be an Earth custom.

He decided it'd be rude to turn her down, even as he cringed to think of other males she may have innocently invited into her home. An invitation into the house of a Clecanian female was usually a signal that she was interested in sex. The way Alice's eyes kept straying around the room nervously told him she, unfortunately, didn't intend the same.

Now within the bright, cool confines of her home, he set the ball near the door and studied her again. Silently, he thanked the unseasonably warm weather for the glimpse of her exposed shoulders and the low dip of her neckline.

She cleared her throat, and his eyes snapped back to hers. He clenched his fists in frustration. At his first opportunity to make a better impression, he'd been unable to keep himself from ogling her.

A pale pink spread over her cheeks, drawing his attention away from his aims yet again. *Would her cheeks flush like that after a vigorous bout of fucking, or would her skin pinken everywhere?*

"Can I help you?" she said without meeting his eyes.

Get ahold of yourself! Luka cleared his throat. "I'd like to apologize for embarrassing you before."

Alice raised a delicate brow. "You're apologizing for *embarrassing* me?" she said slowly.

"Yes, I—" The burning look in her eyes gave him pause. "I didn't mean to speak to you like that in front of everyone."

"Oh!" she laughed. "Did you mean to speak to me like a dick in private?"

"No…" he began but struggled to clarify.

Alice held up a hand. "Luka, I really don't know what you want from me. I'm sorry we're in this mess and that you feel like I'm your mate now, but I don't think we should be together."

His heart leap into his throat, cutting off his rapidly dissolving reasonable argument to the contrary. He tracked her abrupt pacing around the room, her words coming quickly, as though she'd rehearsed her argument.

"When we first met, I didn't really know you. You helped me stay sane in that place, and for that, I'll be forever grateful, but I need to stop putting other people's happiness before my own." She glanced at him beseechingly before resuming. "I was willing to give us a try, but that was stupid of me. Again, I don't know you, and the way you've treated me so far has been very similar to other people in my life who've proven to be toxic."

Indignation roared through him. *She's comparing me to people who have hurt her in the past? She can't think of me that way!*

"I can explain my actions," he barked, more harshly than intended.

She flinched, and he cursed his erratic temper. The only way to win her over would be to go back to being the calm, reserved person he normally was, but his feelings for her and her rejection were making that impossible.

"I'm sure there's an explanation," she said, throwing her hands in the air. "There's always an explanation, but I need to stop letting people treat me badly and then explain it away." She spoke in a low voice, miming someone. "'I didn't mean to yell, I just had a bad day at work.' Or 'I'm sorry, I forgot about your birthday again. It's just so close to Christmas.'"

Luka couldn't follow everything she was talking about, but it seemed like she'd been treated very poorly by someone or possibly many someones, and now she thought he might do the same. "You're right. I should've never treated you that way. There is no excuse for my behavior."

She blinked at him, searching his face. "Well, uh, thank you for that." She ran a hand through her hair.

They stared at each other for long moments. Luka didn't know what to say to help the situation. How could he prove himself to be a suitable male? All of the lessons from husbandry school hadn't prepared him for this. Something Jade had said stuck out in his mind, but he hadn't gotten enough information to know if it'd work. She'd said it was very romantic and although he'd never tried it, he figured it couldn't hurt.

"Can I make it up to you?" he asked, stepping toward her. He took it as a good sign that although she looked at him warily, she didn't back away. When she remained silent, he continued, "I'd like to kiss you."

Alice's eyes widened in surprise. In the next moment, many emotions played across her features. Her gaze flew to his mouth and grew temporarily heated, making Luka growl quietly under his breath.

She shook her head as though trying to dislodge a thought. "No!" Walking up to him until only a few feet separated them, she prodded him in the chest with an accusatory finger. "Didn't you hear anything I just said?"

Before he could stop himself, he snatched her hand, circling her wrist and resting his thumb in her palm. A loud purr erupted from his chest at the contact.

She stared at their connected hands but didn't move. Slowly she raised her gaze to his. "What makes you think I'd want to kiss you?" she muttered breathlessly, belying her question.

Luka didn't know why she might want to, but Jade had made it seem like it was a very important thing done among courting humans, and Alice's reaction told him something he hadn't known before. She may not like him. She may even hate him. But she was attracted to him.

He ran the pad of his thumb down her palm, squeezing the pulse point at her wrist with his other fingers. A quick inhalation of breath showed him that even this small touch was affecting her as much as it was him. When the scent of her arousal wafted between them, it took all of his willpower not to crush her to him.

"Well," he began, his voice scarcely more than a growl, "for starters, your pulse has sped up substantially. Also—" he ran his gaze down her body, not bothering to hide his perusal of her figure "—I can scent your arousal."

Alice let out a small whimper and shifted her stance so her legs were more firmly squeezed together. *Not a denial, then.* He smiled.

He stepped nearer to her, and her brows drew together in concentration. Because his words seemed to drive her anger away, he continued, "I've never kissed in the way Jade described, but if it elicits this reaction from you, then I'd be happy to do it every minute of every day."

"You've never kissed?" she whispered, eyeing his lips and licking her own.

He stepped closer to her still, making sure not to touch her for fear of her shying away. "I'm a fast learner. Top marks in all subjects."

Crooking a finger under her chin, he angled her head up toward his. He inhaled deeply, his eyelids drifting closed. Her natural, sweet scent mixed with her arousal called to something deep within him. His already rising shaft shot hard in an instant. He'd smelled this before. He recognized it somewhere in the back of his mind.

The fact that he'd scented her arousal previously, and now recognized the scent, made his spirits soar. It meant she'd responded to him like this before. Had been attracted to him and couldn't suppress it.

A devious thought entered his mind. He may not be the best with reading her emotions, but he could make her desire him in other ways. If he spent enough time pleasing her, she might slowly come to want him around. If he was around enough, he could learn how to win her over.

This wasn't how he'd wanted their relationship to be—based on sex, just like every other Clecanian's was—but he'd take what he could get. He'd vow to work his way under her skin.

"Top marks?" she questioned absently, her hand rising to fist his shirt. At her touch, his purring intensified.

She'd let him kiss her. He knew she would. But he didn't know exactly what he was supposed to do. Did he kiss one lip at a time the same way he'd kiss the column of her neck, or should he lick and suck the way he'd kiss her nipples? Hoping she'd take the lead once he started, he lowered his mouth. Pressed his lips to hers and held them in place motionlessly.

His eyes still open, he saw hers crinkle in humor. A heartbeat passed, and Luka began to feel like an idiot. This was obviously not right. Before he could pull away, she moved. She pressed her mouth firmly to his, rounding her lips. When he matched her movements, she parted her mouth slightly, letting her breath mingle with his. The sensation was new but not unpleasant. He found this connection to be surprisingly intimate and erotic. He had to focus all of his energy to not push to take charge of the kiss and explore it the way he wanted.

All his self-control shattered, however, when she swiped her tongue across his. Surprise made him rear his head back. Alice peered up at him with a languid smile before her eyes widened in horror. "Oh, you didn't like that. I'm so sorry. I—"

With a growl, he covered her mouth with his and deepened the kiss in the way he wanted, hoping it was correct. Before she could decide to move away, he pulled her body to his, one hand fisting in her hair to hold her in place while the other ran down the small of her back. To his shock and relief, she wrapped her arms around his neck, meeting his fevered kiss with a passion of her own.

A low groan escaped him when he felt her body soften, her curves pressing against his now-aching shaft.

Need to find a bed. Now! he thought, his mind only half present.

The scent of her arousal had strengthened, driving his sense away. Both of his hands reached down to squeeze her round ass. He wanted to roar with pleasure when she moaned into his mouth. He lifted her easily, intending to carry her to the nearest horizontal surface. Her legs wrapped around his waist, putting her pussy in line with his cock.

She rocked against him lightly. How was it possible for anyone to inspire such maddening lust? Luka felt as if he'd die if he weren't inside her in the next instant, but first, he had to make sure she wanted him. He'd please her for as long as it took for her to be ready.

Tucked into a private corner of the large open room, he spotted her bed. Walking them to the edge, he sank onto it. She continued to grind underneath him. If she didn't stop soon, he'd come right there. Forcing himself to pull away from the kiss, he gazed down at his mate.

His chest tightened at the image before him. Her lips were swollen from their kiss, her cheeks flushed. More beautiful yet, she beamed up at him. In between pants, she whispered, "I tried to kiss you before. You pulled away."

He grinned. "I wouldn't have if I'd known what I was in for."

He sat back, running his gaze over her. Pride swelled in him when she laid still, allowing him to look. He scrubbed a palm over his face at the sight of her hardened nipples poking through her thin top. Her thighs were still spread around his hips, giving him the merest glimpse of her underwear just visible under her dress.

Was he ever going to be able to leave this bed? If she'd allow it, he'd happily stay here forever.

Licking his lips and eyeing the hem of her skirt, he knew exactly where he wanted to start this veritable feast. "If I go lock your door, will you move?" he questioned, not wanting to break the daze they were in but needing to ensure their privacy.

A shy smile played at her lips. "I'll be here."

Before she could change her mind, he dashed to the door, engaging the lock with a shaking hand. "I plan to have you in that bed as long as you'll let me, and I don't want those girls to interrupt," he called over his shoulder. After the bolts sounded, he turned and walked back toward her, taking in the sight of her beautiful form reclined on the bed.

She giggled. "What girls?"

He reached the edge of the bed and knelt, eyeing the vee of her thighs. Mind too gone with lust, he answered, "The ones who come in without knocking."

Rising to her elbows and tilting her head at him, she slowly asked, "How do you know they do that?"

Shit!

Luka wracked his brain for a reasonable excuse as to why he'd know that, but none came. He stared at her silently, with dread. Her smile faded, and her eyes strayed to the patio then back to him.

Jumping off the bed, she screeched, "Have you been watching me, Luka?"

Jade had said honesty was best. He slowly rose from the floor. "Yes."

She mouthed wordlessly at him for a moment. He took the opportunity to quickly explain, "After the drugs wore off, the mating bond pulled me here. I had to see you and make sure you were safe, and I didn't think you'd want to see me."

"This is too much," she said, covering her mouth with her hand. "You need to leave."

He stepped toward her, but she backed away. What else could he say? He'd watched her for many days and nights, and what was worse was after being with her today, kissing her, he didn't feel badly about it. She was his mate. Being near her felt so right that he only now understood how wrong being away from her felt. His whole life had been lived with a piece of a puzzle missing that he'd never known existed in the first place.

After experiencing what it was like to have her in his arms, to see her face smiling up at him, he knew he'd watch her every day for the rest of his life. So, what should he tell her? Lie and say he was sorry and wouldn't do it again, or tell her the truth?

Before he had a chance to decide, she crossed to her door. Forgetting the lock he'd just engaged, she pulled on the handle fruitlessly.

He hovered behind her, reaching over her shoulder to unlock it. She stood frozen with him at her back, the door still shut.

"Why couldn't you just have been a normal guy?" she murmured. Swinging the door open, she stood aside. With her eyes trained downward, she said, "Get out."

"I'll leave," he said, waiting for her to meet his hard stare. "But you should know something. You *are* my mate. And even though your human body has learned to forget how to recognize me, I *am* yours. Deep down, you don't want a *normal* guy, and I'll prove it. I'll give you your space, but I won't give up. That's a promise, Alice."

14

∽

Alice paced, fuming. She'd been so stupid. Again. Why couldn't she ever just listen to her brain? Why did she always have to trust her consistently inaccurate feelings?

When he'd first arrived, she'd tried to stay strong and stick to her guns, even as she'd felt herself softening toward him. Then he'd asked to kiss her. It had come out of nowhere, was completely inappropriate, and should've resulted in a hard slap across the face, but Alice couldn't help her body's reaction. She'd wanted to kiss him since she'd first met him. Had fantasized about it.

Her steps slowed, and she ran a hand over her lips absently. But damn it all if he wasn't the best kisser she'd ever had. Fast learner, indeed. She groaned, glancing toward the bed. Part of her wished he hadn't told her about the stalking until after she'd gotten a little more action. Her body burned with unrelieved lust.

She moved to the bed, intending to take care of her wet, throbbing need herself, but then stopped. Glaring at the windows to the patio, fury washed over her anew. He might be watching her even now.

Alice tried to hold on to her anger, but the strangest urge to drop her hand into the waistline of her underwear and torture him a little came over her.

She slumped to the bed, trying to work out how she actually felt. Was she upset because she thought she *should* be upset? Or was she truly offended? She needed to get insight.

Stomping outside, she headed toward Vanessa, Daisy, and Rita's shared home. When she arrived, she found them sunbathing on the patio, reclined in a wide but shallow kiddie pool, florescent drinks in their hands. Squeals erupted from all three upon her arrival, giving any Woo Girl a run for their money.

Alice couldn't help but smile, her anger fading away at the sight of her three very tipsy friends.

"Hey, girl!" Vanessa laughed as she tried and failed to roll onto her stomach without spilling her drink.

"That's a party foul. You have to drink the pool water now." Daisy giggled while grappling to find her own drink's straw with her tongue.

Alice chuckled and took a seat near the three women sitting waist-deep in the small pool. "I see you guys are having a fun day."

"Well," Rita slurred, shielding her words from the other two, "Vanessa was feeling a little down, so we decided to cheer her up."

Alice focused on Vanessa, who was attempting to drink the dregs of her glass while lying on her stomach. She'd been so wrapped up in her own drama with Luka that she hadn't taken the time to be there for her friend.

Since their arrival, Vanessa had put on a brave face, but she knew how much the woman wanted to return home. She often talked about her sister, whom she'd gotten in a fight with shortly before she'd been taken. Earlier, Vanessa had said Lucy had a lead for her. Alice nibbled her nails.

It must've not panned out. Alice tried to stifle the selfish wave of relief that came over her. Of course she didn't want her friend to be in pain, but if Vanessa somehow found a way to leave, it'd be a difficult loss for her to cope with.

Alice readied to ask what had happened, but from the corner of her eye, she saw both Daisy and Rita clumsily shake their heads. Daisy put a finger to her lips, almost poking herself in the eye. Alice would make sure to come by and see what was going on later, but for now, she'd try and lift Vanessa's spirits as well.

"How did you guys get all of this stuff?" she asked, studying the hard, plastic material of the pool and the bright-pink liquid in a pitcher close to her foot.

A wide grin spread over Vanessa's face. "Izzo got everything for us. He works here, you know. And for some strange reason," she said, raising her voice unnecessarily, "he keeps hanging around this section of the Temple."

Daisy blushed and grinned, biting her lip. "I saw them using one of these tubs to check on some of those glowing fish and asked if we could have it when they were done with it. He was just being nice," she argued quietly.

Rita chuckled. "That boy almost tripped over his own feet when you gave him our supply list, and I can tell you, it wasn't because I asked."

Daisy smiled wider. "Anyway, how did your meeting go? Did you talk to Luka?"

Alice's smile faltered. "Yeah."

Even inebriated, Vanessa noticed the change in her demeanor. Her brows knit in concern. "Oh no, what happened?"

She didn't want to spoil their good mood, but she was bursting to talk to someone about this. She took her time retelling everything that'd happened between her and Luka. The women gasped and scowled in all the right places, and when she finally described how they'd left it, they sat in silence.

"So, wait," Vanessa said, looking around. "He's been watching you? Like, all the time? Is he watching us now?"

Alice stared out into the tree line, feeling a rush of…excitement? "Maybe, I don't know."

"Kinky." Daisy giggled, sinking into the pool of water until she was half submerged.

Rita threw a hand over her heart in mock surprise. "Daisy, my word. Has that shy little exterior really been hiding an undercover freak this whole time?"

Vanessa rose to her knees. She cupped her hands around her mouth, yelling into the tree line, "Luuukkkaaa! Are you out there, you big perv?"

"Vanessa!" Alice shushed the woman with a laugh.

She turned back to Alice, refilling her drink. "So, what's the problem? If you really thought he was a dick, you wouldn't be talking to us about him. You like him, but you think you shouldn't. Is that it?"

That's exactly it, Alice thought, surprised by the woman's candor and intuition.

It wasn't that she didn't like Luka. She liked him a lot, but she knew, from experience, what she'd be getting into with a personality like that. She'd told them about Luka so they'd persuade her away from him. Talk her off the ledge, not make her question herself more. "Is it wrong that I do? He's controlling and possessive and…"

"And makes your lady parts rejoice," Rita chimed in.

Was that it? Was she just insanely attracted to Luka and only thinking it was more because she couldn't separate her emotions from sex?

"There have been so many red flags, though. Back on Earth, this guy Randy did creepy stuff like this. He didn't stand outside my house, I don't think, but he'd randomly show up at my work, or he'd take a class I was taking, even though he was working towards a communications degree. I didn't think anything of it at the time, but later on, when he got really controlling, I started to put it together." Vanessa quirked a brow, looking unconvinced, and leaned over the edge of the pool to refill her drink. Alice continued, "And another guy, Jorge, he was always so sweet to me in private, but whenever we went out, he'd treat me like crap. Like he was embarrassed to be seen with me."

"Jesus, you have really bad taste in men," Rita said, wincing.

Alice threw her hands in the air. "That's what I'm saying! My instincts are never right."

"Do you really want my advice, or do you want me to tell you what you want to hear?" Vanessa asked, reclining on the hard edge of the pool.

She bit her lip, unsure if she *did* want her advice. Alice had learned that, although Vanessa didn't always soften her words, she was actually really good at reading people and giving advice, even if it was hard to hear. Vanessa had admitted that, in another life, she'd have liked to have been a psychologist.

Alice tensed. "I want your real opinion."

"It's true, you've picked a lot of duds in the past, but this isn't Earth, and you can't base your decisions on what you know about Earth men. You're comparing apples and oranges. He's an alien. A mated alien. From what we've learned, that means they have some seriously crazy shit going on in their brains, and despite being trained for everything else in husbandry school, they weren't trained on how to deal with and manage the mating bond, because no one thought it existed anymore." Vanessa gave a small hiccup then resumed. "For all you know, stalking is normal. It's not like he can come knock on your door like a regular person. You've only talked to him a handful of times and, yes, he hasn't been the best, but you still like him for some reason. If it's just attraction, then get to know him more. If he's really an ass, your attraction will wear off in time, but maybe he'll end up surprising you." She smiled. "There's something endearing about a guy who makes you the center of his world. As long as he's not trying to control you, I don't see a problem in how you feel about him."

"So, you're saying I should just ignore how he acted at the meeting and him watching me?"

Vanessa sighed. "No. I'm saying you have to put that stuff into context. Take it from someone who says stupid shit without thinking all the time." Suddenly, her eyes turned glassy, and she downed her drink in one gulp.

Alice slid to the ground, sympathetic tears springing to her eyes at the glimpse of pain she saw on her friend's face. She reached out to her, but Vanessa shooed her away.

"I'm fine. Really. And if I thought you were in danger of ending up with an asshole, I'd tell you, okay? Keep your guard up, but give him a chance. That's all I'm saying."

"You go get that ass." Daisy smiled dreamily, sweeping her arms and legs through the water as though making a snow angel.

The women all dissolved into laughter at the outrageous comment coming from the painfully shy girl. "I think you guys broke Daisy," Alice wheezed.

The rest of the afternoon passed happily. After migrating indoors, the women joked and drank long into the night. After Daisy and Rita drifted to sleep in a mountain of pillows and blankets, Alice took the opportunity to talk to Vanessa.

"What happened today? Do you want to talk about it?" Alice whispered.

Vanessa let out a sigh and turned toward her more fully, tucking her legs under her on the couch. "I just... I need to get back to her, Alice." Her smile faded. "I've been talking to anybody who'll listen, trying to get them to tell me how I can find a ship to take me home, but no one will do it. Today, I thought I had a good lead. Lucy said one of the guards knew someone, but it turned out the ship he had in mind had already left. It's just not fair. Most of the non-human women that Jade helped rescue got to go home months ago! Just because some of our planets are Class 4 that means we can't? It's not right."

"Are you and your sister really close?" The pain she saw in Vanessa's eyes was heartbreaking.

She chuckled sadly. "No. We can't stand each other. She's so uptight, and she's always complaining about how I can't just settle and find a good job. We don't even see each other that much, but...she's my sister. She's a part of me." Her eyes grew watery. Alice reached out to squeeze her hand in silent support. "I said some really terrible things to her before we were taken. I can't stop thinking about it. I know her—she'll ruin her life trying to find out what happened to me, and I won't be able to live with myself if I stopped trying to get back to her."

"We'll figure it out," Alice said softly, not knowing how but knowing she'd do everything in her power to make it so.

"Anyway." Vanessa sniffed. "After the guard told me the ship was gone, I lost it." She smiled over at the two quietly snoring women. "I don't know what I would've done without them." She looked back at Alice. "Without all of you."

Alice leaned forward, wrapping her in a tight hug. Eventually Vanessa relaxed, and before long, she drifted to sleep as well.

Trying her best not to wake the women, she placed glasses of water on the table in front of them, then tiptoed to the door and left. How could she help Vanessa? Every Clecanian she'd met so far had been adamant they weren't allowed to return home. If they waited long enough, Alice reasoned, the Clecanians might decide to reveal themselves to Earth. Alice shook her head absently. Vanessa hadn't gone into detail about what'd happened, but there seemed to be an unspoken urgency in her need to return home.

She meandered along the wooden platforms that connected the five houses in this section of the lake, lost in thought. As she turned onto the walkway that led to her house, she stopped short. Luka was sitting in front of her door, silently watching her.

It'd been a long day full of emotional ups and downs, alcohol, and the sun. Alice was exhausted, and didn't have the mental strength to deal with him right now. Not until she worked through her feelings some more.

She groaned. "What are you still doing here?"

Standing, he let his gaze roam over her before answering, "I left my pass inside."

Ignoring the heat spreading through her at his hungry stare, she moved to open her door. "Why didn't you tell me earlier?"

He shrugged. "I wanted to give you space." Rather than stepping out of the way to give her clear access, he hovered, crowding her with his large frame. Heat radiated off him, as did his intoxicating scent. Pine? No. Definitely earthy, though.

Well, he has been hiding out in the woods, Alice!

She kept her gaze trained on the door while unlocking it. Her skin tingled as if it could feel his eyes on her. The door finally swung open, and she reached in to retrieve the ball.

"Here," she said, dropping it into his upturned hands unceremoniously.

Never taking his eyes off her, he murmured, "It's been deactivated."

"Of course it has," she grumbled. Uncomfortable with how much she liked his warm gaze, Alice activated her hand clock, then scowled at the symbols.

"It's twenty-four before humista," he said, eyeing her with his hands behind his back. "May I come in and wait for a guard to come by? They should be making their rounds in about a half hour."

No! Say no! her mind screamed.

"Fine." *Idiot.*

He gave her a small smile and waited for her to enter before following. "I'd like to ask you for a favor," he said, tucking the ball under his arm.

Making her way to the food synthesizer, she remained silent. What would he ask for now?

Weariness pulled at her. *What won't I give him?*

A thump behind her made her jump. She wheeled around and saw the red pass he'd been holding was now on her small dining table, his hand resting atop it. She'd forgotten how fast he could move.

"What?"

He wet his full bottom lip with his tongue, then ran a hand through his messy hair.

Alice subdued the sigh that bubbled up in her. God, she wanted to kiss that lip again. "What favor?" Her words lacked the venom she was so desperately trying to inject them with.

As it turned out, not being a pushover was hard work, and Alice was tired. Tired of fighting against her instincts. Her mother had always told her she couldn't stand people who "buried the hatchet." Alice was one of those people. She didn't like dwelling on arguments or holding grudges.

On the one hand, this had resulted in people treating her badly, knowing she'd forgive and forget by the next day. On the other, she found she was able to get back to "happy" much more quickly than other people.

Dwelling on something that was done and gone didn't make sense. Why couldn't she just find someone who wouldn't take advantage of that?

"Can you tell me what happened…in the cell?" His fists clenched at his sides. "I can't remember much, and the little I do remember…well…I'm not sure I'm recalling everything accurately."

Alice let out a slow breath. He wanted to do this now? Programming the synthesizer to produce a hot beverage similar to tea, she thought about what to say. Over her shoulder she asked, "Do you want a drink?"

He jerked, crossing to her in an instant. "I can get this for you. Please sit down."

She tilted her head at him, trying to figure out his angle. Slowly she retreated to the table, too exhausted to scrutinize his actions for long. "What do you remember?"

He leaned back against the counter, clearing his throat. "I remember being chained and alone for a long time. Then, I remember you. Talking to me…touching me."

Heat crept up her cheeks. "Sorry," she muttered.

"Sorry?"

Glancing up at him and noticing he wore a confused expression, she explained, "It wasn't right for me to touch you when you were in that state. I'm sorry. Helas threatened to electrocute you if I didn't, so I hope you understand." It was a lie. She knew it. Eventually, even without threats from Helas, she would've touched him.

He began walking toward her then stopped, rushing to the counter to fetch her drink. Setting it on the table, he sat catty-corner to her. "You should never apologize for that."

She clutched her glass, raising her eyes to meet his.

A wolfish grin spread over his face. "Never."

Heartbeat picking up speed, she hid her smile with her cup, taking a long sip. A weight had been lifted, knowing he didn't despise her for what she'd done. "I thought you were mad about it."

He laughed, displaying perfect white teeth. "You thought I'd be mad about a beautiful female, my mate no less, running her hands over me to keep me from being tortured?"

Charming. What a dangerous quality. She focused on her tea.

"I have a proposition for you concerning your work with animals."

She eyed him. "If you tell me again that I can't have a man teach me to read your language, then—"

"No. No," he said, shaking his head. "As part of my research, I have access to a wildlife reserve open only to me and a few others in my field. If you'd like, I could take you there. You could see some of the animals for yourself."

"I..." She was lost for words. On the surface, his suggestion seemed very thoughtful. What was the catch? "And in return?"

"I'd like to have dinner with you."

"Dinner. That's all?" she said with narrowed eyes.

He licked his lips again, his gaze flashing to her mouth for an instant. "I can't promise I won't attempt more, but dinner is all that's required."

She felt a pang of pleasure shoot to her sex at his admission. Would she be able to resist his attempts? His nostrils flared, and a low purr sounded in his chest. A predatory grin spread across his face. "Just dinner," she said shakily.

This was too much. The effect he had on her was too visceral. She needed to bring up his stalking. Because it had to stop, but also because she needed a reminder of why she should be cautious around him. "Are you planning on being a peeping tom again?" At his confused expression, she amended, "Watching me. Are you planning on hiding in the woods and watching me again?"

Leaning back, he regarded her for a moment before finally answering. "I could say no. You wouldn't know one way or another if I did. But I don't want to lie to you. I can't promise the mating bond won't force me back."

Alice scowled. Why hadn't his answer dampened her attraction? "It's obsessive. You don't even know me."

"My very DNA has been altered by you. I'm stronger now. Faster." Like lightning, his hand shot out and gently gripped hers. Immediately, her heart rate sped up, and a purr rumbled through him. "Do you feel that? It's physical. Biological. I may not know much about you, but my soul recognizes yours." She tugged at her hand. After a moment's hesitation, he released it. "When I'm not near you, I feel...wrong. I walk around all day, unable to concentrate. Like I've forgotten something but can't recall what it is. It's maddening."

Warning! Warning! Keep your guard up! Hadn't she always felt an oddly intense connection to him? Did what he say make sense, or was he just really good at forming an argument in favor of his bad behavior?

His eyes bore into hers as they silently stared at each other, her breaths coming quickly. "What if I end up hating you?" she whispered.

Leaning toward her until only a few inches separated them, he rumbled, "Do you hate me, Alice?"

A loud pounding on the door made her jump.

Luka let out a low growl, holding her gaze for a moment longer before rising and walking to the door.

While his back was turned, Alice took a few calming breaths. *Well, that didn't go my way.*

In the open doorway stood Zed. He glanced between them. "Metli sent me to find you. Figured you'd be here."

"Hello, Zed," Alice said, walking to the door.

"Zed?" Luka said, clenching and unclenching his fists.

"Yes, I told Alice she may call me Zed."

Alice watched as the two men seemed to have a silent argument. "Do you guys know each other?"

Luka's eyes softened when he looked at her, making warmth spread through her. "Yes, he's my brother."

"Your brother?" That's why Auzed looked so familiar to her. "I thought this planet had an infertility issue. How many siblings do you have?"

Both men relaxed, shoulders dropping. Luka answered, "Our mother wasn't Clecanian. She didn't have as much trouble reproducing."

Zed stepped backward out of the doorway, indicating it was time for Luka to leave.

"I'll have Au-zed," he began, emphasizing Zed's full name, "collect you and bring you to me in a few days so I can take you to the reserve."

Around his brother, Alice noticed Luka's demeanor was much more formal. It seemed he kept his emotion on a tighter leash around others.

Does he only show a soft side with me? She inwardly cringed at the juvenile thought.

She nodded her agreement. With one final longing glance at her, Luka left.

***

"You couldn't have waited a little longer to get me?" Luka grunted once they were out of earshot of Alice's home.

They'd been making great progress. She may not like him very much, but she was at least willing to give him a chance to redeem himself during dinner. How much of her decision to see him again was based on his bribe to take her to the research reserve? He didn't know, and he didn't care. Winning her over would take time, and he'd use any tools at his disposal to acquire that time with her.

When he'd had the idea to let her visit the reserve, he'd been both overjoyed and frustrated he hadn't thought of it sooner. A visit would make her happy and help her career. He wanted to punch the air in triumph, knowing he had something to offer that almost no other male could.

On top of the fact that it'd be of interest to her, the Huil Research Reserve was also quite romantic. He could get her away from prying eyes, and knowing that no one else would be able to access the reserve while he was there, he'd be able to relax.

"You should've never let the time on your pass run out. Metli was furious," Zed replied without looking at him.

Finding that he was having trouble hanging onto his anger, he shrugged. "Still, you interrupted at precisely the wrong time."

Reaching the long stretch of water between the main building and the exit, Zed escorted him across. "She's agreed to see you?"

A wide grin spread over his face again. "Yes, I'll send you the details on timing later. You can escort her, correct? I don't trust anyone else to do it."

"You know I will." Zed leaned in, his expression serious. "You know, Metli asked me to retrieve you *yesterday* afternoon." A small smile pulled at the corner of his mouth, and he winked before retreating back across the lake.

15

"Alice, are you listening?" Rhaego snapped.

A few people snickered.

This morning the Queen had sent word that Rhaego would be stopping by to give whoever was interested a lesson in the Tremantian language. For what Alice assumed was about an hour, Rhaego had been patiently explaining the name and pronunciation of each letter in the Clecanian alphabet. Within that span, he'd had to get Alice's attention five times.

Soon, she was supposed to leave with Zed to go see Luka, and she found she could concentrate on nothing else. This was important, dammit, so why couldn't she pay attention?

"Yes, I'm sorry, Rhaego. I'm just a little distracted today."

Lucy, who'd sat next to her, rested her chin on her hand and gazed dreamily at Rhaego. "She's going on a date."

"It's not a date," Alice quickly argued. But it was. Wasn't it?

The more she'd thought about what Luka said, the more she started to agree with him. They did share some kind of connection. Was it possible humans still had the ghost of a mating bond somewhere deep down? She'd always known she'd felt an unusually strong connection to Luka, but she'd just assumed it was because they'd gone through something traumatic together. Looking back, however, she recalled feeling drawn to him from the very first time she'd seen him.

When people on Earth talked about soulmates, could this be what they were referring to? Some long-lost connection only certain people shared and were able to recognize. If so, how many humans had missed out on finding their mate because they were separated by a galaxy? And then, if all of that was true, who was Alice to spit in the face of fate? Had she found her honest-to-goodness soulmate?

Rhaego grunted. "I think we should just call it a day."

Alice flinched, realizing she'd once again stopped paying attention, lost in her own thoughts.

As the six women, who'd come to the class left, Alice rushed over to Rhaego. "I'm really sorry."

He waved dismissively and gave her a small smile. "It's okay. I wish I had someone who made me that distracted."

Alice had guessed as much. When she'd learned Rhaego had volunteered to teach the class, she'd wondered why. The tight shirt and combed hair he'd sported upon arrival had told her more than enough.

"A few of the women were definitely checking you out today. None of them distracting enough?" she said, grinning at the deep maroon blush spreading across his cheeks and horns.

"Jade advised me some of the females might like this clothing choice." Rhaego smiled sheepishly. "It was nice to be looked at without fear, but I didn't recognize a mate."

"You could still go on a date with one of them—you never know. It took Theo a while to recognize Jade, right?"

He shrugged. "What if I become involved with a female and recognize my mate in another? Human females approach sexual relationships differently than Clecanian females do. I wouldn't want to hurt anyone."

Alice shook her head and wondered how she'd ever been afraid of the giant, horned softy. "Whichever female you do recognize is going to be so lucky. You're a great guy."

"Thanks," he mumbled, walking her to the door.

Outside in the bright sunlight, Lucy was talking quickly to a flustered Auzed. His arms were crossed over his chest, and his expression turned bewildered when she slowly traced a finger over his bicep, leaning toward him suggestively.

When he caught sight of Alice and Rhaego, he dashed toward them, leaving Lucy to pout in his wake.

"Why did you do that? Lucy seems to really like you."

Zed's jaw clenched, something it did very often. "She likes everyone. She's always flirting with one of the guards. I don't like being toyed with. And our males don't understand that flirting is common to Earthlings. They have begun to assume the humans are attempting to court a husband and are getting their hopes up. This week alone, I've had to issue three citations to my males for unprofessional behavior."

Alice shrugged. The men here were turning out to be a lot pickier than she'd thought men from a planet low on females would be.

"We're leaving as soon as you're ready," Zed announced, causing Alice to pick up speed.

When she approached the door to her home, she spotted a beautiful plant floating on a clear round platform. The leaves of the plant were bright green and bushy and cascaded over the edge of the glass bowl they were planted in.

Quickly, she grabbed the plant and brought it inside, leaving the floating platform to fly away. She placed it on her dining table, along with three other beautiful plants she'd received. There was never a note, but she could guess who they were from. Asivva, who'd come to tell her about Rhaego's lesson, had explained they were common courting gifts from a time before the Ceremony existed.

She stared at the plants for a moment, trying to squash the materialistic joy she felt at having received a present. She wanted to get to know Luka and didn't want these presents to sway her emotions. A grin spread over her face. *But I do love gifts.*

Biting her nails and rechecking her hand clock, she crossed to her wardrobe and glared at her clothing. Her outfit had to be functional, that was all she knew. Should she try and look nice? Should she dress down? She couldn't decide.

After several agonizing minutes weighing the pros and cons of trying to look attractive for Luka, she settled on shorts, boots, and a long-sleeved top. The outfit was utilitarian while still showing off her figure. She allowed her hair to hang loose but decided to tie a ribbon around her wrist just in case. After a few minutes futilely struggling to tie the ribbon one-handed, she gave up, sticking it in her pocket instead.

My kingdom for a hair tie.

Butterflies started to dance around her stomach as she and Zed made their way to the exit. She needed to distract herself. "Zed, isn't this against the rules? Someone in the city might see me, right?"

His eyes continued to scan the lake. Although off duty, he seemed unable to stop keeping everyone safe. "You're allowed to be seen. The Queen doesn't want the other females seen because they could potentially call forth a Clecanian's mating marks."

Anxiety and excitement still coursing through her, she blurted, "Is Luka a good guy? Does he…watch a lot of girls?"

He shot her a sidelong glance.

"Oh, come on. I know you know about him doing that. You saw him in the woods that day, right? I won't tell anyone," she urged.

"I don't know what you're talking about."

She scrunched her mouth to the side, tsking.

"Luka's always been very driven. He's always thinking, always working, and very rarely does he fail. If he wants something, he goes for it, and he doesn't stop until he succeeds." Zed aimed another smile at her. "I've never seen him want a female like he wants you."

Brightening, she remarked, "Is that right?"

"You've been good for him." A knowing smile on his face, he added, "He needs to fail every so often. He gets too cocky if he doesn't."

They walked in silence the rest of the way to the transport, and once inside, they remained lost in their own thoughts.

Alice hadn't seen the city yet and was frustrated with the lack of windows in the mirrored vehicle. "Why aren't there any windows? Don't people like to look outside when they travel?"

"I haven't given it much thought." Zed frowned, staring at the ceiling of the cab. "I know there are thousands of tiny cameras all over the cruiser's surface to allow it to steer without hitting anything. The shell of the vehicle is very strong, as well. It may not be as visually appealing, but it's safer."

His explanation made sense, but even so… An alien city, and she couldn't see it?

Before long, Zed announced they'd reached their destination. He reached for a communicator, but when he made no move to leave, Alice grew confused. "Aren't we getting out? Where are we exactly?"

"We are in Luka's building. He asked me to bring you here, then let him know. He'd like to come down and meet you, rather than us going to his home."

"Why?"

Zed sighed, likely tired of answering questions about his brother. "He's very private and pretty messy. He probably didn't want to straighten up."

Alice smiled mischievously. "Have you told him we're here?"

He narrowed his eyes at her. "No, not yet."

"Good. I want you to take me to his place."

"Why?" he asked, brows drawn.

"Because!" she cried. "He gets to hide in the trees and watch me and sit outside my house, but I'm not allowed in his? That's crap!"

Auzed laughed loudly, an odd sound coming from the normally stoic man. "I agree. Let's go."

They exited the transport and made their way to a set of doors a few feet away. Beyond the doors lay a large winding staircase.

"How many floors up is he?" she asked, craning her neck.

Walking over to a control in the wall, he replied, "The seventy-ninth floor."

Alice groaned, wondering if this was a dumb idea. Without warning, the ground began to move. She screamed, clawing at Zed.

He let out another loud laugh. "Did you think we were going to walk up each floor?"

Relaxing, Alice thought back to the spiral staircase in the outpost. Had that been able to move too? Was this their version of an elevator?

After a nauseating ascent, the stairs slowed to a halt in front of a deep-red lacquered door.

"This is him. He owns the floor." Zed reached out and placed his hand on the door handle rather than the door itself. A familiar buzz and grinding of locks sounded. "Luckily, he gave me access in case of emergencies." Alice waited to follow him inside, but he remained stationary. After a moment, he crossed to a panel on the wall near the door. "Ask Luka to contact me when you're ready to leave."

"You're not staying?" she said, suddenly nervous about being alone with Luka again.

"I need to get back to the Temple. Don't worry, you'll be fine. Just remember, it'd do him some good to fail a little," he whispered the last, and Alice had to stifle a giggle.

Turning back toward the door, she nodded, straightening her spine.

"Oh, and one other thing," he said, waiting for her to meet his eyes. "You should know that right before the meeting a few days ago, Luka broke a bone in his lower leg. His fibula. He tried to ignore it so he could make it to the meeting. Walked all the way around the lake just to see you."

Alice thought back to the pained expression she'd seen cross his face many times throughout the meeting. It all made sense.

Why didn't he tell me? Alice wanted to slap her palm to her face. *Because I told him not to make excuses, that's why!*

She groaned. "Thanks for telling me."

Zed shrugged. "It was sort of my fault. I thought it was just a sprain and told him to suck it up. Don't let his behavior, at the meeting at least, color your opinion of him."

Alice crossed the threshold; the sound of the grinding stairway spiraling downward confirmed Zed had set off. She stood for a moment in the entrance, absorbing what she'd just learned. This new information changed things, but she didn't have the time or privacy to really think through what those changes meant.

For now, Alice decided, she'd try to get to know him again. No broken bones, no chains, no fooling around. There were definitely aspects of Luka's personality that concerned her, but she could admit that while those things were red flags on Earth, they might not be here. Yes, the best plan now would be to get to know Luka as a person and then decide if he was dating material, and she desperately hoped he was. Giving herself a mental high-five, she peered around.

The lighting provided by the familiar glowing orbs in the large, open, semicircular room was dim and warm. It took her eyes a moment to adjust. A grin tugged at her mouth and relieved some of her anxiety.

The wall before her curved along the length of the room. Pictures, scribbled notes, and a variety of papers were stuck all over it. As she took in the various pieces of furniture scattered haphazardly throughout, she saw piles of books and papers strewn across almost every surface.

He's messy. Alice smiled, thrilled she now knew this intimate detail.

To her right, she saw a small kitchen, the barest area of the house by far. It looked like no one had cooked in it, maybe ever. No utensils or spices sat on the black stone counters. There was no visible sink and no stack of dirty dishes, waiting to be cleaned. Alice found it odd that the area of her home most likely to be messy was Luka's cleanest.

Near the kitchen, there was a set of polished wooden double doors. A matching pair could be found on the opposite side of the wall. Both sets large and imposing. Both firmly closed.

She should call out for Luka, tell him she was here. Alice grinned wickedly. *He thinks it's okay to watch me because I'm his mate, then he should be okay with me snooping around his house too.*

There were no windows in the room, and although large, the lack of light from the outside made Luka's home feel like the crowded study of an eccentric professor. A guilty pleasure washed through her. She knew she was invading a very personal space.

Two worn armchairs and a low table situated in front of a fireplace called to her. The area would make a wonderful reading spot if the fire were lit. Rather than being attached to a wall, as most fireplaces were, this one stood freely in the middle of the room. A metal bowl large enough to take a bath in held a pile of glittering, jagged black rocks. Hanging from the ceiling, about five feet above the bowl, was a vent.

Tilting her head at the large firepit, she laughed under her breath. It wouldn't have been out of place in the old tv show *The Jetsons*. That's if George Jetson also had a sexual magnetism that made her want to lay naked on a fur rug while enjoying the fire.

Alice approached the large basin, hoping to see the black stones in more detail. Suddenly, tall flames roared to life. Alice shrieked, snatching her hand away from the now-red stones.

The sound of doors being flung open briefly flashed through her consciousness before a deep voice rumbled behind her. "Alice?"

Heart still beating a mile a minute, she turned, intending to berate him for his dangerous insta-fire. What she saw had her words melting inside her, sliding down until they settled hot and heavy in her sex.

He was naked except for a small towel. Rivulets of water ran down his broad chest and chiseled abs until they vanished into the fabric hanging low on his hips.

She'd seen his body tons of times, touched it too. But the vision of him unchained, wet, and glowing in the firelight made her feel like she was seeing it for the first time.

"Fuck," she moaned.

She clapped a hand over her mouth when she realized she'd uttered the curse aloud.

Gaze meeting his, she groaned. His brows drew together in confusion, then he glanced down at his body. When his head rose again, the most masculine, confident grin she'd ever seen came with it.

He stepped toward her, smirking. "What are you doing here, Alice?"

She frowned when she noticed the tight grip he'd had on his towel had loosened. Flustered, she said, "Zed let me in. I wanted to see where you lived."

Movement from his towel drew her gaze. The thick fabric slowly tented. The answering clench and flood of heat to her core made her stifle a whimper and back away from him.

Like a flash, he crossed to her, throwing an arm around her waist. His scent and warmth permeated her senses. The hot touch of his hand on her lower back was like a brand.

He pulled her body into his, leaning down to rumble in her ear, "Careful, love. You almost stepped into the fire."

Love? Alice had to concentrate on breathing. He was proving she didn't need to step into the flames to feel as though she were on fire. Trapped under the material of his towel, his hard length pressed against her abdomen. The one part of him she'd never touched.

The deep purr that sounded from his chest reverberated through his whole body. The vibration from his shaft hit her stomach and shot to her clit like a lightning bolt. Without thought, her body arched into him.

His other hand, which had been holding his towel, sank into the hair at her nape, clutching firmly. The pressure of their bodies pushed together was now the only thing holding the towel between them. If she moved away, it would fall, exposing him completely.

Gripping her hair hard enough for her to feel a pleasurable sting, he tilted her head to the side, exposing her neck. She could feel his hot breath on her ear, his lips ghosting over the skin of her lobe.

Voice gone ragged, he said, "I can scent your need, Alice. Let me help."

Oh God, he can't mean… How was she supposed to tell him no? Her nipples hardened, oversensitive in the now-damp fabric of her shirt. She clamped her arms to her sides more tightly, fingers curling into her palms in a tight fist.

Get to know him first. Get to know him first.

"I…I don't think that's a good idea." Her voice was barely a whisper.

Directing her head to point toward his, she saw a predatory smile darken his features.

Slowly he let his mouth drop until it hovered a breath away from hers. "But you smell good enough to eat. Let me relieve you. I won't do anything more, I promise," he crooned.

She gasped as his hand on her back dipped to roughly knead her ass. He took her momentary surprise as an opportunity, expertly kissing her parted lips.

This time when a moan tore from her, she wasn't surprised. Luka's intelligence and confidence were so fucking sexy. When he kissed her, he didn't do so sweetly. He didn't tease her with soft lips and quick passes of his tongue. He kissed her like a starving man, deep and rough and frenzied.

The thought that he might kiss her pussy like this made her hands shoot out to clutch at his strong, damp shoulders. He growled into her mouth, lifting her against his body with one arm. The towel between them dropped as his leg shot out, his foot swiping away the contents of the low table.

In a whirlwind, she was lifted and turned until she opened her eyes, surprised to find herself lying on the table. Luka stood over her, completely naked, gazing down at her. Her eyes widened at the sight of his large, thick cock. She'd glimpsed it many times while they'd been locked up, but she'd never let her gaze linger. Now she reveled in the sight. Licking her lips, she imagined touching him there.

"Don't push me, Alice," he growled low in his throat. "Or I'll have to do more than I promised."

***

Luka hadn't thought he'd be lucky enough to feel Alice in his arms again so soon. In fact, he'd decided that certain precautions needed to be taken to make sure he didn't become too aroused while they were together in the reserve. He didn't want to push her away, after all. He needed to seduce her slowly.

He'd sat in his tub, letting the warm water wash over him, imagining she was smiling up at him, running her hands over his shaft. He'd almost thought he could even scent her when he'd started pumping his fist, trying to relieve some of the building pressure before seeing her. But then he'd heard a scream and had raced out to find her…here.

The heated look she'd given him had pushed him over the edge. The scent of her need was so strong, he could tell she burned with it. All he wanted to do was rip off those tight shorts that curved over her ass like a second skin and plunge into her, but he forced himself to go slow. Make her want him.

Looking down at her now, his self-control was shattering bit by bit. The way she stared at his naked body, licking her lips like she wanted to taste him, sent his thoughts spiraling until only instinct remained. He gripped his cock, roughly pumping his fist over it, and ground out, "Take off your shorts, Alice."

Her small pink tongue darted out to wet her full bottom lip again, and he groaned.

"If you don't want them ripped off, remove them," he snarled, making her flinch.

He cursed under his breath, sure he'd scared her away, but then her hands slowly moved down to unbutton and remove the shorts. "Good girl. Now the shirt."

His heart pounded wildly in his chest. Would she do what he said? Allow him to dominate in the way he needed? The mating instinct raging in him told him she would. She was perfect for him in every way.

After a moment's hesitation, she arched her back, lifting the shirt over her head and exposing her perfect breasts.

Luka sank to his knees at the edge of the table, taking in the sight before him. Slipping his arms under her thighs and clutching the tops of her legs, he let his gaze roam over her.

"You're so damn gorgeous," he breathed, his chest feeling tight.

Now propped on her elbows, her breaths were coming in quick gasps. A flush spread over her cheeks and down her chest, almost reaching her pebbled nipples. She squeaked when he gave a sharp tug, dragging her across the table toward him. He released her legs, letting them rest on either side of his hips, and loomed over her.

Placing one hand on her shoulder to keep her from scooting away and one hand sprawled over her small waist, he set upon her dusky nipple. As soon as his tongue circled the peak of her breast, she arched into him, her fingers digging into his hair. Low moans escaped her as he licked and sucked at her delectable breasts.

The scent of her arousal sat heavy in the air, making his mouth water. If he reached lower and touched her there, he'd find her soaking.

My mate, wet for me. At the thought, his purring intensified again. She cried out, squirming down against him more fully and angling her hips toward his painfully throbbing erection.

A sharp yank on his hair made him grin. Releasing her breast, he allowed his little mate to guide him where she wanted.

Most females would've directed him toward their sex, demanding he pleasure them. Instead, Alice tugged his face up to her own, pulling him down for a kiss. He groaned into her mouth, settling his body on hers, his cock trapped tightly against her grinding sex.

Kissing had quickly become one of his favorite things. The connection he felt when their mouths were locked like this was...indescribable. Could she taste her own flesh on his tongue?

Little stifled moans escaped her, smothered by his greedy mouth. The motion of her hips picked up speed, her fingers digging into his shoulders more firmly with each passing moment.

Eyes widening, he drew away. "It's my job and my privilege to make you come. What do you think you're doing?"

Her eyes were heavy, drugged with lust. A groan of protest and frustration burst from her before she clawed at him, trying to drag him back toward her. His chest expanded. Was there a sight more lovely than his mate, maddened by lust, reaching for him?

Grabbing one of her wrists in each hand, he forced her arms to her sides, then sat back on his haunches.

In a throaty voice, she said, "Please come back, Luka. I'm so close."

Her sultry plea was just desperate enough to move him to do what she asked, but then he recalled the tenuous position he was in with her. He needed to show her he could rule her body. "You'll come when I say so, love."

He'd muttered the pet name quite by accident earlier, but the widening of her eyes, and the hint of a smile on her lips, made him think she'd liked it.

She let out a groan and raised her head to watch him. Holding her gaze, he lowered his mouth to her black underwear until he hovered just over the sensitive spot he'd researched. As though the primal part of him knew she loved the vibration from his purring, it rumbled through his chest once again.

At the sound, she let out a small whimper and held her breath. His open mouth landed, wet and hot, on top of the fabric covering her sex. She moaned, head falling back onto the table and hips jerking toward his tongue.

His cock twitched angrily; the blood pumping through it felt like boiling water. Every moment he spent not tending to his own needs was agonizing, but the way she writhed and mewled before him made it all worth it.

Releasing her restrained wrists, he quickly tore apart the area of underwear guarding her entrance and rolled the remnants up her hips and out of the way.

His breath left him. Soft brown curls sat atop her glistening, pinkened sex. *Beautiful.*

It seemed the time he'd spent admiring her stunning cunt had been too long, because she reached down and began quickly circling a small nub at the apex of her sex herself. *A clitoris, clit for short,* he recalled. *She must be hurting if she's willing to do this herself.*

Knowing she wouldn't take kindly to his teasing much longer, he threw her legs over his shoulders, snatched both her wrists, and pinned them on her stomach in one of his large palms. Her cry of protest transformed into a moan of ecstasy when he clamped his mouth over her sensitive bud.

Luka's mind swam with pleasure, almost as if he were drunk. His female lay below him, moaning his name. The sweet taste of her arousal coated his tongue, his face rubbing against the soft skin at her thigh. A thrill ran through him, knowing he was about to hear her come for the first time. The stiffening and quivering of her body told him as much.

With a grunt, hating his own weakness, his free hand flew to his shaft, pumping in time with her rolling hips.

Her breaths hitched, and her body shuddered, making her breasts jiggle. *So close now.* He released her wrists, plunged a finger into her sex, and growled, "Come, female."

Pumping his fist over himself harder, his own orgasm erupted out of him. He snarled and grinned while still licking and sucking her as he felt her tight core convulse around his finger. Her hands clutched the edge of the table, and her back bowed as she cried out, "Luka!"

Continuing to leisurely stroke her with his finger, he waited until her cries faded into soft pants. Then, unable to keep from touching her, but knowing her enticing core was too sensitive, he ran his palms up and down the soft skin of her thighs.

She looked to the ceiling, her hands reaching up to cover her face. *Is she upset?*

He felt her attempt to tug her legs away, so he gripped them tighter, frowning. This was supposed to make her like him more, not less. Why did she want away from him?

She sat up, supporting herself on her elbows, and studied him, brows drawn. The dark pink flush of her cheeks wasn't just from exertion. *Embarrassment?*

Glancing down her body, she toyed with the elastic remnants of her underwear now circling her waist. In a shaky voice, she said, "Can I get dressed, please?"

He ground his teeth. Maybe if he stared at her hard enough, he could glimpse the inner workings of her mind. What had he done wrong?

Had he misread her attraction? Impossible. Experimentally, he leaned forward and gently kissed and bit her inner thigh. She jerked, and he scented her arousal spike again.

No, she was definitely still attracted to him.

She sat up more fully, shielding her sex from view with her hand. All of his Traxian instincts screamed to life, and a low growl erupted from his chest in time with a stab of pain.

My mate is hiding herself from me? He battled the urge to flip her, bend her over the table, and sink into her, proving she could keep nothing from him. But something in her eyes held him back.

Releasing her, he stood, then pulled her up against him. Skin to skin, she struggled weakly. "Luka...I—"

He silenced her by placing a soft, lingering kiss on her lips. After a moment, her body relaxed, sighing into his. The last thing he wanted to do was let her go. His heart clenched painfully in his chest. He knew if he wanted to distract her, he could. If he slipped his hand to her sex right now, she'd become aroused. Lose herself again. But she didn't want him to, and that knowledge was like a knife to the heart.

When he ended the kiss, he saw the dazed expression slowly fade from her face. He gestured to the room he'd burst through. "The bathing room is through there." Now pointing to the doors on the other end of his home, he said, "My room is there. I'm going to go get dressed as well."

"Thank you." Clearing her throat, she moved away from him. His body tensed at the loss.

After she'd hastily gathered her clothing, she retreated to the bathroom, leaving him naked and alone, burning with the need to chase after her.

16

Alice silently berated herself. *Don't I have any self-control at all?*

She clutched the gleaming black countertop in the bathroom, and glared at her reflection in the mirror. *So embarrassing!*

Alice felt as though she'd temporarily lost her mind out there. She'd acted like a nymphomaniac, unable to resist a sexy man. How could she face him again now that he knew the effect he had on her?

Cursing under her breath, she gathered her clothing, laughing humorlessly at the destroyed underwear circling her waist before tugging the ruined fabric off. Shoving her shorts and top on, she crossed her arms and leaned against the counter.

It wasn't right that he could smell whenever she was turned on. A downright dirty, unfair advantage was what it was.

She slumped. Alice didn't want to fall into bed with Luka too fast. Sex always made her feel more deeply and more quickly than she should. In the past, she'd made the mistake of sleeping with men too early and growing too attached before she'd really known who they were.

For both of their sakes, she couldn't let that happen with Luka. A mate wasn't a girlfriend or boyfriend who could be broken up with. Once she consented to be with him, she knew he'd never let go. She needed to be sure about him, about them together, before signing on for forever.

Luka had been showing a thoughtful side of himself, but she didn't know if that side of him was just an act to lure her or if that was who he truly was. Did he only want her because the mating bond told him so? Because he wanted to have sex with her? Alice didn't think so, but her instincts had been woefully wrong many times before. It'd break her in two if she found herself in love with a man she could never leave, only to learn he was drawn to her body and nothing more.

Get to know him. Figure out if you like him!

Already replaying their sexual interlude in her mind and wishing she could do it again, she stomped her foot. Pointing at her reflection, she said, "You will lay down ground rules. You will be firm. You will be strong. You will be in charge of your future."

Nodding, she stormed through the bathroom doors, ready to lay down the law and…he wasn't there. Alice threw her head back and let out an exasperated huff.

"It's fine. I'll just talk to him when he comes back," she whispered.

Muttering to herself and encouraging her nerve to stay in place, she once again explored the room.

The long, curving wall held hundreds of tacked-on papers and pictures. Alice squinted at the text on the papers, wishing she'd paid more attention in class today. Tremantian writing was beautiful. Unlike many western languages on Earth, this writing didn't read left to right or right to left but rather up to down. The letters curved delicately and attached to the letter below, producing a flowing script. It reminded her of an East Asian written language she'd seen once.

As she continued to study the papers, however, she found that not all of the writing looked the same. Some contained the Tremantian symbols she was learning, but others were vastly different. She raised her brows. *How many languages can Luka read?*

Not wanting to feel impressed by any more of his talents at the moment, she began studying the pictures. The romantic in her gave an unwelcome swoon as soon as she realized what she was looking at. Mated couples.

Hundreds of pictures of mated couples of all kinds were scattered around the pages of text dotting the wall. She frowned and walked along the room, surveying the happy, glowing faces of past Clecanians.

One picture made her steps falter. A tall, blonde beauty stood regally in a red Grecian-style dress. A large man stood next to her, dressed in what Alice assumed was Clecanian formal wear. Blue mating marks were visible on their intertwined hands. They were a gorgeous couple, but what made Alice pause was the look on the man's face. While the woman beamed toward the camera, the man gazed down at his mate. The love and pure joy in his eyes made Alice somehow feel both full with empathetic joy and hollow.

She stiffened when she heard the soft sound of a door closing. The warmth that spread over her back told her Luka was behind her well before he spoke.

"Do you like this picture?" he rumbled, sending chills through her.

Did she like it? It made her heart ache. "Why do you have all of these pictures?" she asked instead. "Come to think of it, why do you have so many pieces of paper? Isn't this a technologically advanced planet?" She gestured to the room at large. "Shouldn't all these books and pictures be digital?"

"They've been loaded to many databases, but I've always found physical pages to be easier to organize in my mind. I enjoy the feel and smell, as well." He moved to stand next to her, hands clasped behind his back, nodding toward the image of the happy couple. "They're all pictures of Clecanian mates from the past. Whenever I find an account of a mating, I gather their story along with their picture and put it on this wall."

She glanced at his handsome profile. "For research?"

"My field is modern reproduction, not mating," he said after a moment.

"Then why do you have these everywhere?"

His jaw clenched and his brows drew together as though he was wondering why himself. After a long pause, he turned to her, peering down into her eyes. "I suppose," he began slowly, "I like to have a reminder of what could be. I liked to imagine a world in which coupled Clecanians could go back to being happy together. Their stories push me to work harder."

Crap. He is a goddamned closet romantic! She could barely handle her sexual attraction to Luka as it was, but now he revealed that he had a romantic side? She could practically feel her ovaries yelling at her to say, *"We can be happy together!"*

"So, what's their story?" she grumbled, forcing her gaze away from Luka's intense stare and pointing to the picture of the handsome couple. She could feel Luka looking down at her for a moment longer. Their stance felt like the unhappy mirror of the man and woman in the photo.

"They were mated for eighty years, a long time in those days, before our medical advances. He was a gardener, growing plants for use in our medicines. She was a soldier. At the time, Clecania was at war with the Tagion species. During a particularly brutal battle, she was injured and had to be hospitalized. He saw her while delivering plants and recognized her as a potential mate. She recognized him as well but didn't want to abandon her fellow soldiers, so she refused to be near him, knowing if she was, her mating marks would appear, and she'd never want to leave."

"You can choose like that?" Alice asked, enthralled.

Luka shrugged. "It's been known to happen. Mating is an instinct, but we still are who we are. We still have goals and ambitions."

"What happened next?"

"She returned to the front lines. He stayed in Sauven, another city near here. He couldn't communicate with her often, but he'd sneak into her home to feel close to her. Every time he did, he'd bring a flower or plant." The corner of his mouth lifted in a small smile. "She said when she finally returned home, she felt like she'd walked into a forest."

Alice's chest swelled and her throat grew tight. Luka had given her plants every day too. She took a few calming breaths, and something he'd said jumped out at her. "She *said* it was like a forest? Was this paper written by her?" Alice reached out to gently graze the yellowed page with her hand.

He gave her a lopsided smile then pointed to the man in the picture. "His name was Atheon." His finger moved to the woman. "And her name was Illukia." Raising his eyebrows at Alice, he added, "I was named after her."

Alice gasped, glancing from Luka to the picture. "Those are your ancestors?"

"My grandparents. I never met them, but my father told us endless stories about them when we were children." He grinned back toward the picture.

Out of all the pictures on the wall, how had she found the one connected to him? Unsettled, Alice asked, "What happened to them?"

He exhaled slowly. "They were happy and mated for eighty years, but then the plague swept through. Like many females, she was taken."

Her head snapped back toward the elated, loving gaze of Luka's grandfather. Tears sprang to Alice's eyes. How devastated must he have been?

Luka glanced toward her, then did a double-take. He grabbed her gently by the shoulders, twisting her body to face him.

Along with all of her other weaknesses, Alice was also a crier. Movies, shows, Hallmark cards. Give her a sappy commercial, and watch her start to well up. She kept her head turned, eyes focused on the picture, not wanting Luka to see how silly she was being.

Turning her face toward him with a soft hand on her cheek, he gazed down at her, worry in his expression. "They spent a happy lifetime together. That's more than any Clecanian alive today can say."

She nodded, tears running down her cheeks. "That's really sw—sweet," she said, her voice breaking.

Luka grinned down at her again, the corner of his eyes crinkling, then pulled her into a hug. "You feel everything so deeply, don't you? That's wonderful."

Alice stood stiffly for a moment, emotion still clogging her throat. When he tucked her head under his chin and began petting her hair, she relaxed, pressing her cheek into his chest. A low purr emanated from him, soothing her frayed nerves.

She hadn't prepared for this caring, sweet side of Luka, and she didn't quite know how to handle her feelings. He hadn't laughed or mocked her show of emotion, and he hadn't clammed up or become uncomfortable, either. He acted exactly the way she wished people would act with her, and that scared the ever-loving shit out of her.

Pulling away, she wiped at her eyes. With a deep inhale, she glanced up at him, trying to be stern. "We need to talk about some things."

"Okay." He absently ran his hands up and down her arms, and she regretted that she'd need to put an end to the affectionate gesture.

"If you want to keep seeing me, you're going to have to follow some rules. I want to get to know you, and you're making that very difficult for me." When he made to argue, she held up a finger, quelling him. "One, no more touching me." She glanced pointedly at his hands.

The motion of his hands stopped on her shoulders, and his contented smile morphed into a frown. She felt his fingers briefly squeeze before he removed his hands, as though he'd had an internal battle to do as she'd asked and almost lost.

Emboldened, she continued, "And two, no more watching me. I mean it. No more."

His brows drew together and he clenched his fists at his sides, but said nothing.

Her gaze hopped around the room nervously while she waited for his response.

Finally, he stepped back, crossing his arms over his chest. "I can't do both," he said simply.

"What?"

"No touching and no watching? I can't do both." He shook his head. "It's an instinct, and what you may not understand is that it's painful to ignore." He gestured toward his grandparent's photo again. "That's why she didn't allow their mating to go further before leaving. After the marks appear, it physically aches to be away from you. The feeling lessens when I'm near you and when I'm touching you. So…I can manage one of your requests but not both."

Alice stood with her mouth hanging slightly open. She hadn't expected a negotiation. Realistically, she'd expected him to ignore her rules entirely and do whatever he wanted. That's what she was used to from other men, but Vanessa was right—he was different and this situation was different. Her brows drew together. She didn't want to cause him pain.

What did she care more about? His watching had been unsettling at first but now oddly made her feel safe. Touching her was dangerous, though. He knew exactly how to make her resolve weaken, and she couldn't have that. Maybe there was a third option.

"Okay," she said slowly. "You can't watch me from the woods, but you can come visit me once a week, and you can touch me, but only in the places I say are okay. Everything else is a red zone."

He raised his brows expectantly, waiting for her to continue.

"You can touch my arms and hands."

"And your back and face. Also, I want to visit you every other day," he argued.

Face equals lips. One kiss, and she'd be begging him to touch her everywhere. *Can't have that,* she thought quickly.

"Just my back. No face. Every three days. Final offer."

"Fine," he grunted.

Instinctively, she stretched out her hand, then recalled Clecanians didn't shake hands.

Before she could lower it again, Luka snatched it, gently massaging it in his hands. Stepping closer to her, voice as smooth as silk, he said, "You are more than welcome to touch me anywhere you want." Bringing her upturned hand to his mouth, he slowly kissed her wrist, her pulse jumping at his touch.

Her sex clenched. *I've made a terrible mistake.*

17

⚭

What had she gotten herself into? Shortly after their negotiation, Luka had announced that if she wanted to go to the reserve before dark, they'd need to leave soon.

He'd been touching her arms and hands nonstop since then.

Arms and hands. That's a safe bet. How sexual could holding hands be? Idiot. When it came to Luka, Alice apparently felt every brush of his hand was sexual.

They rode in silence for a while. Luka seemed lost in thought, and Alice was clenching her entire body, forcing herself not to lean into his touch.

Her hand rested, upturned, on his thigh, almost close enough to his shaft to make her pull away. He gently traced the lines of her palm and the soft padding of her fingers. His other hand circled her wrist firmly. The combination of the soft, gentle caresses and the possessive, tight grip was driving her crazy.

She knew he could smell her arousal. He'd been able to identify it through the thick underwear she'd worn before; now that she was without, she could only imagine how easily he understood what he was doing to her. It felt like manipulation, and having been manipulated so often in the past, Alice loathed it.

When he brought her hand up to his mouth for yet another torturous kiss, she pulled away. His hold on her wrist tightened and he studied her. "You said I could touch your hand."

Tugging again, she snapped, "Yes, but I didn't say you could attach yourself permanently to it. You're rubbing it too much. The skin is getting raw."

Releasing her, he chuckled. "Why do you lie when you know I can scent how you're really feeling?"

Heat bloomed on her cheeks, and she petulantly crossed her arms, angling away from him. "Why do you keep trying to turn me on when you know I don't want you to?"

"I'm assuming you aren't presenting your back because you'd like me to rub your shoulders, but I think it'd help you relax."

A backrub sounded wonderful. *Just a small one wouldn't hu—No. Bad Alice!* She crossed to the cruiser bench opposite and sat facing Luka, out of reach.

He leaned forward, placing his elbows on his knees, and studied her again as though calculating what his next move should be. Finally, he said, "Come back, Alice. I won't touch you anymore."

A small smile tugged at her lips and washed away her annoyance. She felt a familiar warmth spread through her, making her chest tighten. "You used to say that to me, you know. At the outpost." She imitated his deep baritone and repeated, "Come back, Alice."

Luka raised his brows. "Did you listen then?" he asked with a teasing smile.

Despite herself, she chuckled, but then her smile faded and she tried to really look at him, past the charm he was trying to wear like a mask. "Do you honestly not remember anything?"

He glanced away and hiked his shoulders. "I remember a little. More and more every day."

"I'm sorry for what he did to you," she whispered.

"I'm not," Luka said seriously. His eyes rose to meet hers again. "If he hadn't, you would've been put in a cell like the others and may have never escaped. Because you did, we have a lead on finding the other outposts, and I found you." He peered at her with brows drawn. "I don't know if you can understand the lengths a Clecanian would go to, to recognize their mate. I'd do it again if I had to."

Alice didn't know what to say, so she just held his stare, seeing the truth of his words reflected in his eyes.

The intense silence was broken when the cruiser gently lurched, alerting them they'd arrived. Luka hunched and retrieved a large bag from the ground. While his back was turned, Alice took a few calming breaths and tried to slow her hammering heart.

He'd do it again? For me?

The hiss of the vehicle door sliding open preceded a rush of warm air. Inhaling, she picked up a familiar scent. Not quite pine, but…it smelled like Luka. *How often does he come here?*

When she emerged from the cruiser, a sprawling forest greeted her. As she looked closer, she found that "forest" wasn't quite right. Luka hefted his large bag, wrapped his hand around hers, and guided her into the tree line.

The foliage here was a verdant green. Not as cool and deep as a typical forest. More vibrant and rich, like she imagined a jungle would be. The ground was covered in large fallen leaves and neon-green moss. Her eyes wide, she tried to take in every detail as Luka pulled her along.

The setting was familiar yet eerily different. The texture of the tree trunks was similar to the trees on Earth, but the color varied from trunk to trunk. While many were the typical hues of brown found on most trees, others were assorted shades of teal swirled with light brown. She also spotted a few farther into the forest that had shades of pink, yellow, and blue.

Animals and insects remained hidden in the dense foliage, but their calls echoed around her in an otherworldly chorus. Calls she would've normally associated with an amphibian were loud. Much too loud. Birdsong rang out from all around her, and when she raised her eyes, she could see bright flashes of color racing across the treetops.

The damp, heavy scent of the forest lessened slightly, and she lowered her gaze to find they were approaching a wide, glittering stream.

Releasing her hand, Luka crossed to an enormous ancient tree at least a hundred feet tall. Its gnarled roots weaved in and out of the ground, creating dark holes for all manner of creatures to hide.

Without warning, he reached into one of those black pits. Alice covered her mouth, her skin crawling to think what might be lurking in there. He shot her a lopsided grin over his shoulder. "Scared for me?"

Alice pursed her lips and lowered her hands. "The fear you're smelling is from possibly witnessing a grown man get his hand bitten off because he was dumb enough to reach into a random hole in the woods."

He gave a chuckle and continued rooting around in the depths of the tree. A small squeak sounded before he withdrew his hand, now holding a small furry animal.

"What are you doing! Put it back," she cried, running over. What was he thinking, tearing an animal out of its home like that?

He sat on the ground, placing the small creature on his lap. To Alice's surprise, it didn't try to bolt as soon as he let it go. "Calm down, female. This guarsil needs medication."

"What?" she said softly, kneeling down to study the creature.

The guarsil, as he called it, was the size and color of a pomegranate, its round body covered with dark red, wiry hair.

As Luka reached into his bag and retrieved a small green tablet, the guarsil snuggled into his lap, trying to burrow between his legs.

"Its mother left recently, but he hasn't moved out of the nest like his brothers and sisters. A few days ago, when I checked on him, I noticed he had a bit of a cold."

"A cold? You're treating him for a cold?"

He held the green pellet out to the animal, and Alice watched as long arms she'd thought were cute little hands shot out from its round center to snatch the tablet. "Guarsils are pack animals, and they're endangered. I know where his nestmates have moved to, but if he doesn't get better soon, I won't be able to return him to their pack. A cold won't kill him, but being alone when he gets better will."

Alice watched as the tiny animal nibbled the edges of the green object. Its small, sharp teeth attacked it the way a human would corn on the cob. "It's kind of cute." She smiled.

Luka gave a humorless laugh. "Cute now, but in about two months when it reaches maturity, it'll be vicious. Their small size is deceptive. Animals will come by sniffling around a waiting guarsil, thinking it's a fallen wanget fruit. When they get close enough, all the pack members attack. They've brought down animals a hundred times their size."

Like some kind of terrifying out-of-water piranha. Alice leaned away from the creature and glanced around.

"Don't worry. I won't let anything get you," Luka said, smirking up at her under dark brows.

The retort that bubbled up evaporated on her tongue. He *would* protect her. She felt it. No man from her past had ever made her feel quite as safe as Luka did.

Unaware of her open regard toward him, he dropped the squirming guarsil back into the roots of the tree.

"Why are you trying to help it?" Alice asked, recalling that healing animals was her passion, not his.

He shrugged. "Because I'm here all the time and I can."

She held his stare. Would all Clecanian men go out of their way to help an unlikeable, vicious animal? She thought not.

"How often do you come here?"

"Before you?" he began, peering at her meaningfully. "Every day or every other day. As often as I can. Sometimes other researchers schedule work, which means I'm not able to visit."

Ignoring his first comment, she asked, "What kind of research are you doing out here? I thought your field was Clecanian reproduction?"

He surveyed the area with a lopsided grin. "I study the mating habits of different animals to see whether there are any noticeable patterns in their rate of reproduction and their mating practices. Do their bodies produce more of a certain chemical while in heat that could be harnessed and used in Clecanians? Does the time of year or their diet result in more or less births? That type of thing. Mostly I just come and watch. I don't know exactly what I'm looking for, but the interesting ways in which they couple helps me brainstorm."

"What kinds of interesting ways do they couple?" she asked curiously. Some creatures on Earth were known to mate in odd ways. Would they be similar here?

"Well..." He pointed to the water. "There are certain types of suu who are hermaphroditic. When they choose to mate, they'll attempt to stab each other with their reproductive organs and inject the other with their seed. They sometimes die from the wounds sustained."

"I think that's very similar to slugs on Earth." She laughed, recalling the first animal science class she'd taken after a year of uninteresting general ed courses. "I don't know how slug mating habits could help your research, though."

With another slanted smile, he hiked his shoulders. "If you look hard enough, you can always find similarities that could lead to some useful piece of information. Hermaphrodites are rare among Clecanians, but battles for dominance aren't unheard of. The Rotun in the East wrestle to decide who their spouses will be. Whoever wins becomes the lead of the marriage and makes the majority of decisions with input from their partner."

She eyed his large frame, glad she hadn't been taken to a Rotun city. There'd be no question about who'd win in a wrestling match between her and Luka. "Seems like the men would have an unfair advantage."

He hissed a laugh through his teeth. "You haven't seen a Rotun female. They may not be as big, but they're strong and are trained to be excellent wrestlers." Squinting into the sky, he said, "Let's go. I thought we could take a walk and see what we can see. I'll tell you what I can about the animals if we spot any."

Alice nodded and began to rise, one hand on her bent knee. Luka took hold of her other hand, helping her the rest of the way.

"Thanks," she muttered when she was on her feet. His hand twitched in hers, but he released her, stepping away to retrieve his bag. She attempted not to ogle his ass as he bent to grab the bag. "What's in there, anyway?"

He tightened the loose strap over his broad chest before giving her a vague answer. "A few things I thought we may need."

Rolling her eyes, she motioned for him to lead the way.

As they traipsed through the forest, Luka kept reaching out and briefly touching her. While she was annoyed at first, after a while she began to wonder if he truly couldn't help it. He'd be in the middle of describing an animal or plant and would suddenly run his hand down her arm or quickly squeeze her hand without any explanation. Alice wasn't even sure he knew he was doing it.

Her awareness of the confusing male ebbed, however, as they ventured further and the wonders of an alien forest revealed themselves. She could see many similarities in the fauna of Clecania and Earth, but some of the animals they came across were completely alien.

Alice was extremely thankful she'd been smart enough to wear boots when little green seed pods on the ground began hopping and biting at her ankles. Luka explained that the little insects had evolved to resemble the seed pods of native bushes. They'd wait on the ground by said bushes and nip at any creatures happening by, hoping to draw blood.

Luka's senses were keen, and every so often he'd branch off and examine a track or a broken limb she hadn't thought anything of. He seemed so at home here.

"Is this what you do when you come here every day?" she asked as he scooped a small amount of sap from a purple vine.

He stashed the sap in his large bag and then walked back over to her, his eyes lit with excitement. "A variation of this. I come to observe and note any differences. After four years, I've finally put together the fact that wadefs go into heat when the wyret vine's sap begins leaking." He threw his hands out, a delighted smile lighting his face. "I can't believe I'd never realized it before. It'll be exciting to see what properties this sap has. I'm wondering if they eat it or if it gives off an undetectable smell of some kind." He held out his hand to her. "Come here, see if you can smell anything."

Alice couldn't hide her smile. Luka's enthusiasm for his work was a palpable thing. She took his hand and let him direct her to the deep purple vine oozing green sap. Leaning in, she inhaled. "It smells like black licorice!"

She grinned up at him, and his eyes locked on her mouth. A heartbeat passed, and then she hastily cleared her throat and moved away.

Damn gorgeous man with his rugged Indiana Jones scientist-explorer thing.

"What's licorice?" Luka asked from behind her, interrupting her internal griping.

"It's a candy. People either love or hate black licorice. It has a very distinctive smell and taste." She glanced at him over her shoulder and fought the urge to glare at the sun for highlighting his chestnut hair so perfectly.

"Do you love it or hate it?" He sped up until he was striding along next to her.

"Hate it. But I like some drinks that have that flavor for some reason. There's this cocktail I created at the bar that has just a dash of anise…" Her words faltered for a moment when Luka briefly placed his hand on her lower back and guided her to the right. She swallowed and tried to remember what she'd been talking about. "Uh, anise is where a lot of the flavor in black licorice comes from, but if you put just a little in a mixed drink with ginger beer, it really brings the whole thing together."

"Did you enjoy creating drinks on Earth?"

Alice frowned. From anyone else, that question might've sounded like he was putting down the profession, but Luka looked sincere as he waited for her answer. The corner of her mouth lifted. "I did. I mean, it wasn't my dream job. The pay sucked. My boss sucked. And some of the customers sucked, especially during the school year when the college kids are in town. But I liked talking to the people who came in, and I liked making up drinks I thought they'd enjoy. Are there bars here?" Maybe she could go back to working in a bar while she tried to become an alien veterinarian.

"There are, but most of them have automated bartenders."

Who did the lonely souls who needed a drink and a listening ear talk to, then?

Luka stopped her with a hand on her arm and pointed to a tree canopy. Thousands of colorful birds, each smaller than a grape, nested in the branches above. He cupped his hands around his mouth, making a loud, high-pitched shriek. The birds bolted from the trees in a mass of bright pinks and oranges. Once in the sky, they re-formed like a school of fish. Their small bodies flying so closely together gave the impression that a much-larger bird was hunting for its prey.

Alice's gaze settled on Luka's face, smiling up at the birds as they flew away. "What do you do for fun when you aren't working?"

He glanced at her with raised brows and then began walking again. "I work more or I exercise."

I bet you do. "Do you have any hobbies?"

He thought for a moment. "I collect stories of matings and I read papers from other researchers in my field."

"What about your family? Do you go and visit them a lot? Do you ever get frustrated doing so much work? Do you take many vacations?" Now that Alice had started to feel more comfortable with Luka, she found she had a million questions for him. "What kinds of things do you do to stay happy?"

He laced his fingers behind his back, opened his mouth, and then closed it, as if unsure what to say. "I've always been very focused on work. Eventually, I'd like to stop working and move out of the city. I'd like to see my family more often, maybe visit my nephews. I haven't seen my sister's children since they were young." He stared at the ground, brows drawn.

"You shouldn't wait to do those things. Family's important."

"What's your family like?" Luka asked, absently running his knuckles down her arm.

Should I get into this right now? Talking about her past was always painful for Alice. *That's why I'm here, right? Give him a chance.*

"My mom was…tough. She worked a lot and wasn't a very happy person. I shouldn't be too hard on her. She was just a single woman trying to be strong and do what she thought would make our lives better, but she ended up missing out on a lot."

Alice felt her throat tightening and tears beginning to form in her eyes, and she blinked them away. Luka reached for her but then dropped his hands abruptly. At that moment she almost wished she hadn't made her rules.

"We had a difficult time understanding each other. She tried, but she couldn't figure out why material things didn't make me happy. I would've preferred to spend a day with her than a day shopping, and that just didn't make sense to her." Alice lifted her hand clock, sighing at the foreign symbols. "I remember always sitting in front of this big grandfather clock we had in our foyer, waiting for her to come home from work."

"I understand what you mean. My father had a hard time raising six of us after our mother died. I knew he loved me and did what he could. I would've liked to have spent a whole day alone with him too."

Alice stopped walking and studied Luka. His muscles were tensed and there was a lingering concern in his eyes. He searched her face with a clenched jaw but didn't say anything. Something told Alice he wasn't used to speaking about things like this, being vulnerable in this way.

She reached out and clasped his hands in hers. A low purr stuttered and then stopped as if he'd quelled it. "I'm really sorry about your parents. Thank you for telling me."

His shoulders relaxed at her words, and a purr rumbled through him. "Would you like me to explain the way we tell time as we walk?"

Alice brightened. "I'd love that. Nobody seems to care about telling time here."

Luka's chest expanded, and he grinned. Over the next hour, they continued to walk and he patiently explained the complicated method for telling time. Alice was becoming flustered. Not only did she have to first understand the movements of the moons in relation to each other in order to understand their equivalent of a.m. and p.m., but she also had to wrap her head around the fact that they didn't count up in hours, but down.

"You don't have time zones, either?" Alice asked, her head pounding. "So if it's four before prime, that means it's getting dark here, but in other places it's light out and they still say the same thing?"

Luka chuckled. "Yes. It's a planet-wide system."

Alice was relieved when they came to a sun-speckled clearing along the stream. She needed a break, and this spot looked perfect. Glancing across the water, she recognized the roots of the tree housing the guarsil. Apparently, they'd made a large arc around the stream and had come to the banks on the other side.

"I guess it makes sense to count down from thirty-two but—"

Suddenly, Luka crouched down, pulling Alice with him. Putting a finger to his lips, he pointed toward a large tree with thousands of reed-like branches arching over the water.

Overall, the tree looked similar to a weeping willow, the spill of leaves creating a curtain around the base. Alice peered at Luka for reassurance, fearful he may have spotted a predator hidden by the tree.

He grinned and grabbed her hand, motioning for her to look back at the tree. Her eyes searched and searched, but she couldn't find any birds or insects lurking that may have prompted Luka's sudden interest.

Glancing at the trunk of the tree, she mused about how oddly shaped it was. The base started out small, but as her eyes continued up, the trunk bowed wildly then returned to a normal width. It looked as though the tree had eaten a very large animal who was now trapped in its center. The trunk also appeared to be split in two vertically. The long halves twisted around each other all the way until they vanished into the canopy.

They crouched there in silence for a few minutes. What was he waiting for? She tugged at his hand, eyebrows raised. He rolled his eyes then retrieved a large box from his bag.

The box rested on his lap, and he grinned at her before flipping the lid open to reveal a mound of small black insects. Alice reared back, losing her balance and landing hard on her ass.

Luka lifted one, showing her they were no longer alive, while his shoulders shook in silent laughter. Unable to stop it, a grin spread across her face too. She pushed on his shoulder, hoping he'd lose his balance as well and spill the box all over himself, but he only swayed in place.

Silently, he held up a hand, telling her to stay, and crept toward the tree, box in hand. When he got within a few feet, he gave the box a hard jerk, sending dead bugs flying all over the leaves, then retreated at a sprint. Alice cocked her head. The bugs should've drifted to the ground but instead they peppered the leaves, like they were stuck there.

When Luka returned, he dashed to sit behind her and quickly scooted forward until her back was to his front, his legs bent on either side of her hips. She turned to him and started to scoot away, not liking how easily she could sink onto his warm, inviting chest, but he grabbed her head in both hands and turned her face toward the tree again. She was just about to scold him for touching a red zone body part when the tree began to move.

Once she sat frozen in place, unable to look away, Luka removed his hands and ran them down her arms, resting his chin on top of her head.

The curtain of leaves started to spin slowly, then faster and faster. An image of a carnival swing ride popped into her head. The once-arching branches became horizontal with the force of their rotation. They kept spinning, now moving upward like a tornado, the tube of the twister growing narrower and narrower until the branches formed two vertical cylinders right above the twisted trunks of the tree.

Alice was both afraid and excited to see what would happen next. She leaned against Luka and gripped his knees. Placing his palms over her hands, he lifted them and crossed their overlapped arms around her abdomen. In essence, he was hugging her against his body without ever touching her waist. A corner of her mouth lifted at the clever workaround.

When the massive trunks of the tree began to unwind, all bets were off. Alice scooted back as far as she could and tried to stand so she could get away from the gargantuan creature emerging before them. Luka held her fast and leaned down to whisper in her ear, "I've got you. They won't hurt us."

"They? What is it?" she breathed.

"A mated manta pair. Our city is named after them."

She watched in astonishment as two separate creatures emerged. Like a shot, the swirling green leaves were sucked down into the trunks. After a moment, the trunks themselves lowered and they stood, quietly ingesting their meal.

Luka spoke again at her ear. "They send their tongues out to catch wandering insects. The green bits that look like leaves are incredibly sticky. Sometimes they'll stay frozen in place for days, waiting until they sense they have a full meal."

Now moving and not pretending to be a tree, she found that the creatures were not so scary. Once relaxed, their long trunks made them look similar to stubby-legged, camouflaged elephants. As she watched, the larger of the two manta rubbed its trunk against the other. Alice tilted her head. The touch almost looked loving.

"When they're alone, their leaves are sparse and they can't catch as much food, but when they find a partner, they stand together, creating a full, thick canopy." He nuzzled her ear gently. "They mate for life."

Ah, shit. She was curled up in his lap, and he was telling her love stories. How the hell had this happened? It's like they were watching a nature documentary together. *This was supposed to be serious research for my job, not Netflix and chill!*

Now done with their meal, she witnessed the two manta inch their way back in place, lifting their trunks and twisting them together gracefully.

Luka gave her a gentle squeeze. "This part is fun."

Before she could ask what he meant, the green shoots exploded out of their trunks like a firework, making Alice jump. If he weren't holding her, she would've probably cleared the ground.

A laugh rumbled through his chest, and she chuckled with him.

This felt good. She liked laughing with him. They'd had a wonderful afternoon together, and he'd kept his word except for a few brushes against her ear and the hands on her head. *He'd definitely bent the rules,* she thought as she reclined against his chest, but he hadn't broken them, and she found she enjoyed his tricksy side.

When her pounding heartbeat slowed, she relaxed into him, allowing his body to envelop her. His arms tightened around her as he let out an exhale. Had he been holding his breath? A purr rumbled through him, and she grinned.

18

Luka's chest felt permanently expanded. *She's allowing me to hold her!* Leaning into his hold, even.

Earlier when she'd told him her rules, he'd been bewildered. His plan was to entice her to be with him through the pleasure he could give her. That plan wouldn't work if she didn't allow him to touch her.

She'd said she wanted to base her decision off his personality. Luka wasn't known for his personality. He liked to be by himself. Working alone in his home was second only to being out in the reserve. He knew how to charm a female with compliments and how to please her, but few females cared to get to know a male as a companion. It would make it harder for them to move on and procreate with others, so he'd never held the fact against them.

The idea that Alice might not like who he was at his core frightened him more than he could say. But, if that was what his mate needed, that was what he'd provide. He'd decided, after his disastrous attempt to court her favor by pleasuring her, to try and be himself. He'd shown her the animals he loved and had talked endlessly about the reserve. Never once had she acted uninterested or bored. He'd even teased her with dead insects.

Making her come had brought him pure masculine satisfaction, but knowing that she liked who he was made him feel...so much more.

They sat there together, watching the swaying manta in silence. Emotion swelled in his throat when he felt her breaths grow slow and even. She trusted him enough to fall asleep wrapped in his arms. If it were up to him, he'd gladly stay just like this, holding her until the sun came up, but the cold creeping over her bare legs forced his hand.

For a moment, Luka sat frozen, not knowing what to do. He wanted her to trust him, and she'd made him agree not to touch her anywhere except the areas she'd mentioned, but waking her rather than lifting her and carrying her back to the cruiser seemed wrong.

A loud baeder croak sounded, causing her to bolt awake. He watched her take in her surroundings, wondering if she'd be upset that he'd held her for so long.

She peered back at him. "Did I fall asleep?"

"You did, love."

His tension faded when she blushed and quietly said, "Oh, sorry. I guess that walk wore me out."

"Let me take you home." Luka shot a glance to his pack, picturing the feast he'd prepared for them.

"What about dinner?" She attempted to stifle a yawn.

He helped her to her feet, loving the feel of her hand in his but hating that the touches were so brief. "I'll come by tomorrow instead. Is that alright?"

After she gave a small smile and nod, he began directing them back toward the cruiser. To his surprise, she reached for him, entwining her fingers with his. It took every ounce of willpower he possessed not to shout with joy and kiss her until her toes curled.

As they approached the vehicle and she released him to climb inside, he worried the return to the real world after basking in the romantic haze of the reserve would cause her to pull away again. To his delight, she didn't complain or argue when he lifted her hand into his lap once more.

Earlier in the day, on the way to the reserve, he'd stroked her hand, learning the type of touch that aroused her. Now, he simply relaxed, contented from feeling her small soft palm in his.

"Thank you for bringing me here today. I see why you love it so much," she said, pulling him from his musings. "I'm sorry I'm so tired. I was nervous and didn't sleep very well last night. Out of curiosity, what did you have planned for dinner, anyway?"

She'd been nervous? "I made us a picnic." He nudged the black bag on the ground with his foot.

When Jade had first given him the idea, he'd thought it ridiculous. Tremantian females wouldn't enjoy eating on the ground in the woods. But after some time, he'd realized this wasn't any female, this was his mate. It made sense that if he enjoyed the reserve she would too.

Still, a lifetime of experience had him holding his breath, waiting for the derision to show on her face at the idea. His breath had caught in much the same way earlier when he'd decided to share a personal fact about his relationship with his father. She'd surprised and delighted him with her tender response then, and he hoped the same happened now.

Alice stared at the large bag with wide eyes.

Dread knotted in his stomach. He'd been wrong. He only hoped the mistake didn't set them back too far.

"You packed me a picnic?" She looked at him with an odd expression.

"Yes. I'm sorry. I thought you might enjoy eating outside and I believed the manta would do a good job of keeping the insects away from us, but I see now—"

"Whoa, wait," Alice interrupted. Surprise lit her face, and he was gifted with a glorious unguarded smile that stole his breath. "Don't apologize. I love it! I'm so upset you didn't tell me about it earlier. I would've rallied if I'd known you'd gone to so much trouble. I thought we were just going to get takeout from a restaurant or something."

Her intoxicating scent washed over him. The happiness radiating from her made him feel drunk from pleasure and had his cock stiffening.

"I didn't know you could cook."

It took him a moment to find his voice again. "Yes. I'm not the best. I only received a score of seven in my cooking exam, but I have a few meals I make well."

Turning toward him and tucking her leg under her, she asked, "Cooking exam? Did you go to culinary school or something?"

Attempting not to eye the seductive jiggle of her breasts as she repositioned herself, he replied, "No, husbandry school."

Her eyes rose to the ceiling, and she squinted in concentration. "Oh, yeah. Metli told us a little about that. I didn't realize you had to learn cooking. What else did you learn?"

How will she feel about my schooling? Jade had recounted her introduction to the concept, explaining she hadn't taken to some of their studies favorably.

"We learn about different things a wife might need or desire from her husband. Cooking, childcare, anatomy, sexual proficiency—" Luka tried to speed through the last, hoping she wouldn't question it, but she interrupted all the same.

"Excuse me? Sexual proficiency?"

He attempted to recall Jade's issue with the practice before speaking, hoping to assuage some of Alice's dislike. "Yes. It's an optional class that teaches males close to graduation how to properly please their partners."

He held his breath, waiting to see if she'd be understanding or disgusted. Jade's response to the class had surprised him, and he'd tried to imagine how a male's schooling might look to an outsider.

While in school, he'd never thought of the practice as disagreeable—quite the opposite. All of the males he knew, including himself, had been a bundle of nerves and embarrassment entering the class, and by the time they'd left, they'd had confidence.

They taught young males how to seduce a female and what to look for in her responses to know whether she was enjoying herself. The males had also learned the importance of consent and how to harness your sexual energy and control it when no willing females were available.

She blinked at him a moment, her beautiful blue eyes searching his face. Unexpectedly, she reached out, cupping his cheek in one hand while gripping his fingers with the other. "And you were okay with that?"

He let out the breath he'd been holding in a whoosh, a purr exploding in him. *She's concerned for me.* Warmth spread through his chest at the thought that his mate was worried about him.

"Yes, love. I was more than okay. Without those classes, I wouldn't be able to arouse my mate with just a touch to the wrist and hand," he murmured, recalling her intense reaction to his ministrations in the cruiser ride earlier.

A pretty pink blush spread over her cheeks, but she didn't deny it. With a smirk, she muttered, "Cocky male."

"Is it cocky if it's true?" he teased.

Suddenly her eyes grew unfocused and her brows knit. She searched his face. "Have..." She nibbled her thumb nail briefly before continuing. "Have you ever been married?"

Could that be jealousy etched on her face? Luka had to subdue the satisfied grin that threatened to spread over his face. "No, love. I've been picked a few times, but never ultimately chosen. I made sure not to be." He snatched her hand away from her mouth and kissed the tip of her thumb. "Would you be upset if I had?"

She pursed her lips and looked away from him. Her voice was falsely casual when she said, "No."

"Liar." He said, allowing his purr to rumble through his and show her his true feelings.

She narrowed her eyes at him, but he saw the corner of her mouth lift in a smile. "Can I see what you made? We could eat together now if you're hungry."

He allowed the subject to shift, but continued to bask in the idea that his mate was covetous of him. "That'd be wonderful." Was this how it would be with her? Easy and happy and intimate in a way he'd never experienced.

Rifling through his bag, he extracted the food and drink he'd carefully packed this afternoon and set it on the table. He programmed the warming lids to heat their food and then handed Alice a glass of tury. "Jade told me she calls this prosecco 2.0 and you would understand what that meant."

Alice licked her lips, drawing his eyes to her mouth yet again. *You've gone your whole life without kissing. You can wait a little longer.*

She took a small sip, and her features lit up. "Mmm. That's really good. I was worried it was going to be too sweet, but it has a tartness I like." Crossing her legs, she took another sip and relaxed against the soft cruiser wall. "When do you have to go back to work?"

He shrugged. Thinking about work would be all but impossible right now. There used to be a rule that allowed for extended absences from work if you became mated, but he wasn't allowed to reveal his marks. "I'm not sure."

"If it's not too distracting, I'd like to go with you to the reserve again. Watch you while you work."

Luka couldn't contain his wide grin. "You're making my life quite difficult, you know."

Her hopeful expression faded. "Oh?"

With any other female, he'd be treading dangerous waters with his teasing, but he sensed Alice enjoyed seeing that side of him. "If you aren't there, I won't be able to get any work done because I'll be thinking about you, and if you are there, I won't be able to get any work done because I'll be thinking about you and looking at you."

Alice blushed. "Thank you."

Luka uncovered the food, making sure to hand her the plate containing the ingredients her taste preference scan had revealed she'd like.

"This is wonderful. Thank you," she said in between small bites of food. "Will you tell me more about your family?"

Luka described his brothers and sister for the rest of the ride to the Temple. He didn't know if there was anyone else he enjoyed talking to quite as much as Alice. She was funny and sincere and talked about everyone she knew with a genuine, open kindness he'd never experienced before.

A dark part of his being twisted when she talked about the males she'd met so far. At her mention of Rhaego and how he'd be returning to teach more of the Tremantian language, Luka had to focus on not shattering the thick glass in his hand. This wasn't good.

His mind started to spin. They were headed back to the Temple now, where unmated males patrolled freely. A savage part of him screamed for him to redirect the car back to his home with so much force that his hand actually shot out before he quickly pulled it back.

It was unnatural to even think about leaving her alone. *I could watch her again*, his mind hissed. *She's my mate; I need to make sure she's protected.*

The cruiser stopped, and the door hissed as it slid open. Luka worked to pull himself together, but he feared the slightest movement on her part to leave him would make him drag her back into the cab.

Alice set her plate down and looked at him expectantly. "Luka, are you alright?"

He set his plate down as well and ground his teeth.

She rested a hand on his knee and caught his hard stare. "You can tell me. What's wrong?"

Could he tell her? He swallowed. "I'm struggling with this, Alice. It feels wrong to let you leave." A guard walking in the distance caught his eye, and his hands fisted.

Her brows drew together, but Luka was relieved to see sympathy in her eyes rather than anger. "I'm sorry this is hard for you. You need to let me go, though. How will we be together if we can't ever be apart? It's not healthy."

He sliced his hands through his hair and tried to calm himself. She was right. If she was going to work as a veterinarian and he was going to continue his research, he needed to be able to be apart from her. He suspected his Traxian half was exacerbating the effects of the mating instinct, and he had to find a way to control it.

He nodded and lifted his head, forcing a smile. "I'll see you tomorrow."

She got up and knelt in front of him, taking his hands in hers. "I can see how hard this is for you, and I appreciate the effort." With a shy smile, she added, "On Earth, it's customary for a couple to kiss after a date. I could lift the ban on face touching for a moment if that would help."

Like lightning, his hand shot out and gripped the back of her neck. He slanted his mouth over hers and kissed her until they were both gasping for breath. Alice's blue eyes were heavy-lidded and focused on him when he pulled away, and some of his stress melted. He leaned forward and kissed her more slowly, languorously, taking his time to learn what made her breath hitch and fingers clench. When he moved away again, he was pleased to see the disappointment in her eyes. He might not be able to have her now, but he felt certain she wouldn't want anyone else.

19

Luka had tossed and turned all night and was in an odd mood. His mind and body were fatigued, his aggression high, yet he was also excited and nervous about seeing Alice for dinner.

To top it all off, unwelcomed, simmering arousal coursed through him. When he'd returned home the night before, Alice's scent had still lingered, driving him mad. He'd stared at the area where she'd lain naked by the fire and recalled the way her body had shuddered when she'd come.

He'd paced, unable to relax. She should've been there with him, not alone in her home. Unable to sleep, he'd decided to distract himself by working through his best course of action. He needed to have a clear plan to make sure Alice eventually decided to stay with him. He'd contacted Theo to get some insight, but it had only led to more frustration.

Humans are impossible! With any other female, he could give gifts to show his sincerity or he could display his skills to prove he'd make a fit husband and father, but when it came to Alice, none of that mattered. Theo had explained that after many conversations with Jade, he believed a human's capacity for love and loyalty were unparalleled, but it had to be won— earned, even. They listened to their hearts rather than cold logic. There was nothing he could do or give to ensure her affections, and the lack of certainty was terrifying.

He clutched the bag of food he'd prepared a little tighter when Izzo began jogging toward him, wide grin in place.

"Hello, brother," he said cheerfully as he neared.

Luka only grunted in answer and snatched the pass out of Izzo's hands. He walked ahead, anxious to get to Alice and experience the soothing relief he felt whenever he saw her.

"I heard all about your date," Izzo said from behind him.

Luka tried to ignore his brother, but he couldn't quell his curiosity. "And?" he growled.

"You did well. She was very happy."

His spirits soared for a moment before darkening again. "How do you know? Did you visit her?"

Luka pictured Alice kindly inviting Izzo into her home, unaware of what that meant to Clecanian males. He'd need to explain the significance to her.

"She wanted my help in surprising you with something. She's been working at it all day, so make sure you put on a damn happy face, because right now you're acting like a sour baeder, and she doesn't deserve that."

Luka's steps faltered and he spun toward his brother, head tilted. Izzo was young and had always been the most lighthearted of the group. He never let his Traxian side dictate his mood, and he always worked to lighten the spirits of his dour brothers, but now his substantial frame and light-blue eyes were radiating authority and aggression.

Pride swelled in Luka for a moment. Izzo was becoming a formidable male. Strong, proud, and honorable. It lessened some of Luka's anxiety to know not only Zed but Izzo was watching out for his mate's best interests, even if that meant standing up to Luka himself if needed.

"I'll be better when I see her. It's difficult being away."

Izzo crossed his arms and huffed, glancing across the water near Alice's home. "Tell me about it."

Alice had been right yesterday in the forest. He needed to start seeing his family for what they were, blessings. Most Clecanians nowadays had few, if any siblings. He shouldn't take their affection for granted.

"How are things with…" Luka tried to recall the name of the small girl with curly brown hair Izzo was infatuated with.

"Daisy," Izzo provided. He hiked his shoulders, and the corner of his mouth turned down. "I haven't technically recognized her, and I don't know why. From the first moment I saw her, I could've sworn she was meant to be mine."

Luka gripped his shoulder. "I've spent a lot of time researching mating the past few days, and I've read many accounts of matings. What I've come to find is it's not nearly as consistent as most people think. I've read about mating marks appearing as soon as an individual scents their mate, before ever even seeing them. Others appear after years of friendship. Asivva believes it took Theo so long because he'd subconsciously built a mental barrier to it. It varies from race to race and individual to individual. Don't lose hope. If your instincts are telling you she's yours, they're likely right."

Izzo slowly nodded in agreement, pushing his shoulders back. "Thank you. I needed that." He smirked at Luka. "Look at you, giving pep talks and going out in public. Alice is rubbing off on you."

Heart picking up speed at the mention of her name, Luka resumed his trek toward her house and grinned. "I sure hope so."

When he finally reached her door, Izzo departed, telling him his pass would expire in four hours. If he needed more time, Alice had to alert a guard and request it.

He softly knocked and straightened, his skin itching with excitement.

She opened the door, and his stomach did a somersault. Her hair was loose and a bit wild, and her skin was flushed pink. A beige smock was tied around her waist. She beamed at him, and he had to control his impulse to wrap her in his arms.

A low purr punctuated with a growl escaped him when she stood on her toes and quickly kissed him on the cheek.

Her smile dimmed as she scanned his face. "Are you alright? You look tired. Did you sleep okay?"

"Yes, love. May I enter?" Luka loved the way her pupils dilated and her body seemed to vibrate with pleasure every time he used the pet name.

Distracted from her worry as he'd intended, she blushed and stepped aside to let him in.

Once inside, she grasped his hand and tugged him toward the kitchen, unaware of the effect the small contact had on him.

"I wanted to repay you for dinner last night, so I tried to make you dinner myself. Izzo helped me pick foods you liked and showed me how to cook them on that weird stove-counter thing. I have to go freshen up. Go sit down, I'll be right back." She waved her hand at the table, then scurried away into the bathing room.

He glanced toward the dining table and his jaw slackened.

Glass orbs had been programmed to hang over the table in a long delicate pattern, and the lights in the rest of the house were turned down, creating an intimate, warm glow. The softly lit table was covered with a large cloth and decorated with the plants he'd given her. On either end sat their covered plates and a soft napkin folded into an intricate pattern. He glanced to the kitchen and saw piles of used dishes and bits of chopped food. She must've been working on this for quite a while.

She'd done all this for him? The door opened again, and she emerged from the bathing room. He felt himself growing hard as he took in her stunning appearance. Instead of the smock, she wore a vermillion dress that was tight around her chest, accentuating her breasts, and flared delicately around her waist, ending mid-thigh. Stuck in the hair by her ear were a few small flowers plucked from the ruhi bush he'd sent to her today.

His eyes couldn't take in enough of her, and after a prolonged silence, she began shifting on her feet. When she raised her small nails to her mouth, a gesture he'd began attributing with stress, he was startled out of his hypnosis.

Dropping the food on the ground, he crossed over to her and ran his palms down her arms. "You look…beautiful." The compliment was not enough, not by a long shot, but she preened all the same.

"I hope you like the food." She dashed to the kitchen and bent to retrieve something from a refrigerated compartment. "I'm sorry I didn't tell you and you brought food too, but I was worried I might mess it all up and if we didn't have a backup, we'd go hungry."

She removed two glasses filled with amber liquid. Setting one by the plate on one side of the table, she moved to take a seat at the other.

He stayed in place, gazing at the scene before him, and tried to temper all the different emotions roaring in him. Nobody had ever done anything like this for him, and he was completely puzzled as to what he'd done to earn it.

"You don't like it?" A look of concern crossed her face, and her gaze darted around the table.

"I'm not used to it," he said, walking to the plate she'd set out for him. He peered over at her. "I can't express how much I appreciate it."

Alice shifted in her seat and nibbled her lip. "It's not that big a deal. The food probably isn't even that good."

Luka snorted. He'd have happily eaten tar if she'd gone to the trouble of putting it on a plate. "There's only one problem."

She scanned the table again, seeking the offending "problem," and frowned. "What is it?"

"You've put me much too far away." He hefted his chair and placed it catty-corner to hers, moving his plate and drink next. He sank into his chair and grinned at her. "How am I supposed to admire all the parts of you I can't touch from over there?"

She blushed. "Sorry. Old habits die hard."

He quirked his brow and thought about the interesting saying.

"I made you a cocktail," she said, eyeing the glass. "I hope you like it. It was really difficult to find the right flavors in liquid form, but based on what your brother said you enjoy, I thought you might like this. It's my closest approximation to what we call an old-fashioned."

He took an experimental sip and savored the velvety concoction as it slid down his throat.

Alice leaned toward him, brows raised.

"That's incredible," Luka said honestly.

She leaned back, smiling, and her shoulders relaxed. "Good. I thought I'd start with a classic before trying to make something more complicated. You have no idea how many different fruits I tried before finally finding a vegetable that worked in place of orange."

A magenta light pulsed in time with a low ding on the house's programming pad.

"I've never seen it do that before." Alice turned an inquisitive eye toward him. "What does it mean?"

For a moment, Luka had the devious urge not to tell her that some impertinent person was interrupting their dinner, but it might be an emergency. Covering her hand with his, he explained, "My communicator connects to your house when I walk in. That color means I'm getting a call."

"Oh," she said. "You should answer, then."

"Let me just tell them now isn't a good time." He snatched the sleek gray communication device from the bag he'd dropped near the kitchen. His brows knit together upon seeing the caller. *Verakko?*

"Hello."

"Are you with Alice?" Verakko asked without greeting.

Luka's hackles rose. The male who'd been making his mate laugh a few days ago was now inquiring after her. "Why?" he bit out.

"We have news and need to see her immediately. Can you bring her to the Queen's estate now?"

"If she goes, I go." Jealousy flared in Luka at the male's question. Logically he knew Verakko wouldn't have called and requested this meeting unless it was urgent, but a less understanding side of him rebelled against delivering his mate into the hands of another.

The sound of an annoyed exhalation rang out before he said, "Fine, but only if she agrees. Put her on."

He held the communicator out to Alice.

Slowly she took it, one brow raised at his stiff posture and clenched jaw. "Hello?" she said softly.

Even with his superior hearing, he couldn't quite make out what the male was saying.

Whatever Verakko's response was caused Alice to break out into a grin and, subsequently, caused Luka to grimace. "Oh, hi, Verakko! How are you?"

He clenched his fists when she chuckled lightly at something the male said.

"Uh-huh." She glanced at him, taking in his stiff posture, and listened. "Right now? Can it wait?"

Alice leaned toward him and ran a soft palm up and down his tense forearm. A rapid purr rang through him at a higher pitch than normal, indicating his internal mix of satisfaction and agitation.

"Yeah, I'm okay with him coming too," she said, smiling at Luka.

His shoulders dropped an inch. At least she'd allow him to go with her.

"Okay, sure. See you soon." She handed the communicator back to Luka, tsking when he issued a curt goodbye and hung up.

20

Six well-armed men with stony expressions stood before them, staring hard at her and Luka, and, for the first time, she was appreciative of Luka's overprotective personality.

Not able to drive the cruiser directly to the Queen, they'd stopped at the border of her property and now waited to be allowed in on foot. Luka stepped in front of Alice, partially blocking the guards' unwavering stares.

She smiled into the dark-green fabric of his shirt and, knowing he enjoyed her touch, laid her hands against his lower back to show her gratitude. A low purr rippled through him before he quickly coughed, pushing the purr away. Grinning, she assumed he didn't want to show a weak side of himself in front of the lethal males.

After their day in the woods yesterday, Alice had realized something. Luka may be able to turn her on whenever he wanted, using the scent of her arousal as confirmation, but she had a superpower of her own. She was confident she could make that delicious purr run through him whenever she wanted, just by touching him in the right way. It felt good. Like she had a small measure of control over his reactions as well.

Feeling more playful with Luka by the minute, she experimentally ran her hands up from his tapered waist to the large muscles of his upper back. His body stiffened, goosebumps breaking out over his exposed biceps. Hands shooting behind his back to snatch her wrists and hold them together accompanied a quickly stifled purr.

Eyes still trained on the men in front of them, he growled, "Alice" in a warning tone over his shoulder.

Stifling the impulse to rest her head against his back, knowing she'd receive another unwelcome purr, she giggled silently.

Instead, she studied the towering metal structure in front of them, wondering how long they'd need to stand here. The surface was solid and looked more like a wall than a gate, as she'd been informed. Without the guards standing in front of it, she may not have identified it as a potential entrance at all. No breaks in the smooth charcoal gray could be seen.

A slow rumble from beneath her feet had her leaning into Luka, her restrained hands blocking her from pressing herself to him fully. He squeezed on her wrists gently and then guided her to stand in front of him.

The vibration in the ground grew, making small pebbles and bits of dirt hop. Before her eyes, a slice of the tall, impenetrable wall slowly began sinking into the ground, leaving a small rectangular opening at the base, just wide enough for one person to walk through.

With an encouraging push from Luka, she dashed through the opening, not wanting to be guillotined in reverse. Turning, she saw Luka stroll through, a barely contained smirk on his face.

She waved a hand at him dismissively and began to walk down the clear dirt path leading away from the gate.

Catching up with her easily, Luka ran a knuckle down her spine, making her shiver. "I'm going to get you back for that, you know."

"Hmm, I can only imagine how annoying it must be to not be in control of your body's responses," she needled.

"I love not being in control, but only with you and not in front of others." The playful gleam in his eyes became soft and sincere.

Alice swallowed a sigh, feeling a flush creep over her cheeks. She returned her focus in front of her and simply replied, "Mmm."

The path leading to the Queen's home was tidy but rustic. Alice supposed they wouldn't pave roads normally since their vehicles floated, but it was still odd to be traveling toward a literal queen using a dirt path.

The surroundings were different than she expected, as well. Although not as dense as the forests of the reserve, the trees here were still numerous and wild. Ages ago, she'd gone to France on a school trip, and she recalled the land near the castles and chateaus being highly manicured.

Trying to imagine what an alien queen's home might look like, she began to get excited. Would the Queen's palace rise out of the forest like a castle in a fairytale book? Would it have turrets and spires?

As they rounded a corner and the pathway dead-ended near a small cottage, Alice's steps faltered. Was this housing for staff?

Rather than angling his steps away from the small structure, Luka walked further toward it. The cottage was small and tan; two large windows and a door dotted the front. A curved roof made of shimmering green tile topped the building. Just in front of the small house was a smaller pathway, lined on either side by large beds of wildflowers.

From the green front door emerged Verakko. Not bothering to walk over and greet them, he waved them forward, disappearing again into the small house.

"Is this where she lives?" Alice whispered.

Luka glanced toward the charming cottage and then back toward her. "Yes. Why?"

She shrugged. "It just doesn't look like a place a queen would live. Little Red Riding Hood or a hobbit maybe, but not a Queen."

"What's a hobbit?" Luka inquired seriously, pulling a laugh from her.

"Nothing. Nothing. Let's go."

Following him inside, she saw that the interior was as small as the exterior, though no less charming.

"Over here," Verakko called from their left.

Through an archway, she could see Verakko and the Queen sat at a small wooden table. Alice and Luka settled themselves at the table, as well.

"Hello, ma'am," Alice said, stumbling over "ma'am," not sure if it was appropriate.

The Queen gave a quick nod in acknowledgment.

Luka bowed, only taking his eyes off Verakko for a second to peer into the Queen's face as he said, "Madam."

"Hello, Alice. Luka. Thank you for joining us. I don't want to waste your time, so I'll dive right in. After spending some more time at the facility, Verakko has made a few discoveries." Nodding toward him, she continued, "I'll let him explain."

He smiled. "Nice to see you again, Alice." Toward Luka, he frowned. "And you."

Luka grunted in response.

"As you know, both outposts were rigged with some kind of failsafe. I continued searching the facilities, looking for any clues but they were both dead-ends," Verakko began.

Alice's heart sank. What would happen to all the people still being held in those places?

"We do have another lead, however," the Queen added. "We've been trying to get information out of Helas, but he's proved to be very loyal to the Insurgent cause. We suspect he was a higher-up within the ranks of the organization."

At the mention of Helas' name, she saw Luka stiffen. For the most part, Alice had put the awful days at the outpost behind her, but despite Luka's argument to the contrary, she wasn't sure he had.

She found his tightly balled fist under the table, and ran her fingertips over his skin until he loosened enough for her to place her hand in his. Body still radiating tension, she was relieved to see his clenched jaw loosen a fraction.

The Queen continued, "Sal, on the other hand, has decided to provide assistance."

"Why? And how does this concern Alice?" Luka rasped.

How does *it concern me?* Alice had become used to the Queen asking for her assistance in regard to humans and what could be done for the human women, but Luka was right, this felt different. This wasn't a large meeting at the Temple to discuss strategy, this was an intimate meeting at the Queen's house. A creeping sensation worked its way up her spine as she took in the briefest flash of concern on Verakko's face.

Verakko held Alice's stare. "Sal has revealed Helas has a secret work area in the woods near the outpost. He said he knows how to find it, and that it contains an operating system of its own that the other members are unaware of. Apparently, Helas was rather paranoid and decided he wanted to be able to oversee the other outposts without anyone else knowing."

"That's great!" But why were they telling her?

Verakko dipped his head from side to side, a grimace in place. "It's almost great. The system is protected by a three-factor identification. In order to log into his feed, we need

Helas' security token, fingerprint, and facial recognition scan."

"And I'm assuming these body parts need to be attached to him at the time?" Luka muttered darkly.

"Yup." Verakko glanced back toward Alice. "We can transport Helas to the house and force him to sit in place, but we can't force him to tell us where the token is. That's why we need you."

"Me?" Alice squeaked, eyes widening. "I don't know where it is."

Luka had gone perfectly still, his face unreadable.

"No, but Sal does, and he says he'll go with us and show us where it is, if you visit him first. He claims he wants to make amends." Verakko leaned toward her, and his eyes seemed to glow more brightly. "If we can get access to their video feeds, their locks, and their speaker system, I can lock in all the guards, unlock all the cells, and explain to the prisoners what is happening and how they can escape."

Helas' henchman? The last she remembered of Sal was when she and Vanessa had dropped the large man on the ground before escaping. In order to free the women being held in cages throughout the world, all Alice had to do was listen to some asshole's apology?

Weighing the pros and cons, she reasoned it might be a good opportunity for her to find closure. She still had so many questions about her missing time. If she and Jade had been transported on the same ship, why couldn't she remember months of her life? On the other hand, this could be a ruse.

"You'd need to accompany us to the prison and stay until we have everything we needed from Sal, and then you never have to see him again." As Verakko pushed, Alice noticed his voice became deep and resonant as though it changed with emotion, and some of his words were punctuated with a slight hiss.

Crap. She knew what she needed to do, and nobody at this table would be happy about it, including her. Her eyes strayed to Luka, and she grimaced. His muscles were bunched, and his eyes were glued ahead of him, but his hand was gentle around hers. If what he'd told her about the difficulty he felt being away from her was true, then he wouldn't like her idea one bit.

"I won't go to the prison to see Sal." She felt Luka's frame relax for a moment before she added, "I want to go with Sal, Helas, and whoever else to the cabin."

"Absolutely not." Luka's head snapped toward her, and she held his furious glare for long moments. "Alice, I'll not have you around those vile…disgusting…." His wild gaze wandered.

Verakko crossed his arms over his chest, his teal skin darkening slightly. "I agree. It's too dangerous."

The Queen stayed silent, but her intelligent eyes were focused on Alice.

"The women in there need to trust whoever is talking to them. I'm sorry, Verakko, but you just sound too…alien.

Everyone here does. It's the way you speak and the words you use—they'll know you're not human. And what happens when you try and talk to the humans who don't have a translator? Do they just get left behind? We can't assume they all have one." She could feel Luka's erratic pulse through the firm grip of his hand. She turned to him. "Luka, we're our own people, right? We have our own goals and ambitions?" she probed, repeating his words from days ago.

He threw his head back angrily, and his knee began bouncing. His breaths were coming quickly while his eyes darted across the room, likely looking for an argument.

Alice, Verakko, and the Queen all sat in silence, waiting for Luka's response. Alice would go regardless. She didn't need his permission, and if he truly thought to fight her on this, he'd lose. But she wanted to see what he'd do. For the last few days, Alice had been holding back from Luka. She could sense she was falling for him, hard, but she couldn't let herself fully trust him yet.

Being abducted by aliens had taught her a few things about herself. Despite her insecurities, she was passionate and resilient and brave. She needed a man who pushed her and allowed her to continue to flourish, not one who decided what was best for her without her having a say.

She didn't mind if he got mad about her decisions. They could scream and fight like cats and dogs, but at the end of the day, she needed to know he wouldn't try to keep her from doing what she wanted.

When he faced her, his eyes and brow were crinkled with worry. "I need to go with you."

Alice felt warmth spread through her, shooting all the way to her fingertips. They could do this. She could make things work with Luka. "Of course you can come." She turned back to the Queen and Verakko. "Sal owes a bigger apology to Luka than to me, anyway."

"Wonderful," said the Queen, her strained smile not reaching her eyes. "I'll need a few days to arrange for the two men to be quietly transported to the cabin. If the other Insurgents don't know of this secondary system, I don't want to alert them."

Verakko picked up a black communicator from the table and held it out to Alice. "We'll contact you on this." He gave Luka a once-over before adding, "Show her how to use it."

They all rose and began exchanging farewells when the Queen addressed Luka. "You received my message about your marks?"

Luka's lips thinned, and he nodded.

"It wasn't a request, Luka, it was a command."

"Understood, madam."

Verakko stayed behind, explaining he needed to assist the Queen in working out logistics. Luka guided her to the door without another word. *What message about his marks?*

Once they were on their way to the gate, she asked, "What did the Queen say about your marks?"

Letting out an annoyed huff, he grumbled, "She reminded me that I need to paint my hands whenever we leave our homes. She wants to keep the marks hidden as long as possible." Flexing a hand in front of him, he frowned. "I'd intended to paint them before I left home today, but…it felt wrong not to be able to look at them."

Her heart pitter-pattered. *Like a wedding ring he doesn't want to take off.*

Alice kept his hand clasped in hers, grinning as they walked back to the gate. The proverbial gears were turning in Luka's head. Brow furrowed and face taut, he looked like he was trying to think through the universe's most complex issues. Alice's worry about the outing to come was buried beneath an overwhelming feeling of joy and affection.

This wasn't right; she couldn't be in this good a mood while Luka looked so stressed. She stopped walking. It took Luka a moment to realize, only turning to peer at her when their connected hands prevented him from walking forward.

"Are you okay?" she asked, standing in front of him.

"I'm…" he took a deep breath, searching her face, "concerned."

Rising to her toes, she reached up and snaked her arms around his neck. "I appreciate your support, anyway." A look of surprise lit his features, and his hands flew to grip her hips before he jerked them back.

Aww, he's still keeping his word. Her chest felt too full at the moment. Finally, she could relax and let the wall she'd been keeping between them crumble. She beamed at him, pulling his face down to hers. Against his lips, she breathed, "No more red zones."

It took him a heartbeat to catch up, but when he did, he threw his arms around her back, crushing his mouth to hers. She felt her feet leave the ground as he lifted her, a strong purr bursting from his chest to tickle her nipples through the thin material of her shirt.

The familiar heat of arousal pooled in her core, and she broke away. "Let's get out of here," she said in an unfamiliar, throaty voice.

A seductive grin spread over his face, and he gave her another slow, hot kiss before setting her on her feet. Mind gone hazy, she wobbled.

Oh, I am sooo ready for this.

21

Once in the cruiser, Luka willed his mind to focus. His mate had suddenly become quite affectionate with him, and he wasn't entirely sure why. Leaning forward, he programmed the vehicle to take them to his home. Even with her underwear in place, the scent of her arousal, brought on by their kiss, was easy to identify under her short dress.

The males at the gate had taken notice, and he didn't want the plethora of guards stationed around the Temple to do the same. The solitary stairway to his floor would be a much safer bet.

He sat back, running his hand over her leg as he went. What had he done so right?

"Alice," he said tentatively.

She smiled up at him. "Hmm?"

"You seem…" He didn't want to say the wrong thing and ruin her mood, but he had to know what had made her so happy. He had to know, so he could be sure to do it over and over again in the future. "… pleased with me," he finished.

"I'm very pleased with you." She beamed.

"Why?"

"Because you didn't try to stop me from going to the cabin to help the trapped human women."

He tensed, reminded of how much he disliked the idea of her around those two filthy cowards. Heads would roll if they tried anything to hurt his mate. He'd never thought of himself as a violent male, but even the mention of Helas had raised his hackles, his Traxian side roaring for blood.

Without warning, Alice shifted in her seat, throwing her leg over his own and straddling him. Cock shooting hard in an instant, he gripped her hips, pulling her down against him.

Cradling his face in her hands, she drew his gaze. "Hey. It's gonna be fine. You're coming with me, right? I trust you."

A torrent of emotions rolled through him. Pride puffed his chest. *She trusts me. And she sees me.* Alice had not only noticed his discontent *again* but was attempting to soothe him. Her sweet, caring personality was what he'd always hoped for in a female but had believed he'd never have.

His mate didn't need gifts or flattery. If support and freedom were what made her smile and glow like this, he'd do whatever it took to quell his possessive instincts.

Her hands moved to wrap around his back, and she kissed him briefly on the cheek before lowering her head to his shoulder, nuzzling his neck.

A satisfying purr rolled through him, making her hips jerk unexpectedly. He pulled her face back, wondering what had happened, before recalling the delicious difference in her anatomy. The scent of her arousal intensified, and he stifled a groan.

"Do you like my purring, love?"

A pale pink crept over her cheeks again, and she scooted further down his lap. No longer pressed against the soft warm entrance of his female, his shaft pulsed angrily. The urge to drag her forward, trapping her against him, welled within him. *Not yet*, he told himself.

He ran his fingers over her bare legs, then burrowed them under the hem of her dress, gripping the sides of her ass. She let out a small moan.

One of his hands moved to snake in her hair. He tilted her head down, forcing her to meet his gaze so he could see her reactions. She let out a small gasp, her wide blue eyes meeting his.

"Do you want to feel my purr while I'm buried deep inside you?"

As he'd expected, her pupils dilated, breaths increasing. He grinned.

Their stare was broken when the cruiser door slowly slid open. He'd been so preoccupied with his mate that he hadn't even realized they'd stopped moving.

"Up. Now," he demanded.

The corner of her mouth lifted, but she didn't move.

She was playing with him, pushing him to take control as if she understood that's what he needed. How could she be this perfect? "Alright, you asked for it."

"Asked for wh—"

Cutting off her question, he simultaneously sat forward and lifted her over his shoulder. Before crouching through the cruiser door, he peered out. Seeing no sign of movement, he bolted from the vehicle to the stairway entrance.

Alice began giggling and tapped on his back. "Luka, let me down. What if someone's on the stairs?"

After requesting the correct floor, the steps began to move. He bounded up the swirling stairs two at a time. "Then they'll be treated to a spectacular view."

She chuckled and wiggled on his shoulder. "Come on, put me down."

A firm smack on her ass, followed by a small gasp, rang through the empty stairwell. "Almost there."

Finally spotting his door, he dashed through the cluttered house to his bedroom. She squealed when he bent, tilting her off his shoulder and depositing her on his bed. In the time it took her to glance around the room, he'd wrenched his shirt off and pressed a knee onto the bed between her legs.

Her eyes wandered over his bare chest, gaze becoming hungry. When her stare lowered to his straining erection, he slowly began to unfasten his pants, letting them fall to the floor.

A swipe of her tongue over her lips pushed him over the edge. He pounced, covering her with his body. Forcing her legs open with his knees, he settled himself between her legs.

He pressed his lips to hers, slanting his head to deepen the kiss the way she liked. Nails scraping down his back made him groan into her mouth. If she kept that up, he wouldn't last long at all.

Her small nails sank in deeper when he began to pull away, so he snatched her wrists, raising her arms above her. In one hand, he held her slim hands together in a viselike grip; with the other, he lifted her dress, pulling it up to her secured wrists.

She writhed under him, arching her body up to lick and kiss his chest.

"Fuck, that feels glorious, but you have to cut it out." He moaned, already losing control of his hips as they ground against the soft fabric covering her sex.

She peered up at him, her eyes heavy-lidded and her cheeks flushed. She grinned, a devious glint in her eyes. "Or what?"

A vicious growl tore from him at her challenge. Jumping off her, he flipped her onto her stomach. Before she could rise, he straddled her, groaning as his dick settled onto her perfect ass still covered by her underwear. That needed to change.

Like a flash, he removed her dress, twisted her wrists behind her back and used the red fabric to tightly bind her hands.

"That's what," he rasped while running his hands over her supple flesh. She bucked under him, making small sounds of frustration.

He kneaded her cheeks firmly before standing. If what he'd read about a human's ability to have sex more than once a day was true, then he'd make sure to take her in this position at least once before the night was over.

Slipping his hands under her hips, he found the edge of her thick underwear and tore it in half. Then he slid the ruined fabric down her legs, kissing and nipping at the backs of her shapely thighs as he went. Standing back, he admired her naked form, immobile and ready for him. Her male.

Not able to use her hands, she attempted to rise to her knees instead, giving him a devastating view in the process. He scrubbed a hand over his face and tried to calm the fire running through his veins. She was so beautiful with her delicate tanned flesh and her long, slim frame. He had to remember not to be too rough—he didn't know what her body could take.

Moving toward her again, he knelt between her parted thighs, wrapped an arm around her waist, and lifted her upright so her back was pressed against his front. Sweeping her hair to the side, he ran his mouth over her neck and shoulder. He brought one hand around her front and palmed her breast, rolling her puckered nipple between his fingers.

She let out a strangled cry, throwing her head back onto his shoulder.

He traced his other hand down her stomach and lower until it lingered just above her clit.

She huffed in frustration, trying to angle her hips to reach his fingers. "Luka…" she pleaded.

His chuckle against her ear turned into a hiss when her hands reached behind her back and circled his aching shaft. She squeezed and stroked as much of him as she could.

Tilting her head against his shoulder, she pressed searing kisses to his neck and whispered, "Come on, Luka. Don't you want to bury this deep inside me?"

He groaned. She'd used his own words against him. Was she trying to drive him out of his mind? *Yes.* He smiled. His Alice was a wild one.

He was one more seductive whisper away from doing as she asked but somehow found the strength to pull away. She wobbled, no longer supported by his body, then turned, still on her knees, to face him.

Wrapping his fingers around her nape, he let his thumb circle the front of her throat. With his other arm twisting behind her backside, he lifted her up against his hips. Then positioning himself so he sat upright at the head of the bed, he lowered her to straddle him once again.

They moaned together as his length slid against her wet folds. She tried to rise a fraction, to sink onto his shaft, but he pulled her back down to rest against him with a firm tug on her bound hands.

"Luka, please," she breathed, rocking her sex and spreading her divine juices along his length.

"Not yet." Hand still at her throat, he angled her so she was forced to peer into his eyes. "Say you're my mate. Say you're mine."

She searched his face, a smile spreading over her own. Would she lose her playful battle? Submit to him? His heartbeat sped up, and he tried to keep the ache he felt from his eyes. A part of him needed to hear her say this. In this moment he'd let his Traxian side free, and it needed the confirmation. *Say it. Say you're mine.*

She leaned in and gave him a soft kiss. "I'm your mate. I'm yours."

The emotion that welled in his chest was followed, as he'd planned, by a deep purr.

"Oh fu—" Her words cut out as her hips jerked and her eyes rolled back.

Her core, pressed tightly against his shaft, grew wetter. The image of his mate trembling before him in ecstasy made his purring intensify. She moaned, and her lower body began to shake, almost looking electrified.

Leaning forward, he took one of her nipples in his mouth, rolling it between his teeth.

"Luka, I'm…I'm gonna…"

He growled, lifting her hips and plunging into her. "I want to feel you, love."

She screamed and bit into his shoulder, sagging on his chest. Her silky core convulsed around his cock as her orgasm tore through her.

High-pitched sighs and moans accompanied every exhalation as she came down from her high. Sweet music to his ears. Untying her dress, he threw it to the side, then massaged her arms and shoulders.

She rubbed her hands over his chest and stomach, then lifted her face. "That was amazing," she breathed.

He rocked his hips against her. "We're not done yet."

***

What a man. Alice licked her lips in anticipation.

Luka had just given her a literal out-of-this-world orgasm, and now she needed to take care of him too. He hadn't come yet. Or at least she didn't think he had.

With her free hands, she gripped his muscular shoulders and took charge, grinding against his gorgeous cock.

Urging her hips forward and back with his hands, he leaned forward to lick and suck her nipples with his lightly vibrating mouth. Already, she could feel a coil in her sex tightening again.

When he'd forced her to stay pressed firmly to his vibrating shaft, it'd felt like her clit had touched a live wire. The sensation was almost too powerful. Then, as he'd slammed into her, his large cock brushing against every nerve ending, she'd come with an intensity she'd never experienced.

Luka began to rock her hips more forcefully, muttering curses while kissing his way up to her mouth. As he devoured her moans with his kiss, he wrapped one arm around her waist and then shifted her backward until her head hit the soft mattress. Sitting on his haunches, he slowly slipped in and out of her, holding her hips high off the bed so they remained level with his.

The speed of his thrusts increased, and the knot in her core tightened even more. Sweat dripped down his taut abs as he pounded into her. *Gorgeous male, her male.*

Alice closed her eyes, her breaths becoming frantic. She wanted to grind against him, but he held her in place too tightly. She felt her body arching off the bed. *So close.*

When Luka's thumb came down to circle her clit in just the way she liked, she broke apart, screaming his name. His thrusts became rough and erratic, prolonging her orgasm, until he finally roared to the ceiling, slamming into her a few more times before stilling.

His body was still shuddering when he laid over her, supporting himself on his elbows. Slipping his hands under her head, he leaned down and ran his mouth over hers. The slow, sensual grinding of his hips and his languorous kiss felt like a claim. And she couldn't get enough.

22

Alice woke the next morning feeling sore in all the right places. Luka had taken her in different positions all through the night. Sometimes he'd initiate, but more often, she had. Each time it'd taken a little convincing to prove she was good to go. Apparently Clecanian women could only have full penetrative sex once per day.

Sucks for them, she thought as she stretched like a cat.

Noise from the other room told her where Luka was. *Need to find something to wear,* she thought, glancing at her torn underwear. She snooped around his room, a spark of joy lighting inside her whenever she spotted a personal item within the bare space. Finding a soft black shirt in his closet that had retained his forest scent, she donned it. Then she used the small restroom connected to his bedroom and ventured out to find her man.

She spotted him looking at a stack of papers on a newly revealed dining table. He wore soft, loose-fitting pants and no shirt. She sighed. Would she ever get tired of admiring his body?

When he spotted her, he grinned, and she felt the skin on her chest flush. Hurtling over the table and landing gracefully in front of her, he wrapped her in a hug. Large palms roamed over her back then curved around her ass before he angled her chin up and gave her a long kiss.

Swaying in his arms, she pointed to the table. "What's all this about?"

"Ah!" he said brightly and crossed to his kitchen. "I made us breakfast and realized there was no place to sit and eat."

Luka carried a few plates of food over to the table, then glanced up at her expectantly, his dark hair mussed. Alice didn't think she could remove the smile from her face if she wanted to.

She joined him and studied the food. Some of the items on her plate were familiar. Foods she'd discovered from fiddling with the food synthesizer in her house. Others were new but smelled delicious. A red, flaky bread caught her eye, and she decided to start there.

Luka proceeded to scarf down his food as though it were going to be stolen. Alice noted that while her plate was full, his was mountainous.

"Hungry?" she teased.

He finished chewing his mouthful, then wheezed, "You worked me hard last night, and we didn't eat dinner."

Taking a small bite of food, she grinned. *Hell yeah, I did.*

"I need to make sure I can keep up with you today."

Donning an innocent expression, she said, "I can always lay off if you're not up to the challenge." Taking another small bite of food to hide her smirk, she added, "I wouldn't want you overexerting yourself."

After chewing through another massive mouthful, he pointed his fork at her. "You'd better watch your words, female."

They sat in easy silence while they ate, exchanging happy glances every so often.

When they were done, Luka spoke first. "What would you like to do today? I can bring you back to the Temple if you'd like."

She glanced at him sidelong. Jaw clenched and eyes blank, he stared at her. Alice thought he might be making this suggestion in order to make her happy, even though he clearly did not relish the idea.

She smirked. "Or?"

His face broke into a wide grin, and her heart pitter-pattered in her chest. "No one requested work at the reserve. I could show you more animals." Gaze turning hungry, he added, "We could go back to the bedroom for the next year or so."

"All fueled up now, are we, tiger?" she joked. "The reserve sounds wonderful, but could we make a detour at the Temple first? I need some clothes."

Her skin heated when he ran his gaze over her body. "I think you look wonderful."

Standing, she began to gather their empty plates.

Brows drawn, he stopped her with a hand on her wrist. "What are you doing?"

Looking from the plates to him, she shrugged. "Cleaning up."

He tugged her forward, dragging her across his lap. "I can do that. Why don't you go take a bath?"

Alice wanted to argue, she really did. He was being so sweet to her and she should help, since he'd cooked, but the lure of hot water on her sore body sounded like heaven. She'd make him dinner tonight, she decided.

"Thank you." Pressing a swift kiss to his lips, she tried to rise.

A small yelp escaped her when he suddenly lifted her, one hand under her knees, the other under her shoulders. "Allow me."

***

The last few days had been some of the best Alice could remember. Luka was revealing himself to be the perfect guy, and with every passing hour she grew more and more sure she'd fallen in love with him.

Every day they'd come to the reserve; sometimes they'd stay for hours and sometimes they'd only stay for as long as it took to feed and medicate the guarsil. The small red creature was becoming stronger each day, and soon they'd have to venture further into the woods and reunite it with its brothers and sisters. Although Alice wanted to make sure they didn't move him before he was ready, she was becoming more and more leery of its ever-elongating teeth and increasingly aggressive swipes of its claws at her mate.

Yesterday, they'd roamed around the reserve for hours. Alice had taken notes on every animal she'd seen, and Luka had patiently described what he knew about the creatures in great detail, then surprised her with a picnic near the still-entwined manta she'd seen her first time there.

To thank him, she'd asked to give him a blow job. A chuckle still ran through her when she recalled his dumbstruck expression. Learning that the women of this planet didn't often go down on their men made Alice even more excited to provide him with that pleasure.

She'd done her best to work his large shaft into her mouth, feeling herself grow wet from his muttered curses and the shudders that had run through his powerful body. After she was done, he'd returned the favor, using that vibrating tongue on her repeatedly until she'd had to beg him to stop.

The rest of the day had passed in a daze. They'd reclined in the dappled sunlight of the forest, eating sweet fruits and talking. She'd told him more about her life on Earth and the troubles that'd come with it. When she'd told him about her past relationships, he'd had trouble calming.

In turn, he'd told her the heartbreaking story of his mother and his brother Theo. Apparently, what she'd assumed were tattoos running all over Theo's body were actually scars. As he'd spoken, she'd offered comfort where she could.

The once-pale markings that ran along Luka's wrists and forearms were still black. It turned out they'd been permanently scarred like his brother's were after Gishen had electrocuted him so violently through his shackles. Tracing the dark markings near his wrists, she now saw them in a new light. She wondered if others found them ugly the way they did Theo's. Running her tongue along one dark marking and smiling at his answering curse, she'd decided to work hard to make sure he knew she loved them.

Whenever they went outside, Luka had angrily painted his hands, curling his lip as he hid the blue marks under a layer of rubbery, flesh-colored liquid. Anytime they were alone, ridding his hands of the covering was the first thing he did. When his marks were visible, he always let out a sigh, and she wondered if seeing them calmed him in some way.

The idea that Luka loved his marks that much made her wonder if he loved her too. Sure, he called her "love," but that was just a pet name. She knew how she felt about him now, and was sure she wanted to be with him, but she didn't want to be the one to say the words out loud first. She'd be mortified if he didn't say them back. She didn't even know if Clecanians said "I love you" to one another.

The happiness she felt with Luka was only interrupted by her building anxiety over seeing Helas and Sal again and the worry she harbored for Vanessa.

She'd seen her friend both yesterday and today. Vanessa's once-bright smile and sarcastic attitude had dulled, and Alice was starting to worry about what she might do if she became desperate enough.

Ignoring Luka's scowl at the idea, she'd decided to spend a few hours alone with Vanessa today. He'd dropped her off at the edge of the lake, and despite her urging for him to leave and pick her up later, he'd grumbled and muttered so much that she'd finally just left him sitting on the grass, looking sullen. She'd arrived at Vanessa's house to find her alone and worn down.

At present, she was mixing two alien gin and tonics for her and Vanessa to sip while they talked.

"So where are Daisy and Rita?" Alice asked as she handed Vanessa a tall glass.

The dark bags under her eyes sagged as she peered at the front door. "I'm not sure. The dome maybe? They like to go socialize." Vanessa sighed and took a long sip of her drink, squinting at Alice's heavy-handed pour. "I think Daisy is hoping if she spends enough time with Izzo, he'll ask her out."

"I don't think it works like that here." Luka had mentioned that the idea of dating before being married was a bit strange and outdated. Normally, women would wait to interact with the men they wanted to marry until the ceremony. He'd told her that occasionally Tremantians would have casual sex, but usually only while waiting for the next ceremony or while they were taking a break due to childbirth or to see to their mental health.

"Do you have your eye on anyone?" Alice asked hopefully. Maybe having a handsome, attentive mate would help Vanessa the same way it'd helped Alice.

She shrugged, her bare shoulder looking thinner than Alice remembered. "They're all handsome, but I'm just not interested in that."

Alice studied her friend. There had to be more to the story than a fight to make Vanessa's fire dwindle to such an alarming degree. Everyone Vanessa had talked to had patiently explained why she couldn't return to Earth. When Luka had clarified it was a galaxy-wide law not to interfere with or contact Class 4 planets like Earth, Alice had lost a little hope as well. "Are you ready to tell me what happened with your sister? I know you got into a fight, and it'll be really hard for her to not know what happened to you, but eventually she'll move on. You said she had a husband, right? Are they happy together?"

Vanessa stared at her glass, nibbling on her lip, then downed the remaining liquid and plastered on a smile. "I'll get over it. You don't have to worry about me, Alice. I'm a big girl."

Alice gave her a hard look, but she knew Vanessa wouldn't budge on this. The girl liked to keep her feelings locked away and buried. She wondered if Vanessa had ever truly let anyone in.

"So tell me about you and Luka," she said brightly.

Alice pinned her with a stern glare. "You're changing the subject."

Vanessa's smile faded, and Alice could see the weariness in her eyes. She was letting Alice see it.

Vanessa sighed. "I need to change it, okay? Make me think about something else."

"Fine. But you'll have to let me in one day." After Vanessa gave her a half-hearted nod, Alice told her about Luka and how she'd fallen for him.

"Well, why don't you tell him?" Vanessa questioned with a little more pep. Maybe she did need a change of subject.

Alice's mouth turned up in an embarrassed smile. "I don't want to be the one to say it first."

Vanessa started laughing. A genuine, hearty guffaw, bolstering Alice's hope that her friend would eventually get through this.

"Where do you think we are, girlie?" she said with a raised brow. "In this city, the women pick their men out of a lineup and rule the roost. It's a matriarchy! He probably doesn't think he *can* say it first."

Alice pondered this. "He's made all the other first moves, though."

"Yeah, to get you to like him and want to stay with him, but he was probably taught not to say stuff like that. I know the women are." Vanessa propped her head in her hand. "We learned all about what the men have to do in school, but do you know what the women's schooling is like? Malie told me, and it blew my mind."

"No, what?" Alice asked, wracking her brain to recall what she'd learned about the women's school. How come she'd never asked about it before?

"A lot of it is about shutting down feelings. They teach the women how to hide their emotions and not lead the men on by being too affectionate in marriages. Crap like that."

"You must fit right in, then. I don't know anyone who pushes their emotions down more than you," Alice said sarcastically.

Vanessa rolled her eyes. "Hardy har. Anyway, do you know Malie?"

Alice tried to picture the Clecanian woman. "Uh, is she the one who has a pink buzzcut?"

"Yeah, exactly! Well, she said all the women are so excited about the humans coming here. She complained about how she's tired of always acting like she doesn't care. I think most of these girls try not to feel anything because they're taught it's their duty to have many partners, not one, but they'd kill to say I love you to someone." Vanessa tilted her head at Alice and lifted the corner of her mouth. "I'm just saying, it seems kind of taboo for people to say that here. Maybe Luka thinks it'll scare you off."

Alice stared at the ceiling in thought. Maybe Vanessa was right. What if he never expected her to say it to him? *He needs to know how I feel.* Suddenly, the urge to see Luka suffocated her.

She stared at Vanessa, jaw slackened. "I—"

"Yeah, yeah. Get out of here. Thanks for the G and T."

Alice dove on her friend, giving her a bear hug. "We'll figure this out, I promise." She grasped Vanessa's face in her hands and forced her to look into her eyes. "Okay?"

"Okay." Vanessa gave a tight nod, her eyes watery. She chuckled. "Now get out of here."

Alice dashed to the door and walked purposefully toward the Temple exit. She needed to do two things. One: she had to ask Luka if he knew a way to help Vanessa, and two: she needed to tell him she loved him. It had to be done in that order, because she was sure that after she told him her feelings, she'd want to sequester them in a private room for many hours. *Work first, play later.*

Rounding the central building, she spotted Luka then bit her lip and grinned. He looked so cute, pacing around the entrance, hands clasped behind his back.

Now that she'd become comfortable with the platforms, she crossed the water quickly, her footsteps sure. He turned at her approach and crossed to the lake edge, teeth flashing in a grin. He stepped forward eagerly, balancing on the shoreline.

She stopped a few feet away, just out of his reach and took a moment to admire his handsome features now cast in a soft orange glow by the setting sun.

"Alice," he warned, pacing back and forth along the shore like a predator tracking prey. "Don't think I won't come in there. I can handle a few stings."

The dark hunger in his eyes gave her pause. *He might actually do that.*

Not wanting to see him hurt, she hurried forward. Before she'd set foot on land, he'd reached out and snatched her, kissing her like he hadn't seen her in months.

He started walking toward a cruiser waiting beyond the entry gate and she trailed behind, her hand clasped in his. It took her a moment to catch her breath.

Once inside, he pulled her under him, pressing sizzling kisses to her neck.

"Luka…" she said in a whisper, lids gone heavy.

Circling the cuff of her ear with his tongue, he murmured, "Hmm."

"I need to talk to you."

Letting his head rise a few inches above her, he pressed a soft kiss on the corner of her mouth. "Then talk, love."

She shook her head to clear it and pushed on his shoulders, managing only to force herself deeper into the padding of the cruiser bench.

He chuckled, kissing the other side of her mouth before rising and helping her to sit upright.

Knowing she needed to be away from him to think clearly, she moved to the seat across from them. His brows lowered and his jaw clenched. Resting his elbows on his knees, he clasped his hands.

"You're worrying me, little mate."

She brushed her hair away from her flushed face, then took a deep breath. "Do you know of any way to transport someone back to Earth?" When his head reared back, hurt flashing in his eyes, she added, "Not me! Vanessa. Do you remember her? One of the women from the outpost?"

His eyes grew distant as he thought. "Vaguely."

319

"Well, she really needs to go back to Earth, and I'm trying to figure out a way to help."

She could see the wheels turning in his mind, but she couldn't wait and nervously babbled, "She left her sister, and she really needs to get back to her. I'm worried if I don't figure out a way to get her there safely, she'll do something crazy. I couldn't live with myself if she tried to hop on some lowlife's ship and ended up hurt or worse. I know it's illegal—"

"I could find a way if it'd make you happy," he interrupted, his expression revealing nothing.

Alice blinked at him. "No, I can't do that. It's my friend, my risk. I didn't want you involved at all, but I don't even know where to start, and you're the only person I trust here."

"I won't allow you to be taken away from me, Alice, and I won't let myself be taken from you, either." He sat back, and his gaze grew unfocused again. "Transporting a Class 4 species to their planet is illegal, but keeping an eye out for a good opportunity and teaching her what she needs to know to take advantage of that opportunity is not." Leaning forward, he clasped her hands in his. "We don't have to do anything illegal to help her. Please trust me with this."

Her heart swelled. His magnificent mind was working through a plan even as she watched. Dashing across the cab, she threw her arms around his neck and stared down into his pale-blue eyes. "I love you," she breathed.

A hesitant purr stuttered through his chest. He rested his palms on either side of her head and his wide gaze searched her face. "Truly?"

Hot tears dampened her cheeks. *Why do I always have to cry at the wrong time?*

Emotion welled in her throat, so she just nodded.

His purr revved to life, full force. He didn't grin or frown, but stared at her seriously, his Adam's apple bobbing as he swallowed. "Over the last few days, I've grown to like you more than I thought possible, but my soul knew it loved you even when I was drowning in the void of my mind. I'm humbled you feel I'm worthy of your love."

The kiss he gave her made her toes curl and mind blank. She had a wonderful, honest, sexy, affectionate mate, and he loved her.

Suddenly, he broke their kiss and stared deeply into her eyes, expression serious. "Are those words taken lightly on your planet? Because, they aren't here. I love you, Alice. I've never said that to anyone else and never will. Are you sure about me? About us? There won't be any going back after this."

Alice couldn't contain the happy tears that streaked down her face. "I'm all yours, forever."

23

Luka gazed down at his mate while she slept. The female who loved him. He still couldn't believe his good fortune. Alice was more than he could've ever dreamed her to be. She cared about everyone and everything. When he was with her, he felt he could finally exhale. She allowed him to be himself. Hell, she allowed him to discover himself. He'd been fixated on work and achievement his whole life, but with her he'd rediscovered facets of his personality he'd forgotten he had.

He enjoyed being playful and teasing her. He liked that she argued with him and challenged his domineering instincts. She allowed the Traxian side of him that ached to keep her close and safe to surge to the foreground when they had sex. She'd fight tooth and nail for what she believed in, but once in the bedroom, she'd submit so sweetly. He'd never felt so free. She saw him for all that he was and loved him anyway.

The corner of his mouth lifted in a smile as he recalled her tearful declaration the day before. He'd never met a female who showed her emotions so readily.

Frowning, he thought once more about his people. He knew Tremantian females didn't show their emotions—not because they didn't have them, but because forming strong attachments to the males they married and the children they bore would only result in their own heartbreak. Humans may be the key to saving their species, but how long would it be before they could be transported here lawfully?

His heart ached for the males and females of his planet. How many would never experience the love he felt for Alice? How many would never rest easy, knowing the one they loved wouldn't leave them as a result of their twisted honor?

It was only a matter of time before it was discovered that humans could be mated and could reproduce. Once that happened, their people would be divided. Some would call for humans to be transported by the droves whether they agreed or not. Others would oppose, seeing the unwilling transport of a Class 4 species immoral and unethical.

What side would he take? On the one hand, an influx of humans would take the pressure off Clecanian females. He knew his sister, for one, would return to her children in an instant.

Across Clecania, courting rituals, traditions, and laws were very different, but one thing was constant. Females were expected to be strong. They were taught to hold their heads high and expand the gene pool by reproducing with many.

There was no easy answer. For now, he'd continue his work. They couldn't count on humans to fix everything. Although he bristled at the thought of leaving her and returning to work, he knew he must. There would be many dark days ahead, but the difficulties they'd been facing for decades hadn't disappeared.

He gazed into the fire, feeling a weight settle over him. How could he keep her safe when their world was on the brink of an implosion?

Earlier, Alice had convinced him to lay out a makeshift bed in front of the fire. He'd done as she directed without complaint. The power she held over him was comical. With a touch of her hand and a soft smile, he'd been tripping over himself to do her bidding. They'd spent hours sitting here while he taught her to read using the stories of the matings he'd collected over the years.

Her interest in the mated couples served as a great motivator. She became so invested in learning their stories that she'd picked up the language much more quickly than he'd anticipated.

He sat back, his mind drifting to yet another problem. How would he accomplish the seemingly impossible task of helping her friend without breaking any laws? He needed her to stowaway aboard a ship that made long journeys. One whose captain was honorable, but also didn't mind breaking laws for the right price.

The image of a male slowly formed in his mind, and he grinned. *I know just the person for the job.*

Alice turned in her sleep, her blanket falling and exposing her side. He ran his knuckles along the gentle curve of her waist and hip. His cock stirred to think how she might repay him if he found a way to help her friend.

***

Alice woke with a shiver, though her skin was warm from the sizzling fire. Cracking her eyes open, she rolled onto her back and found Luka's devastating face looming above her, his fingers ghosting over her exposed skin.

"What time is it?" She arched her back, stretching her hands above her.

When she tried to lower her arms again, Luka shot a hand out, holding them above her head. She relaxed, letting him run his knuckles lazily over her body.

He circled her navel then trailed his fingers up her ribs and around the underside of her breasts. "Night," he answered, gaze fixed on her quickly hardening nipples.

"Are you talking to me or my breasts?" she joked, trying to shift her body away from his maddening caress.

He shot her a lopsided grin. "If I were talking to your breasts, I'd address them with more deference."

A deep belly laugh rolled through her. "Is that right?"

Her laughter stalled when he leaned down and breathed hot air onto each nipple. "Indeed. While the female they're attached to tests my patience daily, they've been nothing but welcoming."

"You're such a weirdo," she teased.

His mouth was poised just over her nipple when a loud growl from her stomach broke the silence. He moved away groaning. "We'll finish this later."

Alice had to stop herself from rubbing her breasts after he finally released her wrists and stood. Luka's mix of goofiness and sex appeal made him a force to be reckoned with.

Rolling onto her stomach, she watched him walk away. His firm ass flexed as he stepped over discarded books. Inserting her forefinger and thumb into her mouth, she whistled loudly.

He wheeled around, eyes wide and brows raised.

Resting her chin on her palm, she made her face serious. "I was addressing your ass, sir. Please, continue on your way."

Slapping his own ass on the way and making her dissolve into laughter once again, he crossed to the kitchen.

Still chuckling, she found his discarded shirt and slipped it on. Her own blue dress lay torn and abandoned near the front door.

Surveying the room, she lifted her hands in exasperation. "How can you tell what time of day it is without any windows? It's going to be hard for me to adjust to never looking outside if I live here." She glanced at her hand clock. It took her a moment to decipher the symbols, but it was becoming easier each day. She tilted herself as a realization hit her. This was the first time she'd checked her clock in days. Knowing the time never seemed to matter when she was with Luka.

Alice felt warmth spread through her belly, and she grinned like a fool.

He cocked his head as she approached, his gaze sweeping the room. "There are windows." Pointing an oddly shaped cooking utensil to the wall running the length of the room, he said, "That wall has windows. I just keep them covered."

Her jaw slackened. "There have been windows here this whole time?" she blurted in exasperation.

Chuckling, he moved to a control panel hidden behind a large stack of books. Before her eyes, the entire wall began to lift and disappear into the ceiling through a gap large enough to accommodate the width of the panel, as well as the many pictures and papers attached to it.

"That wall has windows" was an understatement. The entire length of the room appeared to be nothing but curved glass. Alice's eyes widened further and further as each inch of the illuminated city was revealed.

Mouth hanging open, she approached the expansive view. The sky was midnight-blue, and although light shone brightly from the city, more stars than she'd ever seen were visible. Dozens of buildings, in the form of swirling spires, rose high into the sky. They reminded her of the twisting manta trunks.

In all the cities she'd been to on Earth, lights dotted the skyscrapers, a result of some interior rooms being lit but not others. Looking out, she saw no spattering of illumination. Rather, the entirety of the silver spires glowed brightly, the same color as the moon.

Wait. Her eyes narrowed, and she studied the larger of the two moons. *Is that a ring?*

To her eyes, it appeared the pale, glowing moon had a shimmering band around the middle, too defined to be natural.

Alice was so entranced that she didn't notice Luka approach until he wrapped his arms around her. Planting a kiss on top of her head, he murmured, "What do you think?"

"Is there something on that moon? And how do the buildings glow like that?" she asked in a hushed tone.

"Yes, there are solar panels on Gui, our closest moon. They capture and beam the energy to receivers in conversion facilities. Most of our buildings capture solar and lunar energy, as well. That's what makes them glow. The energy is used to power the building."

Alice's eyes remained glued upward, taking in the odd sight of not one but two moons. "On Earth, there's only one moon."

Luka turned her in his arms. She saw worry flash in his eyes before it was quickly concealed. "Do you miss Earth?"

Alice pondered the question for a moment. "I miss the familiarity sometimes. Smelling my favorite food and feeling warm inside. Saying hello to my neighbor, Mr. Bower. Sitting on my small apartment balcony in the morning to drink my coffee."

Luka's features grew taut, and his head dipped.

"But..." she continued, lifting his chin. "I'm excited to start experiencing those things here. How many people can say they were able to discover a whole new world? I know what I like on Earth, and now I get to learn what I like here. There's also one thing Clecania has that Earth never will."

Luka grinned down at her, his chest puffing. "And what's that?"

Rising up to give him a kiss, she waited until their mouths were only a breath away before whispering, "A second moon."

A bark of laughter exploded from him and rang through the room. Using his shoulders, she jumped as high as she could and wrapped her legs around his waist. He caught her easily, then leaned her against the window.

Planting a soft kiss on his lips, she sighed. "Also, you."

They gazed at each other for a moment, smiling like loons. A soft ping emanated from the kitchen, and Luka's face fell. Lowering her to the ground, they both turned toward the sound of a second ping and froze.

The communicator Verakko had given her was ringing. Alice felt her stomach churn and the blood drain from her face.

It's time.

24

With every second that passed, Luka was less and less sure he'd be able to get through this night without spilling blood. Nerves frayed, he watched his mate pace, muttering to herself every so often.

When Verakko had called, he'd told them they had an opening to move the prisoners tonight and they had to take it. Her face pale and her eyes round, Alice had bravely nodded, declaring she was ready.

She hadn't said more than a few words to him since leaving his home and arriving at the edge of the woods near the outpost. Her attempts to disguise her true feelings were in vain. The bitter scent of fear coming from her was so strong it made him want to tear his hair out. Every instinct he had was urging him to take her back home, but this was her choice, not his. All he could do was be here and help her if he could.

As she paced in front of him yet again, he pulled her into a tight hug, ignoring her squirming until she finally relaxed. Into her hair, he murmured, "I'll be here the whole time."

She gave a few jerky nods into his chest but said nothing.

Movement in the distance had him shoving her behind his body. Two cruisers were gliding toward them. He swallowed a snarl when he felt his mate's shaking hands clutched at his back.

Verakko stepped out of the first cruiser, but the second remained sealed. The Swadaeth male was covered in black. True to his race, the normally green color of Verakko's skin had darkened to a deep midnight-blue. This evolutionary camouflage and his glowing, bright green eyes, were an asset in the pitch-black of the deserts where his race thrived.

"Luka. Alice." He nodded to them both.

Alice stepped to the side of Luka, her fists balled. "Verakko." She nodded, her voice almost too quiet to hear.

Verakko's nostrils flared as he approached, but his face remained passive. "Sal has agreed to help whether or not you speak with him, but if you're willing, he'd like to repent."

A wave of bitter fear hit Luka's nose. He twisted his neck from side to side, the satisfying popping and cracking doing nothing to settle his nerves.

Rounding her lips, Alice took a deep, shaking breath in through her mouth and out through her nose, then said, "I'll talk to him."

Verakko crossed to the second cruiser and gave it a few swift knocks. Alice slipped her hand into Luka's, gripping his fingers with what seemed like all the strength she had.

The first person to exit was Kadion, a military general and member of the Tremantian Council. It made sense one of the Queen's most trusted generals would be assigned this task.

Behind him, Sal emerged, scowling. As the two males made their way over, Sal's yellow eyes scanned his surroundings then settled on Alice.

Luka had to concentrate all his energy on not clenching his fists and pulverizing his small mate's hand. He leaned down and pointed to a thick metal band circling Sal's neck. "Do you see that?" He then pointed to a smaller metal band circling Kadion's large bicep. "It's magnetically attached to the one on the soldier's arm." Alice peered up at him while nibbling on her lip. "He won't be able to walk more than a few feet away from Kadion's band."

Alice pressed a soft kiss to his shoulder and rested her other hand on his forearm. "Thank you."

Kadion halted, forcing Sal to stop as well, about five feet away. Both male's noses crinkled for an instant, picking up the scent of his mate's fear.

She and Sal stood staring at one another, the silence becoming deafening.

"Say what you want to say," he barked at Sal, making Alice flinch.

Sal didn't so much as glance at him but began speaking to Alice in a croaky voice. "I want to apologize for my role in your abduction."

Seeming to find her voice in anger, she snapped, "Why? Why are you sorry? Why are you helping now? You didn't seem to give two shits when you were pushing me into a cell with a stranger."

A vein ticked in Sal's forehead, his gaze swinging briefly to Luka. "I knew he wouldn't hurt you, even drugged, but you're right. I didn't care. I was angry with our world and how our people have been forced to live, but when I found out what Helas did, what they all did, I knew I had to do what I could to make amends."

"What he did?" she repeated quietly.

Sal's throat worked, gaze going distant before he spoke again. "I was told the non-human and non-Clecanian prisoners were transported to another facility. But—" He looked to the ground and shook his head. "I didn't sign up for indiscriminate slaughter. I wanted to help our people. To make a difference. I didn't understand the lengths they'd go to."

Luka glanced between Alice and Sal and inwardly groaned. He could see it on his mate's face. The compassion he loved was welling inside her. This traitorous animal who didn't deserve acknowledgment, much less her pity, would earn her forgiveness.

To his surprise, rather than softening, she dragged her hands onto her hips and nodded imperiously. "You want to redeem yourself? Fine. Prove it. Show us how to free everyone who's still trapped."

Pride swelled in him. His mate was compassionate, yes, but not weak.

Turning, she presented Sal with her back. Instinctively, Luka stepped between them to shield her.

After Kadion and Sal had walked away, Alice faced him. She pressed her hands to his chest and whispered, "Are you okay?"

He gave a humorless chuckle. "I won't be okay until we're gone from here, but I'm content to sit back and admire you for the moment."

"I'm glad." Her smile became nervous. "But I'm worried how you're going to handle this next bit."

"What do you mean?"

"You're not going to like this, but I need to talk to Helas."

"No, absolutely not," he growled, wrapping his palms around her wrists. He would rip Helas apart before he allowed the male to so much as look at Alice.

"Luka," she said, her voice pleading, "I have questions. Questions only he can answer."

"I'll ask him for you. Tell me your questions." A stone dropped in his gut. The look spreading over her face was one he'd seen before. "Why do you think he'd tell you the truth, anyway?"

"Because he's a pompous ass. Whenever he came to talk to me, he'd always talk about himself and his plans. He craves attention, and he probably hasn't talked to many people while locked up. Besides, there'd be no point in lying about the things I want to ask. There's nothing to gain." She pushed her shoulders back and raised her chin. "I need to do this for me, Luka. This is how I'll get closure."

Verakko motioned for the party to start moving through the forest. Sal led the way. Luka glanced toward the second cruiser again, fury and frustration edging his thoughts.

From the dark interior, Helas emerged, face as smug as ever. Luka's muscles burned. His fingers itched to wrap around the male's thick neck.

Alice pulled him back. "I think it'd be better if you hung back and let me talk to him on my own."

Luka felt as though he'd been slapped, and the look of concern that flashed over her features told him she clearly saw his hurt.

"I wouldn't ask except I don't know if you're going to be able to control yourself. You seem like you're ready to tear his head off, and you've only just seen him. I'm worried you'll maim him as soon as he says something negative to me, and he most definitely will."

"He deserves to be maimed!" he snarled.

Alice rested a soft palm on his cheek. "I agree, but right now he's our best chance to free those women. I need to talk to him, and I need for his head to be attached to his body when we get to the cabin. If you honestly believe you can keep your temper in check, you can come with me."

Luka wasn't entirely sure he could keep himself from killing the abhorrent male, but he couldn't leave her alone.

Blood rushing in his ears, he nodded. She searched his face for a moment, then began walking toward Helas, who was bringing up the rear of the group along with a large armed guard Luka had never met.

When Helas caught sight of them, his brows rose and a courteous smile curved his mouth. "How nice to see you both again." Eyes roaming over Luka, he added, "Covering those marks, are we?"

The urge to rip off his paint and rub the male's nose in his marks roiled through him.

Luka decided the easiest way to keep his temper in check was to focus on the one thing that grounded him. Alice. Never taking his eyes from her, he saw her small frame grow stiffer and stiffer until she stood, muscles bunched, mere feet from one of the vilest males he'd ever met.

Alice fell in line beside them as they walked and without pretense said, "I have some questions for you, and I want answers."

"Is that so?" Helas laughed.

She clenched her jaw and, without warning, stood in front of them, halting their progress.

She addressed the guard. "Hey, what's your name?"

The large, older male, glanced to Luka in confusion before answering, "Traef."

"Traef, do you know what he did to me? To hundreds of others?"

Traef swallowed, his expression growing cold. "I do."

336

"Great!" she said, her eyes flashing angrily to Helas, who still appeared amused. "Then you'll have no problem giving him a little shock with that electric prod thing if he refuses to answer me, right?"

The guard stared at a disbelieving Helas for a moment. "I cannot."

A smug grin spread over Helas' face.

"I do, however, have permission to zap the prisoner if he doesn't move fast enough." Traef held Alice's stare until understanding lit her features.

Moving aside, she kept pace as they walked deeper into the dark forest, light from the moons illuminating their path. Helas glanced from Alice to Traef, and Luka couldn't help but grin as he saw the male's gaze grow concerned.

He could only hope Helas refused to answer her questions.

***

"What happened after I was taken from Earth? Why can't I remember anything?" Alice demanded.

When Helas only smirked, Traef slowed his steps, the cuff around Helas' neck forcing him to slow as well. From his side, the guard retrieved and activated the shocker, allowing Helas to see the crackling weapon.

With the metal stick only an inch away from his thigh, he finally sputtered, "You were held in stasis."

The guard picked up his pace again, and Alice swore to find a way to thank him. Peering behind her, she saw Luka a few paces back. His body was stiff, and anger and frustration radiated from him. She had to get through this quickly. It looked like this was killing him.

"Yes, but why was I in stasis for so long?" she questioned.

Helas grimaced but explained, "The Cae were tasked with finding two suitable females. Once they grabbed you, they didn't know how long it would take to find another, so they put you into stasis. They delivered Jade first, and when she escaped, I told them to hold on to you and leave our orbit until I sent further instructions. They ended up leaving their ship cloaked on an uninhabited planet and taking a jumper to a nearby trading port. The pishot revealed too much to the wrong people at a bar and were captured, I'm assuming by your mate's brother, although I can't prove it." Helas' eyes narrowed on Luka then returned to her. "It took us quite some time to find the cloaked ship and retrieve you after we lost communication."

Stranded? She'd lost five months of her life because her captors had decided to go out drinking and ran their mouths? Part of Alice was relieved.

"Why did they pick me? Or Jade? What made us suitable?"

Helas' eyes brightened, and Alice knew she had him on the hook, ready to brag about whatever clever but dastardly way the Insurgents had been able to pluck humans from Earth for this long.

"I perfected the technique, actually." He grinned. "We choose an area we know to be developed, with an intact healthcare system, and then we hack into their records and search for fertile, single females of a certain age with minimal health issues, or at least ones we're able to cure. And…" his eyes twinkled evilly "no emergency contacts. Once we have a list to work from, whoever we've hired to execute the abduction surveils the females and takes any who live alone and can be snatched without attracting attention."

Alice's steps faltered. Her mother was the only family she knew, and before she'd passed away had always been her emergency contact. When Alice had gotten sick last year and had to visit a new doctor in her new town, she hadn't had an emergency contact to put down, so she'd left it blank.

"Why would you care about whether we have emergency contacts? It's not like our family could follow you into space and retrieve the women."

Helas rolled his eyes. "We aren't monsters. We studied Earthlings enough to know that your people remain, more or less, in family units. Taking unattached females seemed the most humane."

"Humane?" Alice growled. *Wait, that can't be true for all the women.*

"What about Rita and Vanessa?" she demanded.

"Who?"

Alice felt her whole body shoot tight with fury, and Luka was behind her in an instant, gripping her shoulders.

A snarl exploded from him. "The females you abducted and caged like animals," he bellowed.

Through clenched teeth, she bit out, "Rita, the older woman, and Vanessa, the tall brunette—she has a sister."

"Ah." Helas stepped over a fallen tree, appearing unconcerned that he didn't know the names of the women he'd kidnapped. "Well, I don't know why Vanessa didn't list her sister, but she didn't. As for Rita…" Helas scowled. "We made the mistake of hiring the Tarfoo to retrieve females after the disappearance of our Cae contacts. The imbeciles didn't learn enough about humans and misread her age." He curled his lip and narrowed his eyes on Sal, walking ahead of them. "Good help is hard to find."

Luka's grip on her shoulders tightened, and she saw a small stone building come into view ahead of them. She had to wrap this up. "How many women are still being held?"

"Many." His matter-of-fact tone made her skin crawl.

"Is there someone in charge of all the Insurgents?"

Helas' face paled. *Interesting.*

Traef slowed his steps again when Helas remained silent.

"You can shock me all you want. There are some things I'll never tell. That zap is like a clippet bite in comparison to what'll happen if I'm found to be disloyal."

Before Alice could argue, Verakko called from the head of the group, "Bring Helas. We're here."

"One more thing," she said, halting Traef, who'd begun to drag Helas toward the cabin. Both men turned to look at her. Helas appeared bored. "Your group—Purity. Reform. Integrity. Clecania." She waited for Helas' attention to shift back to her after angrily flashing toward Luka. "On our planet, PRIC means tiny dick."

She let the unnecessary blow hang in the air and repressed the cruel mirth she felt when undisguised fury roared onto Helas' face. Traef gave a hearty laugh and dragged a glowering Helas away.

Some of her tension lightened. Knowing why and how'd she'd been taken had helped her come to terms with her situation, and she was excited to be able to provide the other human women with some answers as well. Rounding in place, she leapt into Luka's outstretched arms.

As if sensing she just needed his reassuring touch, he stayed silent. Cupping her nape and leaning his cheek against the top of her head, he held her.

Eventually, when her heartbeat slowed and the lingering nausea rolling through her subsided, she moved away. Grasping his hand without a word, they walked slowly to the cabin.

25

The interior of the small building was crowded yet comfortable. A large lavish couch and bed took up most of the small space, leaving only enough room for three or four people to occupy at a time.

Bile rose in her throat to imagine Helas lounging in here comfortably while watching Insurgent members do God knew what to innocent victims.

From the open doorway, Alice peered in and saw Sal directing General Kadion. Pointing at a rough white stone, surrounded by identical stones set into the wall, he explained they'd need to raise Helas' hand and press it to the exact area.

Strong arms wrapped around her chest, locking her own arms to her sides. The curving black designs along the wrists told her they belonged to Luka. Lifting her, he carried her away from the scene.

She squirmed. "Hey! Luka—"

"No, Alice," he interrupted, his deep voice rough. "I stood back while you accepted an apology from Sal. I didn't interfere when you questioned Helas. This is just curiosity, though. You aren't needed right now, and if Sal is leading us into a trap, I don't want you anywhere near that hut."

He was right. Knowing he couldn't see her childish reaction, she pouted. When he'd judged them to be far enough away, he set her down.

They looked on in silence as both guards and prisoners moved in and out of the cabin, Sal directing and Helas unwillingly following directions.

Now you know how it feels, asshole.

Verakko remained inside. *Has he found the computers or systems or whatever they were called yet? Can he see the women? Are they alive?*

Alice couldn't take it anymore. She began walking forward, but Luka stopped her with a hand on her arm.

"I need to know what's happening," she begged. "Helas wouldn't blow up the building with him still inside it. I just want to know if the women are alive."

Luka's lips thinned. His brow furrowed as he studied her. Straightening, he surveyed the woods around them. "*I* will go see what's happening, and *you* will stay here. Do you hear me, Alice? You. Will. Stay. Here."

She frowned, sticking her hands on her hips. "Yes. I understand."

Stomping away, he leaned into the hut doorway, then waited for the guards and prisoners to clear the room before entering.

As he disappeared inside, a seed of doubt sprouted in her. What if it was dangerous? Had she just risked the man she loved because she couldn't wait a few minutes? Feeling her heartbeat pick up, she rocked on her feet.

I promised not to move. She hesitated for only a second longer. *Fuck it.*

She'd no sooner taken two steps toward the house when rustling from above made her stop.

Dropping from the trees in a flash, five winged men rushed Kadion and Traef. Frozen in place, she watched in terror as a pulse of blue light shot from a black glove covering one of the winged men's palms and hit Traef in the head. He slumped, unmoving at Helas' feet.

The small door to the hut swung open, and an infuriated Luka stepped into the fray, closing the door behind him. Meeting her terrified eyes, he held up a hand, motioning for her to stay where she was. She dropped into the tall grass, hiding herself as best she could.

A man with yellow wings flying above dove at Luka. She was just about to scream and draw attention to herself when Luka jumped back, out of the path of the diving man.

Reflexes lightning-fast, Luka shot his hand out and grabbed one of the yellow wings. With a roar, he wrenched the man to the ground, punching him hard until he stopped struggling and lay still.

Four left, she thought, feeling more helpless by the minute.

Two of the winged men circled above, shooting blue pulses of light no wider than a quarter. Kadion, Sal, and Luka dodged the shots as they fought to restrain the other two.

Her gaze flashed to the still form of Traef, and she felt herself heave. Helas, hair and eyes wild, was viciously ramming his boot into the unconscious male's arm. A loud crack rang through the forest, and Helas tried to work the metal band down and off the bloodied, pulverized flesh that used to be the man's arm.

She needed to warn them, but she couldn't risk distracting any of them.

Sal tackled Kadion just as a blue shot of light whizzed past, then sprang up and began wrestling another winged man to the ground.

I guess his apology was sincere.

Kadion shot his legs into the air, propelling his body upward, and landed crouched on his feet. Throwing his hand out, he caught one flying man by the throat while mid-dive toward Luka and the entrance to the hut. With a sickening crunch that carried to her, he broke the man's neck.

Momentarily free of attackers, Sal's gaze swung to her. She waved her hands wildly and pointed to Helas, who was now pulling a black glove and a gleaming knife off an unmoving winged man.

Sal gave a sharp nod and charged at Helas. Just out of arm's reach, Sal's invisible tether to Kadion snapped taut, jerking Sal's head back.

Momentary shock registered on Helas' face before a cruel smile curved his lips. In the blink of an eye, he slashed the air with the glimmering blade. Alice shrieked.

Too late. Falling to his knees, blood gushing from a quick strike above the metal collar, Sal choked. Alice's vision blurred with her tears.

A snarl burst from Luka, his eyes flashing to hers before two of the circling men dive-bombed him from either side. Fighting hard, Luka was a tangle of fists and legs.

Helas dragged each side of his bloodied knife over his pant leg while staring at her, a crazed smile spreading over his face. An icy stab of terror tore through her heart as he started stalking toward her.

Kadion and Luka were now all that stood between the attackers and Verakko. If they broke down the door before he'd freed the women, they might never find another way.

Knowing they couldn't afford to be distracted again, she turned and ran.

Pumping her arms and legs as fast as she could, she made her way deeper into the forest.

Don't look back. Don't look back.

Skidding to a halt, she looked out over a steep cliff leading to a raging river below. She dashed down along the cliff edge. Dodging branches and boulders became more and more difficult as the canopy of leaves above her thickened, swallowing the forest in darkness. Slowing, before she entered into the area of the forest that was completely pitch-black, she ducked behind a grouping of high bushes and willed her breathing to be silent.

Helas was older and stocky, right? He couldn't possibly be agile enough to sneak up on her without her hearing.

An anguished roar echoed through the trees, and she stifled a cry. *Luka!*

"There you are!" a croaky voice said from behind a large tree. "You can't hide, stupid girl. You reek of fear."

Struggling to keep her legs from shaking, she stood. Now only ten feet away, Helas' clothing and pale orange hair looked more disheveled than she'd ever seen them. As he glared at her, his eyes glinted evilly.

No weapons. No fighting skills. No protector. Alice was shit out of luck.

Helas wielded the knife in front of him with one hand and wore the black glove on the other. He crept toward her, and panic tangled her thoughts. *Rush a gun, run from a knife? But what if he has both?*

Behind her lay only black forest. As a Clecanian, Helas had better eyesight and could scent her fear. She had no hope of outrunning him.

The river below churned and flowed, splashing against boulders. Alice knew she'd never survive if she jumped in, and drowning wasn't a death she was interested in.

If she was going to go out, then she'd go out swinging. For once, she'd fight back.

Before she could reconsider, Helas lunged and swung the knife.

He sliced a shallow bloody line across her abdomen and cackled. She jumped back, falling on her ass. Instead of moving in for the kill, he hovered as if waiting for her to beg for mercy.

Fury flowed through Alice when she realized he was toying with her. Grabbing a handful of dirt, she threw it in his eyes, then tried to run around him.

She felt thick fingers slither into her hair a moment before her head was wrenched back. Twisting in his grip, she turned and kneed him in the balls. He threw her to the ground, ripping out some of her hair as he did. While still doubled over, he aimed a vicious kick at her ribs.

Pain radiated from her side, black spots dancing in front of her. She rolled, dragging her knees to her chest. And spotted her only hope of salvation.

Only feet away was a familiar small, round red object on the forest floor, just behind where Helas stood.

She looked back at Helas to see his face was bright red, the veins around his temple pulsing. Knife raised, he stumbled toward her. "You ruined everything, and now you're going to die!"

A loud snarl close by made both of their heads turn. Her heart leapt. A bloody, scratched Luka hurdled in front of her.

Luka's voice was different, deadly. In a calm tone laced with venom, he said, "You're dead."

Alice's lungs froze when Helas raised his black-gloved hand to her mate's face. Both of Luka's hands shot out and wrapped around that hand. With a sickening crack, he broke Helas' wrist.

Helas shrieked and lunged at Luka's side with the knife. Luka caught his other wrist just as the sharp blade sank into his ribs.

"No!" Alice cried. She tried to rise, but a wave of dizziness made her fall back to the ground. She had to find some way to help, and fast.

"Luka!" Alice yelled and pointed at the red object on the ground behind Helas.

His eyes flashed in the direction she pointed. He used his grip on Helas' wrist to slide the knife out of his flesh, a cruel smile curling his lips.

Widening his stance, he suddenly released his hold on Helas and stepped back. Bringing his fists above his head and raising one powerful thigh, Luka landed a hard kick right in the center of Helas' chest.

The man's eyes widened in shock a moment before he was propelled backward, landing directly on the red ball, and she prayed to the heavens it was what she thought it was.

Luka hobbled over to Alice, and they watched. For a moment, nothing happened.

Helas sat up, nursing his limp wrist and glaring at her and Luka with all of the hate he possessed. Then, a deep whine sounded from the shadows. A wave of small, red, snarling creatures exploded from all around him. They leapt from the trees and emerged from under bushes, swarming their prey.

Bloodcurdling screeches met her ears, and Luka quickly turned her face into his chest. The last thing she saw was a bloody, grasping hand, rising from a mountain of guarsil.

***

The forest grew quiet, but the sound of his frantic heartbeat pounded deafeningly in his ears. He flexed his fingers and lowered his head to inhale her scent. The moment he'd looked over to see Alice and Helas gone had been the most terrifying moment of his life.

He'd ripped and clawed at the remaining assailants viciously. No longer a civilized male, he'd reveled in the gore that had landed around him because he'd known the sooner these males were dead, the sooner he'd have a clear path to chase after Alice.

Adrenaline still pumping, he lifted her onto his lap, burying his face in her neck. When she let out a small, pained squeak, he loosened his grip. "You're okay. You're okay. You're okay." Rocking back and forth, he whispered nonsensically into her hair.

Cradling his head in her arms, she scratched her nails over his scalp. "Yes. I'm okay, Luka. Are you okay?"

His purr exploded out of him at the sound of her voice. Gripping her head in his hands, he forced her eyes to his. "You said you'd stay put, love."

Tears flowed down her cheeks, leaving clean tracks in the grime covering her tanned skin. All at once, an overwhelming urge to get her home and wash all evidence of this night away rushed through him.

He bolted up, still holding her in his arms, then hissed when a sharp pain tore through his side.

"Put me down. You're hurt." She wriggled and writhed until he was forced to release her.

Crouching down, she carefully lifted his shirt over his head, then balled the fabric and placed it against the deep slash in his side. Her hands flew to her mouth, and she gasped as she took in the rest of the wounds visible on his chest.

Tears sliding down her face, she spun in place. "We have to get you help."

"Help is coming," a deep voice called from the trees.

Luka wheeled around, ready to rip apart the new threat. Black spots danced before his eyes, a wave of dizziness making him stagger. When he made out the features of Kadion, he allowed relief to wash over him, then promptly collapsed.

"Luka!" Alice cried, rushing behind him and laying his head in her lap.

"He'll be okay. Zed is on the way now with a healer. It'll keep him stable until we get him to a medbay." Kadion sank to the ground next to them with a wince.

"And what about you?" she said, eyeing the deep crimson spreading from his torso and staining his shirt.

Kadion chuckled then wheezed.

The male had fought by his side bravely and taken on the last two attackers on his own while Luka had dashed into the forest. His face was covered in gashes and his once sandy-blond hair was dark and coated in blood.

"Oh, I've had much worse than this. Hazard of the job." Kadion shot her a dimpled smile. "Still, it'd be nice to have a mate care for me like that." One clear and one swollen eye met Luka's. "I hope you realize how lucky you are."

He peered above him. Alice's warm tears were falling into his hair and she ran her hands over his uninjured skin. "I do."

She gave him a watery smile and leaned down, pressing a wet upside-down kiss to his lips. She let her forehead rest against his and whispered, "I love you so much," before rising again.

"Any sign of Verakko?" Kadion asked, interrupting the intimate moment.

Alice's head snapped up. "What happened to him? And Sal and Traef?"

Luka groaned and sat up. "He finally came out and joined in the fight. I didn't catch everything he said, but it seemed like he'd opened all the cells of the outposts and told the prisoners to run, but couldn't do much more than that under the circumstances."

Kadion nodded. "That's what I recall, as well. Then he started fighting. I'd never seen him fight before. He was vicious."

"Then what happened to him?" Alice asked impatiently.

"One of the males—a Strigi, I believe—carried him off through the trees and never returned."

"I hope he's okay," Alice said, tears welling anew. "And the others?"

Luka could hear the heartbreak in her voice and knew she'd already witnessed Sal's fate.

"Traef will pull through, but Sal…" Kadion lowered his head.

A single sob tore from Alice. Luka smoothed her hair back and pulled her onto his chest, letting his low purr soothe her the way it always did. "He redeemed himself, love. Died a proud male."

Alice clutched at his forearms for a moment and then pulled away, sniffing. "What will you do about Verakko?"

"We'll send search parties out to look for him, but Swadaeth are notoriously hard to kill. It might be why they took him in the first place. Probably thought it'd be easier if he were carried off and dropped out of the way."

"And the women? They're free?" she asked, wiping her eyes with the back of her hand.

"We can only hope. Word will be spread among trusted individuals all over Clecania to be on the lookout for wandering females, but we have to assume not all of them made it out. Speaking of…" Kadion scanned the trees. "Where's Helas? Did he escape?"

Luka pointed over his shoulder to a bloody clump in the grass, all that was left of Helas.

Kadion peered at them, brows raised.

"Alice was brilliant. She spotted a guarsil." Luka coughed, feeling his vision waver.

Kadion hissed air through his teeth. "Ouch."

"I took a chance." She grimaced. "Let's all just be thankful it wasn't a harmless piece of fruit."

Yells echoed through the trees, and Kadion rose unsteadily to his feet. Auzed and Izor emerged, ready to tend their wounds.

Luka lifted Alice to her feet and gazed down into her eyes. "Don't worry. I've got you."

Epilogue

One month later

"Keep your eyes closed," Luka demanded from behind her.

"My eyes are closed, and what does it even matter anyway?" she argued. "You have your enormous hands covering my face. Even if I opened them, I wouldn't see anything. Remember, we can't stay...wherever you're taking me...for too long. We promised to go meet your niece today."

Alice didn't know how many more surprises she could handle. Ever since their terrifying attack in the woods, Luka had been repeatedly giving her presents and surprising her with romantic tokens.

"Don't get me wrong, I love presents, but you're going overboard. I asked you to stop, remember?" she said while continuing to stumble forward down an uneven path. The sounds of the forest played all around her, and she wondered if he had another picnic planned.

"I remember I specifically tuned out that request."

Alice huffed. The impossible male had received not one, but three nearly fatal wounds during their attack. He should be the one receiving gifts and surprises, not her.

He whispered into her ear, making her jump. "We're here. Open up."

It took her eyes a moment to adjust to the bright light. When they did, she found herself staring into a small copse of flowering trees.

Keeping his voice quiet, he said, "Have I ever told you about the weshuin?" He pointed up to a small orange bird flitting among the blossoms at the top of the tree.

"No."

"Well, the weshuin spends years and years gathering strong material to build his nest. He starts by finding sticks and small rocks, then builds a tall covered structure." He pointed to a large, impressive stick house, set atop the juncture of two converging branches.

"Wow, that looks more like a small house than a bird's nest." She whispered up to the orange bird, "You're doing great!"

"Next, he finds soft material to line the inside, and finally he flies all over, finding pretty things to decorate the nest with. Flowers, shiny pebbles, buttons."

She watched as the small bird swooped to its nest, pale pink flower in beak, and placed it near the entrance.

"Does he ever actually live in it?" She chuckled, leaning her head against Luka's shoulder.

"Only when he finds a mate." He peered down at her with a warm smile. "It sometimes takes years, but after he's done building the nest, he'll bring the female bird he's courting here to show her. If she goes to sit inside, then she's agreed to be his mate."

Alice sighed. Luka was a hopeless romantic, and she loved it.

"I want to show you something else."

She was just about to complain that she wasn't closing her eyes again when he whirled her around by her shoulders. Emotion tightened her throat, and her heart stuttered.

A beautiful, rustic home stood in front of her. The sides of the two-story house were covered in large picture windows and gleamed in the late afternoon sun.

"Do you like it?" Luka asked, his shoulders bunched.

Alice had to choke out her words through the lump in her throat. "I see you learned some tricks from those weshuin."

His face broke into a grin, and he tugged at her hand, leading her into the house.

Once inside, she only caught glimpses of warm-toned furniture and piles of books. His insistent tug on her wrist forced her to jog through the house and up the stairs.

"Am I allowed to look at the house?" she halfheartedly complained, laughing.

His smile was infectious as he pulled her through a large, comfortable bedroom and onto a...

"A balcony," she exclaimed, hands flying to her mouth.

The small, raised balcony overlooked the forest, and the two familiar, old armchairs from Luka's apartment were placed on either side of a deep-green table, set with two cups.

Luka glanced briefly at her, then rushed over to sit in one of the chairs, leaning forward to sweep away the floating bulbs hovering over the cups to keep them warm.

"I asked Jade what coffee was, and I think this might be close." He motioned for her to sit in the other chair, holding out a steaming glass.

Her lip trembled. She made her way over to Luka, curling up in his lap. "How did I get so lucky?"

A low purr rumbled through his chest, and he brushed his cheek against her hair. "I'm the lucky one."

Tilting her head, she pressed her mouth to his. Their kiss was slow and sensual and utterly full of love.

"Watch it, female. You want to see the rest of the house before retiring to the bedroom, don't you?"

"I want to stay right here." She sighed, taking the cup from his hand.

Reaching forward, he grabbed the second glass. "I hope this helps when you miss your home."

She took a small sip and choked, then began to laugh.

"It's terrible," she squealed.

He took a sip of his own and grimaced.

Replacing their cups on the table, she turned back to him. "It doesn't matter, though. I can't miss home, because I am home." She ran a hand through his hair. "You're my home. I love you."

He beamed. "I love you too."

About the Author

Victoria Aveline has always enjoyed immersing herself in a good romance. Alpha males are her weakness but, while possessive dominating heroes have always been titillating, she craved something more. So she decided to create a world in which devastatingly sexy men could be aggressive and domineering but still bow down before the matriarchy.

Victoria lives with her husband, dog, and about sixty thousand badass honey-making ladies. When not writing or fantasizing about future characters, she enjoys traveling, reading, and sipping overpriced hipster cocktails.

victoriaaveline.com

Made in the USA
Middletown, DE
23 October 2021